JET IX

†

Escape

D1557357

Russell Blake

First edition.

ISBN: 978-1519314857

Published by

Reprobatio Limited

CHAPTER 1

A balmy evening breeze drifted across Port-au-Prince bay, carrying with it the taint of decaying marine life and the stink of diesel fuel. The only lights visible were the faint lamps on cargo ships anchored far offshore from the port. The sun had set two hours earlier, sinking into the western sea, a crimson fireball extinguishing itself in a daily ritual of renewal. The warm Caribbean washed onto the rocky shore in gentle breaking swells, swirling around the few fishermen still standing in the shallows with makeshift nets, hoping to catch dinner so they wouldn't have to go home empty-handed to their impoverished families.

A smallish cargo vessel, its seams weeping russet down the welded plates of its navy blue hull, pulled at the dock lines lashed to one of the concrete jetties that jutted into the water. The battered craft was still plying its island trade decades after the end of its useful life, like a fighter in the tenth round, unwilling to go to the mat no matter how many punches land.

Three islanders stood at an iron gate that protected the jetty, laughing and talking as they watched the sparse traffic pass on the waterfront road. A United Nations armored personnel carrier rumbled along, transporting members of the de facto occupation force both resented and feared by the locals.

Music pulsed from a band playing on the seaside terrace of an open-air restaurant down a spit of beach from the wharf. The establishment was little more than a concrete enclosure with a broad overhang crafted from dried palm fronds and scavenged lumber, but popular with the islanders. Steel drums trilled melodically to a reggae rhythm, playing in time to the flickering torches that surrounded the packed dining area.

The patrons smiled and chatted easily in the welcome relief of the trade winds. The beer was cold and the fish fresh, and everyone a local – tourism in Port-au-Prince had declined to an anemic trickle even before the disastrous earthquake that leveled many of its landmarks in 2010, and had now all but vanished. Haiti had been compared unfavorably to a war zone, which wasn't far from the truth, given the squalor and rampant violence that visited the tropical paradise on a daily basis.

But for the lucky diners, a collection of some of the most prosperous Haitians, those concerns might have been a million miles away as ebony-skinned waiters drifted among them like wraiths, watching for empty bottles or finished platters on the brightly colored tables.

A large man in an oversized red silk Hawaiian shirt clapped enthusiastically when the band finished its number, and his companions joined in, the gold of their watches and necklaces gleaming in the torchlight and their smiles so white as to be nearly luminescent. Two young women, dressed provocatively in shorts and tank tops that left nothing to the imagination, toasted each other with the last of their rum and Cokes, beaming at their host. The big islander, Jon Renoir, gave the band leader a thumbs-up and cupped his hands to his mouth so his shouted encouragement could be better heard.

"You boys crazy-good tonight, you are," Renoir yelled in the Creole that was the predominant language of the island. The steel drummer held up his mallets in salute – Renoir was a powerful figure in Haiti, a crime lord who ran the nearby slum of Cité Soleil, easily the most dangerous enclave in one of the world's most deadly ports.

Renoir dealt in human traffic, providing children to the clandestine pedophile tourists who braved the nation's dangers to satisfy their forbidden hunger, as well as methamphetamines and cocaine to the Cité Soleil inhabitants, transshipment of weapons and drugs to and from the U.S., murder for hire, kidnapping, torture, slavery – the full gamut of every imaginable criminal activity. He was an island fixture, a multimillionaire in a land of extreme poverty and, as such, received respect from the staff and band, as well as furtive, averted looks from his fellow diners.

The man next to him, a whippet-thin Rastafarian with a carefully trimmed goatee, wearing a yellow shirt with a graphic of Bob Marley on it, nodded as though Renoir had revealed the secret to eternal life. "They on fire, all right, those boys is."

Renoir downed the remainder of his bottle of beer and slammed it on the wooden table, glanced at his watch, and signaled to the waiter for the bill. The man scurried over. Renoir threw down a wad of American dollars and then pushed back with a wave to the musicians. The girls drained their drinks with practiced ease, and the one on his right clutched his hand possessively. Renoir's entourage stood, the distinctive shapes of pistols in the bodyguards' waistbands barely covered by their shirts, and the band struck up another song as Renoir's group made their way to the entrance. The restaurant owner, a heavy woman with a scarlet head scarf and a white blouse, approached with her arms outstretched.

"Jon, bless your heart. Always good to see you, it is," she said with a smile.

The big man hugged her. "Got to do this more often, mama."

"You come back soon as you want. Always got my best table for you, I do."

Renoir pressed a twenty-dollar bill into her palm and turned to his goateed companion. "Ate too damn much again, I did."

"Man got to keep up his strength."

The young woman who'd been holding Renoir's hand now took his arm and pulled close to him. Her head barely reached his shoulder. "Tha's right, honey child, you going to need all of it tonight, you are," she slurred in a loud stage whisper.

The front of the restaurant was dark, its neon pink and yellow façade barely visible in the gloom. As Renoir's entourage moved to two copper-colored SUVs, the rumble of a big motor from the end of the street drew their attention. The three bodyguards who framed

Renoir and his female company reflexively reached for their pistols. Both SUV engines were running, having gotten a warning call a few minutes earlier, alerting them that Renoir was ready to depart, and the driver of the nearest reacted to the unexpected sound by reaching for a machine pistol that rested on the passenger seat.

Bright spotlights blinked on across the street, blinding the gunmen, and a voice called out over a megaphone.

"Renoir, this is Lieutenant Ponchet of the Port-au-Prince police. Drop your weapons."

Renoir ducked behind the SUV's front fender with his date as his gunmen whipped their pistols free. An assault rifle barrage barked from across the road as the police opened fire. The nearest bodyguard screamed as two rounds slammed into his torso and he fell back, squeezing the trigger of his handgun reflexively as he went down. The young woman screamed at the sight of his bloody form next to her, and then the driver emptied his machine pistol at the muzzle flashes and there was a lull in the incoming fire.

Renoir worked a Glock 19 pistol from his belt and signaled to his remaining bodyguards. One of them nodded and took a deep breath. He poked his head from around the fender of the adjacent vehicle and was instantly pummeled with rounds. Renoir swore – the police had to be using night vision scopes, taking no chances, which meant he and his crew had no chance.

The side of the SUV shredded as dozens of slugs tore through it, killing the driver, cutting him nearly in half. Renoir got off several shots of his own, and then the girl screamed again – a stray round had ricocheted from the pavement and hit her in the stomach. She clutched the spreading stain and stared at Renoir with wide, pained eyes, and then closed them with a groan.

Renoir grimaced and moved a few feet to his right, where the engine block and steel tire rims would shield him as he considered his next move. His Rastafarian associate clutched a chrome-plated Desert Eagle .45-caliber pistol, and watched Renoir for a signal of how he wanted to play the situation. All the men in Renoir's entourage were veterans of countless shanty-town gun battles, so exchanging fire was nothing new to them, but this was the first time they'd been ambushed by heavily armed police. They would all give their lives if he gave the nod – that was how they rolled – but the signal was his to give, and nobody else's.

Renoir glanced behind him at the restaurant entrance, calculating whether he could make it back inside without being hit. It was a fifty-fifty proposition, but better than the certain death that awaited across the road. He understood how things worked on the island, with as many enemies as he had – the all-out assault on his men told him that he would be summarily executed by his assailants, whether or not they were actually police.

His only hope was to take refuge in the restaurant and then make a break for it down the beach, perhaps swimming to safety to avoid any shooters lying in wait by the water.

The decision was an easy one. He pointed first at the entrance, then at himself, and then motioned to his gunmen to continue engaging the police, his message clear: lay down covering fire while he made his move.

A pause in the onslaught was followed by Renoir's bodyguards firing at the shadows as he dashed back to the restaurant. Plumes of dirt sprayed the ground where bullets narrowly missed him. The façade erupted in a spray of colored mortar beside the crime lord, goading him to greater speed. He darted through the entryway as rounds whistled around him, and then he was safely behind the cinderblock wall, the panicked eyes of the diners and waiters glued to him: a mountain of a man clutching a gun, panting and sweating as he sized up his escape route through the tables.

More gunfire boomed from outside the entrance, driving him forward toward the band, which had stopped playing as the musicians scrambled behind overturned tables. Gunfire was nothing new in Port-au-Prince, to the point where there was a certain laissez-faire to hearing it a few blocks away; but an armed assault at the front door was a different story, and everyone took cover as best they could.

Renoir pushed through the dining area and hurried to the stage.

He stared out over the beach, which was empty save for the fishermen knee-deep in the surf. With a final glance behind him, where the shooting was slowing – presumably as his men died – he ran across the strand toward the water, returning his pistol to his belt as he moved with surprising speed for such a large man.

Fountains of sand geysered next to him and a burst of automatic rifle fire sounded from the side of the restaurant. He ducked instinctively and clumsily zigzagged the remaining way to the water's edge. The rounds followed him, and when he hit the gentle swell, they tore at the sea around him before stopping as he waded to his chest.

"Renoir, no more warning shots, you hear? Hands up, or the next one's between your eyes. Serious, I am. You want to die tonight, big mon?" Lieutenant Ponchet's voice rang out from the darkness.

Renoir stopped. If the cop had wanted to kill him, he'd have already blown his head off. So he wanted Renoir alive. Why, Renoir didn't know, but now that he was in full view of the restaurant's diners and staff, it was unlikely he'd get a bullet in the spine on the ride to jail.

A wave surged past him, and he took the chance to pull his pistol from his waist while the water obstructed the cop's view of his hands. He debated a final shoot-out for a split second and then dropped the gun into the sea – leaving the crooked Haitian cops to arrest an unarmed man guilty of nothing but running for his life.

Renoir slowly turned until he was facing the restaurant, hands high over his head. "Ain't got no gun, I don't," he shouted.

Three members of the Haitian police's elite SWAT team materialized from the side of the building, M16 rifles trained on the big man, and as they neared Renoir, he could see the tension in their faces. The lead man, obviously Ponchet by his bearing, hung back as they approached.

"Come on outta the water, Renoir. We got to cuff you, we do," Ponchet ordered.

"What's the charge?"

"Littering. Now out of the water, you. Let's get this over with."

"You boys making a big mistake here, you are."

"Yeah? Maybe."

"Ain't got no gun. My people thought you was gangsters trying to kill us. Got no beef with the police, I don't," Renoir said as he made his way back onto the beach.

Ponchet nodded, and one of the officers pulled a pair of handcuffs from his belt, the M16 still clutched in his other hand with its ugly snout pointed at Renoir's head. "Turn around and let's do this."

Renoir obliged and stood patiently as the man searched him. Finding nothing, the officer clasped Renoir's wrists behind him and locked the cuffs in place. Renoir turned toward Ponchet and eyed him in the faint light as the moon peeked between the clouds. "You shot my girl. She wasn't doing nothing, she wasn't – just eating dinner."

Ponchet shrugged. "Plenty more where she came from, what I hear about you."

"She was special."

"She should a been more careful 'bout who she opened her legs for." Ponchet tilted his head, studying Renoir's dripping form, and then reached down to his belt for his radio and held it to his mouth. "We got him."

The cop on Renoir's left nudged the crime lord with his gun barrel. "Come on, you. Nice and easy."

"I want my lawyer," Renoir said, his tone resigned, as he took lumbering steps forward on the sand.

"Oh, yeah. Bet you do," Ponchet agreed.

"You gonna regret this."

The blow to the back of Renoir's head stunned him. For a second the sky tilted, the torchlight from the restaurant pinwheeling as he reeled, but he didn't go down. Ponchet moved close to him and whispered in his ear, "Any more threats, you gonna have broken bones by the time we get to the station, you."

Renoir bit back the insult that sprang to his lips and instead grunted, his eyes flat and dead as a shark's, revealing nothing. The little group continued up the strand to the restaurant, which was now silent, the gunfire having died down while the crime boss was bolting for the water. When they reached the concrete stage, Renoir spotted the restaurant owner, and before Ponchet could stop him, yelled out to her, "Call Antoine and tell him what happened. We going to the station. Tell him be quick about it."

A savage blow from Ponchet's truncheon caught Renoir in the temple and his knees buckled as he dropped. The surroundings and the horrified expressions on the faces of the band and the diners faded as his vision blurred and he lost consciousness.

CHAPTER 2

La Virginia, Colombia

Jet squinted in the predawn gloom at the bank on the far side of the river. The leaky boat they'd commandeered after escaping from the monastery had taken them as far as she dared hope, and as morning light glowed beyond the eastern peaks, she made her decision.

"We'll stay on this side of the river. I remember seeing a decent-sized town on the map. We must be near it by now," she said.

Jet, Matt, and Hannah had spent the long night on the water, allowing the current to carry them south at a crawl, and had come up with a plan as they'd meandered toward the little hamlet of La Virginia. They would find a computer and contact one of Matt's old agency acquaintances – a black sheep former analyst named Carl, who had long ago retired to Cuba in an effort to be free of the U.S. intelligence community, his patriotism having waned as he'd seen too much over his years with the CIA. He'd set up shop there and was now an accommodator – helping the locals with forbidden currency and equipment, facilitating illegal transactions, and generally playing middleman on anything that paid in the black-market economy that was the byproduct of communism.

Matt nodded groggily, and Hannah stirred beside him. Jet motioned to the primitive rudder. "You take the helm. Pull in anywhere that looks good. How's she doing?"

"She feels a little hot to the touch, and you heard her coughing. She's definitely coming down with something," Matt said, half-standing as he moved in a crouch to the stern and took the tiller from her. Jet edged forward and sat next to Hannah and then laid a cool hand on her forehead.

"Not too bad," Jet murmured, as much to herself as to Matt.

"She's been through an awful lot," Matt whispered.

"Yes, she has. We all have. But we have to keep moving. We don't know who's after us, only that one of the cartels is helping them, which means it's not safe anywhere in Colombia."

"It has to be because of the diamonds. Nothing else makes sense."

"Maybe, but knowing that doesn't help us. We have to get to either Ecuador or Venezuela. Panama is out of the question after what I went through there. The police will be looking for me for a long time."

"Venezuela is hostile to the U.S. – I vote for Venezuela," Matt said. "If it's the agency after us, they'll have a hell of a time getting any help."

"True, but it's also way too unstable to live there, Matt. I've been to Venezuela. It's always been dangerous, but I hear it's getting way worse."

"We'll talk to Carl and see what he can do for us. Maybe one of the islands? Aruba?"

"Too close for comfort. This all started for me on Trinidad, remember?"

"That's right. I keep forgetting." Matt pointed at a spot on the bank. "Let's hear what Carl has to say, and we can go from there. It's going to be daylight soon, and if they're still looking for us, the more distance we can put between ourselves and the monastery, the better…"

"You can bet they'll be looking. Whoever sent them is still out there. And don't forget the shooter at the base of the mountain." She hesitated. "We have to assume that even though we bought ourselves some time, they'll figure this out eventually. By then we need to be anywhere but Colombia."

The boat drifted toward the river's edge, and the wooden hull scraped on the rocky shore. Jet hopped out and pulled the bow further onto the spit of land, and Matt handed a still-slumbering Hannah to her before climbing out himself. She waited as he pushed the boat back into the current, and they watched it slowly float into the fog.

Matt took in a small circle of stones surrounded by broken glass by the brush line and leaned into her. "Come on. We can take turns carrying Hannah. There's a trail I can just make out by the fire pit. There's probably a road somewhere close by."

Matt led the way, and after several minutes they climbed up a steep grade to a two-lane strip of asphalt. Near a far bend the first rays of dawn glinted off glass – a window set into a building, barely visible in the shadows.

"We must be close," Jet said.

"Let's hope so."

Twenty minutes later they were on the outskirts of town, the area all recently plowed fields, the air redolent of fresh earth and dew. A single cart drawn by a swayback horse bounced along the road. The farmer at the reins in faded coveralls looked ancient, his skin the texture and color of rawhide, a hand-rolled cigarette smoldering between his thin lips as he waved at them in passing.

Day broke over a sorry collection of sorry dwellings arranged haphazardly around the town center, marked by a towering church spire. A few motors sputtered to life in the distance as morning in the rural river town began. Jet and Matt were surprised as they made their way toward the church – the primitive hovels transitioned into a neighborhood of stately two-story homes, and then into a commercial area, the architecture colonial, but the cars surprisingly new.

"There's more money here than I would have guessed," Jet said as they walked the quiet streets.

"That's good, right? It means the likelihood of finding transportation and an Internet café is better."

"Speaking of which, looks like there's one on the corner," she said.

Matt nodded. "Right. You call Carl. We don't want to risk me being seen. I'm afraid with this cast, I kind of stand out," he said, holding up his broken hand.

"That and your skin color, white boy. Stay here with Hannah. I shouldn't be long. You sure he'll answer his phone?"

"I haven't talked to him in a couple of years, but he should. I mean, where else is a seventy-year-old going to be at this hour in Cuba?"

Jet handed Hannah to him and stroked her brow with obvious concern. The little girl's eyes fluttered open and she appraised her mother sleepily. Jet offered a smile. "I'll be right back, honey. You go back to sleep."

Hannah coughed and closed her eyes. Matt held her head against his shoulder protectively. "You're on. Let's hope they're open."

"They are. They've already set out a couple of tables on the sidewalk."

Jet made her way to the café and pushed open the door. A thick man with a mop of unruly gray hair looked up from the counter, surprise painted across his hangdog face. He quickly recovered when she ordered a cup of black coffee and asked about the computers.

"I need to call a friend on Skype. Do you have it here?" she asked in fluent Spanish.

"Of course. There's a headset hanging on the side of the case. You can call and I'll bring your coffee to you, if you like."

"Ah. That would be perfect."

"Take the station nearest the wall. It's the newest."

Jet strolled past four makeshift computer stations, whose flimsy partitions offered slim privacy, and sat at the end unit. To her eye it looked prehistoric, but after a few mouse clicks she was connected, and the line was ringing in her ear. A few moments later, when a gruff male voice answered, the sound was as clear as though he was standing next to her.

"*Sí?*" the voice growled.

"Carl?"

"Who's this?" the voice demanded suspiciously.

"A friend of yours told me to call. Victor," Jet said, using the code name Matt had said he'd recognize.

"Who?"

Jet's heart sank. Either he didn't remember the sequence, or this wasn't Carl.

"Victor."

He hesitated. "I can take a message."

Bingo – that was the correct response. She was speaking to Carl. "Victor really wants to ask about a fishing charter today."

"He does, does he? Then why doesn't he call me himself?"

"He's indisposed. But he told me that if I mentioned Bangkok and a card game, you'd be able to help."

Carl didn't say anything for several long seconds. "What kind of trouble are you in?"

"We're in Colombia. Need to get somewhere safe, where we won't be asked for a lot of paperwork."

"Colombia? What part?"

She could hear computer keys tapping in the background as she described their location and situation, and when he spoke again his voice had lost any trace of irritation.

"Looks like you're about fifteen hours' drive time from the Ecuadorian border, and maybe twelve to Venezuela. Think you can make it to Venezuela?"

"We'll do whatever we need to do."

"How many?"

"Three. Our friend, myself, and a little girl, almost three."

"Victor's gone nuclear family on me?"

"A long story."

"Okay, I'm not sure I want to know. Here's what you need to do to get to Venezuela. Looks like the closest crossing point is a town called Cúcuta. Northeast of you. Probably take all day to travel there, depending on what you're driving. Call me once you're on the ground. In the meantime, I'll see what I can do. You going to need passports, the whole works?"

"Yes."

"Won't be cheap."

"Nothing in life is."

"How hot is the water you're in?"

"Hot enough that we need your help getting to wherever."

"All right. You have my number. Call when you can. How are you fixed for cash?"

"We can come up with whatever you need."

"That could run in the quarter mil range. Figure, buck apiece for adults, half for the kid."

"I understand."

"Sounds like you do. I'll get to work and see what can be done on a rush basis." Carl paused. "I'm assuming this is a rush job?"

"Good guess."

"I'm intuitive that way. And who should I look forward to speaking with when you call back?"

"Me."

"Right. And what's your name?"

"Victoria."

She could hear a trace of a smile in his voice. "Of course. Okay, Victoria. Safe travels."

The line went dead just as the proprietor arrived with a steaming cup of fresh brew. Jet thanked him, took several sips, and then pulled up a map of Colombia onscreen and studied the roads leading to Cúcuta. It looked like there weren't too many options – either head north toward Medellín or east toward Bogotá. Either way, they'd have to get over the Andes Mountains to reach the border, which no doubt accounted for the long drive-time estimates she was seeing online.

She finished her coffee and ordered a cup to go for Matt, bought a bottle of orange juice, and paid. Matt and Hannah were waiting at the end of the block, which was still deserted. She approached and swapped Hannah for the coffee. The little girl didn't wake up, and Jet let her daughter sleep. The stress of the night escape and being in an open wooden skiff on the river had taken its toll, and if her daughter could catch a few winks before things got crazy again, so much the better.

"I reached him," Jet said, and gave a quiet report of Carl's instructions. When she was done, Matt frowned.

"So all we have to do is cross the country without being caught, with the cartel and the authorities actively searching for us."

"That about covers it."

He drained his cup and straightened. "Then we better start looking for something to beg, borrow, or steal."

"I..." Jet froze as a police cruiser rounded the corner at the end of the block and pulled to the curb. "We've got company," she warned, her hand moving automatically to the pistol at the small of her back — a memento from the monastery shootout.

"Easy. Could be routine," Matt said, gathering Hannah up and handing her to Jet. "Let's just go on our way."

"Which is?" Jet whispered as two uniformed officers got out of the car.

Matt looked up the street. "When in doubt, go to church."

CHAPTER 3

Matt led them away from the policemen with calm, measured steps, the cast enveloping his hand hidden by his windbreaker, which he'd draped over the plaster. Jet could feel the eyes of the officers scanning her as she followed him down the cobblestone street with Hannah in her arms, the little girl's head on her shoulder.

Another police vehicle, this one a pickup truck, swung onto the street ahead of them, and Jet stiffened. They were boxed in. If she hadn't been carrying Hannah, she'd have felt more confident, but as it was, if there was shooting, her daughter would be at risk – which meant that gunfire was off the table.

"Easy," Matt cautioned from ahead. "Nice and easy. Just a family out for an early morning walk, that's all," he said as the vehicle neared.

Jet fought the urge to draw down on the truck as it rolled to the curb just ahead of them. She kept her expression blank as she passed the front fender, unable to make out anything through the filthy windshield, but stiffened when the driver's door swung wide as she drew alongside. Her hand crept to the pistol nestled in her waistband.

"*Buenos días*," a scratchy male voice said from within the truck cab.

"*Buenos días*," Jet replied softly, hoping that she didn't look too rough from her night of monastery assaults and river escapes.

A plump man with sergeant's stripes on his short-sleeved shirt climbed from behind the wheel and stood next to the truck as his companion stepped out and stretched. Neither looked particularly alert, and Jet kept walking.

The policemen sauntered over to where the squad car was parked. A surreptitious glance over Jet's shoulder found the other cops leaning against it, smoking, waiting for the newcomers to arrive. After some jocular greetings, they all made for the café she'd only moments before exited, laughing about needing extra-strength coffee to fully recover from the prior night's excesses.

Matt disappeared around the corner, and she followed. Two blocks down the smaller street lined by bright green and red buildings, they arrived at the town church. Matt slowed as Jet caught up to him, and they wordlessly approached the bell tower, a beige monolith jutting into the air with an ornately crafted iron clock just below the spire's roof, showing six forty.

"Now what?" Matt asked.

"We either steal a car or hitch a ride. Either way, we need to be well clear of this dump. They'll figure out we're not on the mountain, if they haven't already, and then the search will be on."

"Maybe we should split up?" Matt suggested.

Jet shook her head, her emerald eyes flashing. "Not a chance in hell."

"Okay then. Just a suggestion. Because if they're looking for a white guy with a cast and a little girl, we wouldn't be that hard to spot..."

Jet moved to the park across the street from the church, where a decades-old split-axle bobtail truck with Venezuelan plates was parked. As she neared, she saw a short man wearing a sweat-stained baseball cap, eating breakfast from a paper plate. He was standing beside an old woman in peasant garb, whose makeshift cart held several large pots and an assortment of containers. Jet sniffed cautiously and was rewarded with the mouthwatering aroma of pastry and some sort of egg stew.

She struck up a conversation with the man as the crone loaded a polystyrene bowl with the breakfast concoction, and quickly learned that he was headed back to Venezuela with a cargo of produce and coffee purchased from his cousin in the nearby town of Cartago.

Fifteen minutes later, Jet and Matt were crowded into the truck cab with Hannah in Jet's lap as the truck lurched along the winding streets toward the main road. The driver, Oliveros, had been amenable to making some easy cash by giving them a ride as far as

Cúcuta, where they'd be on their own – he'd hinted that he had a relationship with a particular customs inspector who would be working the following morning, and Jet knew better than to ask whether they could cross the border with him, jeopardizing his transaction.

He killed time by describing their route, which would take them north toward Medellín, and then cut over toward the Andes a hundred and thirty kilometers before they reached the city. From there they would be on Highway 45, which ran north, paralleling the mountain range until they veered east to Pamplona, a burg on the far side of the summit that was known for its university. From there it would be north again, a few hours' drive along torturous roads, and then they'd be in Cúcuta, with any luck at all, by sunset.

They learned that Oliveros, married with three children, hailed from Valera, a hill town built in the ridged valley that ran between the Cordillera de Mérida mountains, and had lived there his entire life. His modest import shipments paid for a simple life in Venezuela, but he wished he had more money so he could move – the country had changed radically since Chávez had died, and was now run by criminal cartels that used violence and murder as their stock-in-trade, extorting simple businessmen like Oliveros by threatening his family if he didn't engage in smuggling for them.

"You…you aren't carrying anything we could get in trouble for, are you?" Jet asked after he'd told his story.

Oliveros laughed, displaying a flash of primitive dental work, gold-crowned teeth catching the morning light. "Oh, no. I wouldn't give you a ride if I was playing mule. No, I refused after my last shipment – it was a close call, and I don't ever want to repeat that."

"What will happen now that you refused?" Matt asked.

"I plan to sell this load and see about moving, maybe to the coast. Wait for things to calm down. These gangs come and go, and if you have time, the best thing you can do is let them kill each other and then return once it's safe. The group that I'm tangled up with is relatively new, less than a year. I give them six more months before their rivals wipe them out."

Jet nodded quietly. She understood perfectly how Oliveros must feel – in danger, through no fault of his own, torn by powerful forces he couldn't control, his family at risk, and difficult decisions that could cost them everything a daily occurrence.

It wasn't an unusual story in the region, but one that was poorly understood in first world countries, she knew from personal experience. She'd experienced firsthand the culture shock of going from a society where death was a daily, unremarkable companion to a civilized area of Europe or North America where the annoyance of slow Internet or unpleasant rush-hour congestion was more real than being summarily executed by the side of the road. It was impossible to explain to someone from a modern society how precarious life was in much of the world, how random and pointless it could seem.

The poverty and desperation of a country like Venezuela, where basics like bandages and vitamins were impossible to obtain, was simply unimaginable to someone in a mall in Miami or London. But that didn't make it any less dangerous, and she was keenly aware, cradling her daughter as they traversed a country that was half under the rule of rebel warlords who were little more than cocaine-producing gangsters, of how quickly everything could disintegrate into violence and death.

She was jarred from her thoughts by a slowdown just outside of La Dorada, a port town on the muddy brown Rio Magdalena. As they neared the bridge that spanned the wide river, they saw the flashing red and blue of police vehicles, where an impromptu roadblock had been created, one of many ineffective methods employed by the authorities to curb the rampant cocaine trafficking for which the region was famous.

They crawled forward for thirty minutes before arriving at the barrier. The officers ultimately waved the truck through without inspecting it – figuring, Oliveros said, that it would be searched at the border, so no point in duplicating effort.

"Most of the coca moves along the waterways and by plane, anyway," Oliveros explained matter-of-factly. "Besides, any shipments larger than a few kilos are paid off well in advance, so the authorities know which vessels to avoid. It's a system that's been in place for decades. These things are just an annoyance: make-work projects so the politicians appear to be doing something to combat the cartels."

"Do they arrange things for you when you're running a shipment?" Jet asked.

"Oh, no. I pick the stuff up in Cúcuta. I don't ask how it gets there. I don't want to know."

They stopped for lunch at a roadside shack that sold fixed-price plates of stew and beans for the equivalent of a dollar, and sat in the shade of a grove of trees as they consumed the questionable fare. Hannah was listless and Jet could tell she had a fever, but other than giving her aspirin, she couldn't do much for her besides sympathize.

"When we get to Cúcuta, we'll need to find a doctor," Jet said to Matt. "I don't want this spiraling out of control."

Hannah smiled weakly. After a few swallows of water, she went back to dozing by Jet's side as the adults finished their meal. Matt considered the toddler and nodded. "Agreed. Let's hope the town's big enough to have someone competent."

Oliveros rose and dumped his empty plate into a plastic garbage bin, and when he returned, Jet asked him about doctors.

"Oh, there's a very good clinic there. But you'll probably have to wait until morning. We won't arrive at this rate until well after dark."

"What about the hospital?" Matt asked.

"It's not as good. And it will have a lot of paperwork to fill out. It's state operated."

Jet and Matt exchanged a quick look at the mention of paperwork. They were on borrowed time, they knew, and any encounters with the Colombian authorities were best avoided.

The overladen truck chugged north, the river frothing alongside it, and Jet watched the landscape rush by with a sinking stomach. She had believed, before this nightmare, that they were finally on the way somewhere safe, to a new life in Panama, where they would be left alone to raise Hannah in peace. Instead they'd been ruthlessly attacked and hunted across two countries like animals. And perhaps worst of all, they still had no definitive idea who was after them, or why.

As much as Jet wanted to believe that they could have lost their pursuers for good, leaving a dead-end trail with Carl's help, she didn't buy it, and it was with a buzz of anxiety in her core that they continued toward the border, the Colombian jungle seeming to press in from all sides, the future as perilous as any she could imagine.

CHAPTER 4

Frontino, Colombia

Mosises paced angrily in the great room of his remote hilltop estate home, an unlit Cuban cigar clamped between his teeth as he eyed the gathering of men seated on the sofas and chairs assembled around a towering stone fireplace. It had been thirty-six hours since he'd gotten confirmation of his beloved son Jaime's death at the monastery on the outskirts of Santuario, and after sending the Brazilian assassin Fernanda back to the scene in his helicopter two hours earlier, he'd called an emergency gathering of his most trusted subordinates.

Jaime's passing created a power vacuum that the older Mosises would have to step into if his cartel was to survive. A veteran of decades of iron-fisted rule, he knew that any sign of weakness or lack of leadership would be interpreted by those searching for vulnerability as evidence that there was nobody at the helm – which spelled opportunity for the ambitious. But he was too old to operate the cartel on a day-to-day basis for more than a short time, and would need to appoint a new acting head if he were to stave off a disastrous internal civil war.

"I want to understand exactly what went wrong. My son's death will not go unavenged. We will find those responsible if we must scorch the earth to do so," Mosises snarled at the men. "What do we know so far?"

"The police have conducted a thorough search of the entire monastery. His killers are nowhere to be found," Renaldo, Mosises' top capo, said.

"How is that possible?" Mosises snapped.

"It's a mystery we're trying to get to the bottom of, but there are no obvious answers."

"Of course there are. They slipped past the police somehow. We simply need to understand how they did it, so we can pick up their scent." Mosises paused, chewing at the stub of cigar in his mouth with impatience. "I have enlisted the help of the woman I told you about. She has personal business with Jaime's murderers." He withdrew the cigar and stared at the mangled butt, then tossed it into the fireplace with disgust. "She's a hired assassin and highly competent, but she was also there when Jaime was killed. So while I'm confident in her abilities, I don't want to depend on them. Every asset we have – every cop, soldier, customs official in our pay – I want them all on the lookout for these people. A man with a broken hand, a woman, and a child. We should be able to find them. This is our country – how far could they get?"

Renaldo nodded. "Time is not working in our favor. It's been...too long for my liking. I'll put the word out, but as you know, our reach diminishes as we get further from Medellín, and with over a day having gone by with no leads..."

Mosises' eyes blazed. "They are not to escape! There is no price too high for their heads. I want this Brazilian, Fernanda, given anything she wants, but I also want an eye kept on her. Trust no one. There is too much we don't understand about this situation, and what we don't know could get us killed." His tone softened. "I have already spoken to a few of my best contacts and informed them that there is a handsome reward for the first to bring me information about these people. Make sure that message circulates to everyone in the field."

The men rose, the meeting over, and Mosises motioned to two handsome, impeccably groomed men near the back of the room, decked out in obviously expensive clothes and arrogant expressions. They joined him as the rest trooped out, and he moved to the bar in the corner of the room and poured three glasses a quarter full of amber rum.

"I'm sorry for your loss," said Felix, the younger of the pair.

"You and Ramón are my choices to run the cartel once Jaime's killers have been punished. Do not fail me," Mosises said. Ramón and Felix were his nephews, and they were smart, ruthless, and dependable – and most importantly, entirely loyal.

"We won't," Felix assured him. "How would you like us to proceed?"

"Give Fernanda all the room she wants, but assume she has her own agenda. And I want you to make it clear to our allies that there is nothing more important than ending this quickly. I will not tolerate any more slip-ups."

"Where should we begin?" Ramon asked.

"Ramón, go to the monastery. Use whatever means you like to extract the information we require. Felix, I want you in Bogotá come morning, working every contact you have. Between the military, the police, the intelligence service… These people will be trying to escape. They'll be tired, in a strange country, looking for a way out. I want all the seaports watched. There are only so many ways for them to get out of Colombia. I want those sealed off."

Ramón nodded. His black hair was slick with pomade, and his otherwise handsome face was marred by a cruel mouth and eyes slightly too close together for comfortable symmetry.

"I shall do as you ask." Ramón took a moment, thinking. "What if they've gone to ground? If they head south, toward Ecuador, there are hundreds of places they could disappear."

"A white man, woman, and child?" Felix snapped, his tone derisive. "You don't think they would be noticed by someone?" He looked at Mosises. "We should get their descriptions broadcast to every cop in Colombia. And plant news stories in the media. The more people looking for them, the better our odds."

"I already considered that, but rejected it. If someone outside of our sphere of influence captured them, it would decrease our ability to exact a swift vengeance. We want to find them, not have to deal with them in the system," Mosises said dismissively.

"If the police are lucky enough to stumble across them, then it would be just a matter of price for us to take them," Felix pressed.

Mosises regarded him seriously. "Maybe you're right. Put the word out however you think best, but don't come and tell me that we can't get to them because the courts have them. That will not be an acceptable outcome. Am I clear?"

Felix and Ramón exchanged a look. Mosises was distraught at losing Jaime, and neither of them wanted to incur his wrath. Felix shifted from foot to foot nervously. "Perhaps we should keep it within our group for now. You have a valid concern – depending upon which jurisdiction they were arrested in, it could be difficult, and if one of our rivals heard about our troubles, it could bring unwanted attention our way…"

"This Fernanda is our best bet at this point. It's personal with her now as well. I trust she'll find them or die trying," Mosises said.

Ramón rose with determination. "I'll be back at the monastery in an hour. The plane is full and the pilot's waiting for my arrival."

"I want regular reports."

"You shall have them."

CHAPTER 5

Medellín, Colombia

Drago stood on the street corner, watching the entrance of the restaurant where one of his top informers worked – *La Parrilla Brasiliana*. He had arrived back home to Medellín the night before, and had already visited a half-dozen watering holes where the unsavory gathered to commiserate or deal. Aside from the usual scuttlebutt, he'd picked up nothing of note. But he was patient, although keenly aware that the clock was ticking.

He'd traveled to Panama after interrogating the Chilean crime boss and found the skipper of the fishing boat that had been ordered to bring Matt from the huge cargo vessel that had later been found adrift off Nicaragua. Once Drago had exerted his powerful form of persuasion, he'd learned that his quarry hadn't been on the ship as expected – a Brazilian who was pursuing Matt had taken his place.

That made no sense to Drago, although his alarms were triggered at the mention of the Brazilian. Was it possible his client had hired another contractor to pursue the same target? That was a massive professional no-no, but Drago was an adult, and he knew the group he was working for well enough to understand that it was capable of anything.

Before the skipper died, he revealed that he'd overheard the Brazilian telling one of the Panamanians that their target was in Colombia, and that the key to finding him was to lure his girlfriend to the boat and capture her. That hadn't gone as planned, which confirmed Drago's experience with the mystery woman who'd shot him at the river in Chile. Whoever she was, she'd shown herself to be beyond lethal. He still had the stitches to prove it.

Drago's sources in Panama hadn't been able to come up with any further information beyond a photo of the woman being circulated by the police – which might or might not prove worth the paper it was printed on if she ever surfaced there. Highly unlikely, in Drago's professional opinion.

But at least now he had a face. Admittedly one that probably little resembled her now, given the woman's apparent knowledge of tradecraft, but it was a starting point. He'd spent the prior evening putting out feelers, showing the photo around and gauging the responses he got like a connoisseur evaluating a rare wine. That everyone would lie to him was a given, and it was often in what went unsaid that value lay. A telltale flicker, a blink, a sidelong glance, a twitch – these were the clues around which the game revolved.

His temples pulsed with a headache that had been coming and going since Panama, occasionally accompanied by dizzy spells. He'd researched blows to the head and concluded that it was an expected byproduct of the trauma he'd endured in Chile, and had shrugged them off. He'd endured far worse and still carried out his assignments. This was an annoying wrinkle to the disaster that had so far been this contract, but it wouldn't stop him. Nothing on earth would, at this point.

Drago crossed the darkened street and pushed through the wooden doors into the foyer of the restaurant, whose walls were painted in Day-Glo colors and adorned by concert and album release posters of long-forgotten new-wave bands from the eighties. The restaurant specialized in grilled meat, Brazilian style, on skewers brought tableside from a wood-fired grill by fawning servers. The food was good, not great, but the attached lounge was one of Drago's staples for information gathering, primarily because the restaurant owner could be found tending bar from twilight to closing time.

Drago ignored the hostess, a breathtaking beauty who was holding a menu with a blank look on her gorgeous face. He pushed through a beaded curtain adjacent to a DJ booth, replete with thousands of vinyl records and a lighting rig that flashed and strobed to rival the

27

trendiest discos in town. Depeche Mode blared from JBL speakers loud enough to make most of the diners wince, and Drago wondered to himself for the thousandth time how the place stayed in business.

The owner, Isaac, a forty-something geek with five days of salt-and-pepper grizzle on his lean face, his sparse beard compensating for the thinning sprigs of hair atop his egg-shaped head, looked up from his position at the bar. Isaac was a fixture in the restaurant, which prospered in spite of him rather than due to his throwback musical stylings and lackluster menu. Framed flyers behind him announced raves from decades earlier, featuring Isaac in his incarnation as DJ Ice – a period when the young man had transitioned from being a nerdy shut-in wannabe who wore black at all times and for whom the forgettable music of androgynous Brits was a kind of gospel, into a semipopular Medellín club DJ who had enjoyed a decade-long run in the nineties.

Drago knew Isaac had taken his savings, mostly accumulated from his inheritance when his parents died, and opened the restaurant as a kind of shrine to his glory years, a place where the music of Flock of Seagulls and The Cure was always blaring and the good old days had never faded. At least that was his vision. The result had proved to be less than popular as diners objected to the din, especially so when complaints were universally met by an indignant Isaac inviting them to find the door if they didn't enjoy his theme. He seemed uniquely blind to the effect his attitude had on business, and was now the lord of a kind of musical purgatory, forced to augment his income by dealing psychedelics and ecstasy, and acting as a repository for rumors and trends in the Colombian underworld.

"*Hola*, Isaac. How goes it?" Drago asked as he walked across the empty black and white tiled barroom floor to where Isaac stood, stork-like, his eyes slightly bugging out of his ferret face, looking for all the world like a guilty child molester – which wasn't far from the truth, Drago suspected.

"Ah, you know. Fighting the battles. Doing what I must to survive." Isaac lowered a headset he'd been using to queue up the next set of songs remotely and smiled humorlessly at Drago. "What can I get you?"

"Bottle of water and a shot of Jack," Drago said, waiting for the expected outraged response, which wasn't long in coming.

"*I. Don't. Sell. Water.* That's a scam. I have purified water in a glass. No bottles. Clean as anything the megacorporations peddle. Cleaner, actually."

"Oh, that's right. I forgot. Then a *glass* of water and a shot of Jack."

Isaac cared passionately about some unusual things. The first time Drago had dined at the restaurant he'd been chastised by Isaac when he'd asked for a bottle of water – a staple anywhere else in Latin America, but not so on Isaac's turf. The experience had secretly amused him to the point where he asked for one whenever he came for a drink, always with the same result. Isaac's lack of self-awareness was stunning to Drago, and he never tired of twisting that knife.

Isaac slapped a shot glass onto the bar and poured it to the top with bourbon, and then went to a cooler by the side and poured a glass of water. When he returned, Drago grinned humorlessly and toasted him.

"So what have you heard? You called?"

Isaac had phoned Drago that afternoon and told him to come by. He'd refused to talk on the phone, which was par for the course with them both.

"Yeah. It may not be related, or it might be."

Drago nodded and drained half the Jack. This was the usual gibberish preamble he knew he'd have to tolerate before Isaac spat out whatever he'd heard. "I understand."

"There was a big shoot-out last night. South of here." Isaac lowered his voice, even though the bar was empty at the early hour. "They say Mosises' son, Jaime, was killed."

"Mosises?" Drago knew the name. Everyone in Medellín knew it, but he played dumb, forcing Isaac to talk. The more he spoke, the better Drago could evaluate how much of his account was lies.

"Head of the cartel that runs the area. Ruthless. His son, Jaime, had been the face guy for years, but Mosises built it from nothing, and he's still the power behind it."

"What does that have to do with the people I'm looking for?"

"Maybe nothing. But the rumor from my sources in the police is that there was a woman involved."

Drago's eyes narrowed. "Involved how?"

Isaac looked away. "I don't know. Just that a woman was part of the fight. This comes third hand."

"Any description?"

"Not really. You know how that works. But this is where it gets really interesting: there was also a male shooter with a broken hand. A gringo. You mentioned your guy had one, right?"

Drago held Isaac's stare. "I might have."

"Word on the street is that Mosises is looking for them. But that's all I have."

"Bullshit. What does that mean, word on the street? You're either looking or you aren't."

"It's weird. Just a few whispers. I tried to find out more, but it dried up. Seems like only the top dogs in the Mosises cartel know what's going on. They're on red alert now that Jaime's taking the dirt nap."

Drago nodded again. Of course they would be. Information in this case was power. When a major crime figure went down, everyone's position in the organization was in question. Drago expected Mosises' operation was no different, which meant that getting more details was going to be difficult, if not impossible. He could find someone and torture them, but they'd have to be pretty high in Mosises' crew to know anything, and it sounded like right now the cartel was where Drago was: looking for phantoms.

"Who's next in line for Jaime's spot?" Drago asked.

"There are a number of contenders. Two nephews – Felix and Ramón. A cousin: Renaldo. Those are the main ones. Then there's Paulo and Estéban, but they're not as tight, at least as far as I know."

Drago chewed on the information for a while and then slipped a hundred-dollar bill to Isaac. "That's for the water." He slid another four hundred folded tightly. "And the drink."

"If I'd have known you were willing to pay those kinds of rates, I'd have offered you the bottle. You like the new girl working the door? She can be arranged." Isaac winked conspiratorially. "I hear she's a virgin."

Drago smiled. "I'm sure she is, every night."

Isaac laughed, and then his face grew serious. "I'll call if I hear anything more."

Drago made for the beaded curtain as The Cult's "Love Removal Machine" blasted over the speakers. He waved nonchalantly, unwilling to display his excitement at the lead, and called out to Isaac over his shoulder as he exited.

"Do that."

CHAPTER 6

Santuario, Colombia

Fernanda paced outside the crime-scene tape draped from wooden poles encircling the tram station at the base of the monastery hill, Ramón by her side. "How is it possible that the police still don't know how they escaped? Or where they went?" she seethed.

"You know everything I do. They've been interrogating the monks all day, but there's a practical limit to the amount of leverage the police can exert. They're cooperating, but their stories are basically the same. It all happened fast. Nobody had any idea what was going on, then the lights went out, and then there was shooting…" Ramón shook his head. "Our man will be down shortly. He's stepped in and is now overseeing the investigation. The locals aren't up to the challenge, and they were eager to hand it off."

"Who is he?"

"Alberto Viega. Captain. From Medellín. The federal police have taken over the case, and he's the top official in that group who handles fieldwork."

"You had a hand in him getting involved?"

Ramón smiled slightly. "Let's just say that he took an immediate interest once he heard that Mosises' son had been murdered."

Fernanda looked around. There were several dozen officers of various stripes loitering near the base of the monastery, and at least fifty more up top, she knew from Ramón's reports. If the ones above were as useful as these, they might as well be deaf and blind. Nobody was getting anything done, and every minute that went by was another advantage for her quarry. "When can I talk to him? Privately?" she snapped.

Ramón shrugged. "He said shortly. That was twenty minutes ago."

"What about the equipment I requested?" Fernanda asked.

"We're working on it."

"But you can get it?"

"Of course. But if you don't mind me saying so, some of it's rather…I mean, it seems like hunting squirrels with heavy artillery."

Fernanda's expression was stony. "You don't need to understand my methods."

"I meant no disrespect."

Fernanda softened. Ramón was about her age, certainly no older, and wasn't the enemy. "I'm sorry. I haven't slept in two days, my…friend…was killed by these people only a couple of nights ago…I didn't mean to bite your head off."

"Maybe you should get a few hours of rest? Nothing happens quickly in Colombia."

"Right. So I've heard. But I need to accelerate things. We're losing them – they could be anywhere by now."

"Well, not really. I mean, in theory, yes, but there are roadblocks in place, and the police have mobilized and are on the lookout for anyone suspicious…"

"Suspicious. But you haven't circulated the woman's photo or the description of the man?"

"No. Mosises feels it would be ill-advised. He's the boss."

"I suppose I have to agree with him, to a point. These are professionals. Our best odds lie in tracking them from their escape point, not shotgunning out a description and hoping for the best. Besides, if some local cop runs across them and tries to take them, they'll kill him in seconds, and then any element of surprise we have will be lost."

"You still believe they'll make for one of the borders?"

"Think about it. They're in a strange country. Being pursued. They were just involved in a minor war here. Wouldn't you want out as soon as possible?"

"Sure, but it's not as easy as it sounds. We've put word out at all the ports along the Caribbean and Pacific coasts, and if strangers start nosing around for passage north, we'll know in seconds. And we have people watching the airports – Mosises has clout there. He agreed to circulate their description among the airport security force and the immigration people, so the borders are effectively locked down. They try to get on a plane, we'll be all over them."

"They could charter one. They wouldn't be stupid enough to try to fly commercial. There's no chance they make a mistake like that. These people are smart. And they've got skills. As a half dozen of your best cartel badasses lying dead up there should tell you."

"The only thing left are the land routes, and we're watching those, too."

"Borders can be porous."

"True, but these aren't superhighways we're talking. And there aren't a hundred crossing points – only three. Easy enough to watch them."

She frowned and peered up at the monastery. "So far, nothing about this has been easy."

The cable car station began humming as the overhead cables fed through giant metal wheels. Moments later the car arrived from above, and four men hopped down from it, two in uniform, two wearing civilian clothes. Ramón turned and touched Fernanda's elbow. "Come on. Let's go for a walk," he whispered. "Viega will join us when he can."

Fernanda allowed him to lead her down the hill to where the vehicles were parked. He unlocked the doors to his SUV and moved to the driver's seat. "Get in."

"Are you sure he'll join us?"

"Hundred percent."

They didn't have to wait long. Three minutes later a figure emerged from the shadows and climbed into the rear seat. Ramón twisted toward him. "This is a friend of mine, Fernanda."

"Pleased to meet you," Viega said, taking her hand in his, maintaining the contact just a little too long.

"I'm helping our acquaintance in this sad time," Fernanda said, hoping the reminder of Mosises would force the inspector's attention back to business. It worked, because Viega released her, any trace of good humor gone.

"Here's where we stand," he said. "We've been through the complex with a fine-toothed comb, we've interviewed everyone in triplicate – and other than a handful of bodies, some of them shot with an old crossbow, we've got nothing. Nobody knows who the man and woman were, nobody knows what they were doing at the monastery…" Viega snorted in frustration. "Nobody knows anything."

"That's impossible," Fernanda said.

"Yes, but knowing and proving are two different things, and there are limits to how hard we can push the priests."

"Why?" Fernanda asked quietly.

Viega hesitated. "Because they're…they're holy men, young lady. That affords a certain protection."

"Not from me, it doesn't." Fernanda turned in her seat to fix Viega with a cold stare. "Who's your most promising lead?"

"There's one monk I think knows more than he's letting on. He's polite, answers all our questions, but the others defer to him, and I get the sense he's leaving a lot out. His name's Franco."

"I want him," Fernanda said. "Now would be good."

"I…I can't just haul him somewhere and let you go to work on him," Viega protested.

Fernanda's eyes glittered like obsidian in the faint light. "You can, and you will."

Viega shook his head. "I don't know who you think you are, but this meeting is over," he said, reaching for the door handle.

Ramón cleared his throat. "I understand your reluctance. But these are unusual circumstances. Mosises will be most unhappy to learn that you could have assisted us but chose not to. Most. Unhappy," Ramón said, over-enunciating each syllable.

The blood drained from Viega's face. "There are limits. Even for me."

"No, there aren't," Ramón corrected. "There are only limits to what you're willing to do for us. Let me frame it another way. If you don't bring this Franco to the location of our choosing within the hour, I'm going to make a call that will almost certainly ruin your life. Alternatively, you'll cooperate, and at the end of it, you'll walk away a wealthy enough man so nobody will dare touch you, and with Mosises' full backing. I think you understand what that means. Worst case, a priest dies of a heart attack while helping the authorities with their investigation. It's unfortunate, but is certainly plausible. Some won't be happy, but their protests won't amount to much. Whereas you will have your every fantasy realized. To me it's not a hard choice, but it's not mine to make."

Viega was frozen, and for an instant Fernanda could see the fear in his eyes. It was then that she knew he would agree.

When Viega trudged back up the street to the waiting officers, his shoulders were hunched and he was a different man than the arrogant official who'd met with them.

Ramón glanced at Fernanda and then at the dash clock. "It will be more than an hour. We both know that," he said. "Perhaps two, just to get our hands on the monk."

"Yes, but once we have him, it shouldn't take too long."

Ramón studied her as he started the big motor. "There's a building nearby we can use." He paused. "Are you sure you're comfortable doing this?"

Fernanda smiled, genuinely amused by his question. "I live for it."

CHAPTER 7

Cúcuta, Colombia

Jet and Matt watched Oliveros' truck rumble away after it dropped them on the outskirts of the border city. Hannah was snuffling, having spent much of the trip crying; her temperature had slowly climbed as they worked their way toward Cúcuta, which had taken longer than they'd thought. Jet looked at her watch – it was already ten p.m. Engine problems had afflicted the truck when it hit high altitude crossing the Andes, and they'd spent three hours by the roadside as Oliveros worked on the carburetor, eventually succeeding in coaxing it back to life.

Matt scanned the surprisingly modern buildings.

"At least we aren't in the boonies anymore," he said. "It should be easier to stay anonymous here than in a one-horse town."

"You'd think so, but so far our luck hasn't been running that way, has it?"

Matt shook his head. "No, unfortunately it hasn't. Somebody wants us pretty badly, don't they? I've been thinking about it all day. It has to be related to Tara and the diamonds. If I'm right, you're only in danger because you're with me…"

"You're guessing, and I already told you we're not splitting up, so that's not up for discussion." Jet bounced Hannah gently against her hip as she held her. "Let's find someplace for the night."

They set off down a large boulevard and passed a shopping center, the only cars in the lot presumably those of the security guards and cleaning crew. At a busy intersection, Jet flagged down a taxi and asked the driver to take them to the downtown area.

He eyed her doubtfully as she slid into the rear seat. "It's dangerous at this hour," he warned.

"Our hotel lost the reservation. We need someplace inexpensive and quiet," she explained.

"Oh, in that case, there are several near the cathedral. But I wouldn't go for an evening stroll."

"We weren't planning on it."

The drive took five minutes and went by in silence, other than Hannah's occasional mewl. The driver dropped them in front of the church, and after telling them where the hotels were, left them standing on a crumbling sidewalk, the only pedestrians on the street.

"Which one you want to try?" Jet asked.

Matt shrugged. "Doesn't matter to me. Something with two exits, though, just in case."

The first hotel was unsuitable – a three-story colonial building with only a front entrance. The second was better – single-story sprawl, a line of units in bungalows built around a parking area. Jet handled the transaction in the office while Matt waited out of sight with Hannah, and soon they were in the room, which was spare, but serviceable. Jet laid Hannah on one of the two beds while Matt went to the bathroom and wet a hand towel to put on her forehead.

"She's definitely feverish," Jet reported. "We need to get to the clinic first thing tomorrow."

"We can always try the hospital."

Jet shook her head. "Can't risk it. We've come too far to screw up at this point with a document check."

"Then it's aspirin, plenty of water, and rest." Matt checked the time. "Think any markets will be open at this hour? I'm not sure I trust the tap water."

"I'll ask at the office."

"No, I'll go. You stay here with Hannah. A woman on the street at this time of night, alone…would be begging for it."

Jet gazed down at her daughter, the towel soothing her, her eyes

38

closed against the dim light in the room. "No, the hotel people think it's only me staying here, so you can't suddenly appear, asking for directions." She moved to the door. "Don't worry. I can take care of myself."

Matt laughed. "Armed and dangerous. I don't like the odds of anyone trying to mug you."

"Let's hope the local criminal element shows better sense than that."

The woman at the office directed her to a market two blocks away, and she hurried along the sidewalk, her strides long and fluid, covering a lot of ground though she seemed to move normally. The exercise felt good after being crammed into the truck for fourteen hours, and she made it to the shop in a few minutes.

The shopkeeper sold her four one-liter bottles of water and a container of Gatorade for Hannah, along with a collection of candy bars and chips – the only packaged food in the store – and she set off back to the hotel, anxious to get back to her daughter.

At the corner a low-slung sedan with a burbling muffler rolled to a stop next to her, and a face leered from the half-lowered passenger window.

"Hey, Mami. You looking for some action?" a pimply-faced youth called to her.

Jet ignored him and continued walking.

"Come on, sugar. Don't be that way," the punk tried again.

Jet's instinct told her to keep her pace measured and stay quiet. Most troublemakers who were stupid enough to say anything wanted attention, not conflict. Then again, if he got out of the car, she'd be forced to take action. He wouldn't unless he planned to assault her – which would be the last thing he ever tried.

The driver muttered an insult and the car pulled off with a screech of rubber. Jet continued walking, her breathing measured, her heart rate relaxed. The pair of toughs had just made the smartest decision of their lives, although they couldn't know how close they'd come.

Jet didn't tell Matt about the near miss, preferring to remain quiet when she reentered the hotel room. Hannah was awake, and Jet's heart lurched when she saw Matt sitting by the bedside, holding the little girl's hand, blotting her head with the towel.

"I brought you something," Jet said as she approached.

Hannah managed a weak smile. "Hot," she said, her voice hoarse.

"Yes, you're sick. Drink this all gone and you'll feel better," Jet instructed as Matt moved away from the bed to make room for her.

Hannah drained the entire bottle of Gatorade but waved off the junk food. Jet and Matt exchanged a worried look. For Hannah to turn down candy…

Jet tried a smile. "All right, darling. We're going to take you to the doctor tomorrow and make you all better. Try to get some sleep, okay?"

Hannah nodded and closed her eyes.

When she was resting quietly, Matt joined Jet at a small wooden table near the only window. She whispered to him as they eyed Hannah. "I'm going to take a shower. Will you be heartbroken if I sleep with her tonight, instead of you?"

Matt gave her a tired grin. "I'm flattered you have such faith in my stamina after two nights with no shut-eye."

"I figure it never hurts to play to your ego."

"Can I have a rain check? I feel like a zombie right now."

"Of course."

Matt brushed a lock of hair from Hannah's hot, dry forehead. "What's the plan for tomorrow?"

"We take her to the clinic. Hopefully it's nothing. Kids get sick all the time, and her immune system is probably low with all the stress and sleepless nights."

"And then? How do we cross the border without bringing the wrath of the entire Colombian and Venezuelan military down on us?"

Jet shrugged. "I'll do some research in the morning once I can get online. But one thing at a time – first we see to Hannah, and then we'll think of something. We always do." She turned back to Matt and tiptoed to kiss him softly. "You're a good man, Matt."

"You deserve better. I'm lucky to have you."

A smile tugged at the corners of her mouth. "There might be room for two in the shower."

Matt held up his cast. "The doctor said to avoid getting it wet."

"Then we'll have to be careful."

CHAPTER 8

Medellín, Colombia

Drago sat in the back of a neighborhood bar near the edge of the renovated old town, waiting for a return call. He nursed a warming beer that had been on the table for a half hour and took in the shabby crowd of workers and lower-middle-class men sharing the watering hole with him. Though they grew increasingly loud and boisterous as the night wore on, he nonetheless felt at home among them – hiding in plain sight.

He'd called his agent, fed him the details of Mosises' cartel, and asked for some assistance from the client, whose resources were massive and whose reach was global. That had been hours ago, and after circulating through Medellín's seedier boroughs in fruitless search of information, he'd decided to wait for the agent to contact him again.

When the phone buzzed, he took a pull on his beer, forcing himself to wait until it had rung four times. It was the little things that served as giveaways, and it wouldn't do to appear to be too anxious.

Drago answered, and his agent's familiar voice purred in his ear.

"I did as you asked. The client agreed to flex some muscles and just called back. They have located the new cell phone registered to the maid of one of your men, but judging by the traffic on it, she's no ordinary housekeeper."

"Really," Drago said, unsurprised that the NSA would be able to pinpoint a cell in Colombia within a matter of hours.

"She's on the phone an average of six hours a day. Spread out over twelve hours. So it's a safe bet she's the front for your man's comm system with the cartel."

Registering cell phones to maids, drivers, gardeners, and the like was a time-honored tradition for cartel honchos in both Colombia and Mexico. "Which one is it?" Drago asked.

"Renaldo."

"Ah. Where is he?"

The agent gave him an address whose location Drago knew from experience. "That's a whorehouse."

"I don't judge. Although it's hardly surprising that a drug kingpin might enjoy a bit of slap and tickle, is it?"

"Can they intercept his calls and messaging?"

"Negative."

"I thought they could do anything."

"This model phone requires a piece of malware to be downloaded to it in order for anyone to bypass the latest Korean security technology."

"Then what good is knowing he's in the whorehouse?" Drago fumed.

"I've sent you a link where you can download the malware worm. If you can get your hands on the phone, you can load it from your device onto his, and presto."

"And I would do that how?"

"With a micro-cable. The instructions are in the email I sent to the usual address. Read it, download the program, and best of luck. If he moves from the whorehouse, I'll call you back."

"How do I intercept the calls or the messages?"

"You define where you want them forwarded, and it does so in the background without leaving a trace. It's like a Trojan horse. Invisible to the user, but you can either listen in or read along, anonymously. Law enforcement uses it all the time."

Drago hung up and quickly finished his drink. He was only a few minutes from his apartment, where he could get his notebook computer and the cable and be on his way in seconds. What could prove to be more difficult would be locating Renaldo inside the brothel, and then getting to his phone without being discovered.

A refreshing challenge after days of tedium. He hated information gathering, which always seemed like a waste of his time and talents – a necessary evil in his vocation, but uninspiring even under the best of circumstances.

He paid for his beer and slipped out of the bar, just another unfortunate local who'd numbed the worst of the pain for the day and was returning home. As he walked in the crisp high-altitude air, a headache that had been lingering for the last day suddenly worsened, and he sucked in breath as the sidewalk seemed to tilt. He reached out to steady himself against a building until the spell passed. He resumed walking, his pace slower now, and the crude outline of a plan began to form in his mind.

The good news was that the whorehouse Renaldo had chosen was a refurbished colonial mansion in the old section of town, not a defended complex somewhere Drago would have to get past a dozen gunmen. This was a better situation, in that if he was successful, Renaldo would never suspect that Drago was listening to his every word – and right now, the cartel finding Matt and his companions was Drago's only shot.

Drago stopped at his apartment to collect the necessary gear as well as a sound-suppressed Ruger with the serial numbers filed off and two magazines of subsonic ammunition that would make hardly more noise than a champagne bottle popping open. He gulped down three aspirin and dropped the box in his pocket, and then stepped out onto the street and took a taxi to within a block of the whorehouse.

After wandering apparently aimlessly for a few minutes to confirm he hadn't picked up a tail, he covered the rest of the distance on foot. A knock at the ancient door brought a hatchet-faced man in a deep purple suit with a black shirt and matching tie. After a brief discussion, the doorman stepped back so Drago could come in.

He hadn't visited the brothel in almost half a year and didn't recognize anyone but the doorman. The bar downstairs in what had once been the mansion's living room held several dozen young women of varying degrees of beauty, some with skin so light it was almost translucent, others with dusky caramel complexions. Drago ordered a vodka and tonic and swept the room with his gaze, his laptop bag still hanging from his shoulder with the pistol and notebook hidden inside.

A stunning example of Colombian womanhood clad only in black stockings, a garter belt, a thong, and a skimpy top sidled up to him. The aroma of cinnamon and vanilla announced her arrival, and when she smiled, her teeth shone as white as polar ice.

"Hello, handsome. See anything you like?" she asked in a musical voice.

"I do now," Drago said. "What are you drinking?"

"What are you?"

Drago held the sweating glass up in a toast. "Vodka and tonic."

"Can I taste it?" she asked.

"Among other things." He handed her the glass and she took a sip, considered it, and handed it back to him.

"I like that."

"Then you should have one. What's your name?"

"Alana."

Drago nodded to the bartender. "Alana would like one of these."

"Very good, sir," the young man replied.

Five minutes later Drago was following Alana up the stairs, marveling at the view. He'd requested the brothel's most luxurious suite, and when he was told it was occupied, he'd appeared disappointed but was secretly delighted. He'd spent time in that room, and the odds were nearly a hundred percent that Renaldo was there tonight – it carried a considerable premium, which few of the bordello's weeknight clientele would have been willing to pay for an hour's diversion.

When they reached the third floor, Drago pointed at a door near the end of the hall – one down from the master, outside of which a sour-faced young bodyguard sat in a folding chair, scowling at them suspiciously. Drago waved with his drink hand, pretending to be tipsy. "Let's use that one," he suggested.

Alana smiled professionally and teetered over to it on translucent plastic stripper heels. "Perfect."

You have no idea how, Drago thought, and followed her inside under the watchful eye of the bodyguard. When the door closed behind them, Alana twisted the lock with a loud snap. "Nice and private," she said with another grin, and Drago mirrored the smile as he moved to the bed, noting with satisfaction that there was no sound coming from the room next door.

CHAPTER 9

Havana Harbor, Cuba

The lights of Havana twinkled along the shore as a matte gray Cuban navy patrol boat cut through the light wind chop. Two dozen marines sat on steel benches as the vessel made its way toward the harbor mouth, past deteriorating commercial piers that hosted the darkened hulks of cargo ships.

The half century of American sanctions against the island nation had drained the port of much of its prosperity, and the waterfront buildings that lined the *malecón* were weather-battered and decaying, many dating from the 1800s or earlier, veterans of countless hurricanes and generations of neglect.

Major Luis Fuentes stood beside the helmsman as the boat neared a commercial fishing vessel moored in the anchorage by the fort that guarded the harbor approach. The boat was low in the water, obviously overloaded, and in poor shape even by Cuban standards. Fuentes squinted in the gloom and nodded to the helmsman.

"That's it. *El Limon*," Fuentes said, and then called out to one of the crewmen at the bow, where a .50-caliber machine gun that was older than the gunman stood on a support rod next to a spotlight. "Showtime. Hit it."

The high-wattage beam blinked to life and settled on the fishing boat. Fuentes could make out five fishermen on deck, all of whom were dazed, blinded by the light as the military vessel pulled closer.

Fuentes spoke into the hailing system handset and his voice boomed overhead through amplified speakers. "Vessel *El Limon*. This is the harbor patrol. Prepare for boarding."

The men on the fishing boat froze in place. The Havana harbor patrol had a nasty reputation for being trigger happy, and nobody wanted to be tomorrow's obituary – or slipped over the side several miles offshore with a few cinderblocks chained to their ankles.

Havana Harbor had a long and colorful history as a Spanish port that had been plagued by pirates, brigands, and scoundrels of all shapes and sizes. The current political masters, for all their rhetoric, had proved no better than the island's earlier leadership, and the country had suffered while those in power grew rich, all the while trumpeting equality with the fervor of the newly converted.

The fishermen were accustomed to the rule of the sword, and didn't question being boarded in the middle of the night while at anchor. It was the captain's problem, ultimately, as long as nobody got heroic while the authorities went about their business.

The gunboat pulled alongside the fishing scow, and Fuentes' nose crinkled at the stink that wafted from the deck.

"Jesus, that's foul," he said, and coughed into his hand. Once the lines were secured, the marines rose from the benches, their rifle barrels gleaming in the moonlight. "Stay here," Fuentes growled, and made his way over the gunwale to the fishing boat.

The old captain poked his head out of the fishing boat's pilothouse and his expression set in a frown of resignation and annoyance. Fuentes walked to the door and nodded to him. "Inspection. Routine."

"I already handled this with one of your people – Gomez."

"Nobody told me. So you'll have to handle it with me."

Fuentes pushed past the captain and entered the small pilothouse, and then moved to the stairway leading belowdecks. The captain sighed as the major eyed the passageway. Fuentes cleared his throat. "If I go down there and find dozens of stowaways bound for a run to Florida, you're done, old-timer. But if I decide to have a glass of rum with you and sort things out right now instead, well, you can live to fight another day and be on your way whenever you like, with my assurance you won't be disturbed."

"I told you, I already paid Gomez."

"He died this afternoon. Massive heart attack. Why do you think I'm out at this hour when it would normally be his shift?" Fuentes shook his head. "But if you already paid, we can work something out. Frankly, this isn't a negotiation. You either pay or go to prison. However, I'm a fair man. So we can cut the usual figure in half."

The captain slumped onto a bench seat beside the chart table. "That means I'll lose money on this run."

"Think of it as an unexpected surge in the price of fuel. A tax. That's really all it is."

Ten minutes later Fuentes returned to the patrol boat, his pocket fatter by two thousand American dollars. He knew the captain would still turn a profit, but it would only be hundreds of dollars for his trouble this time out. Not Fuentes' problem. Some months were better than others in all businesses, and the world wasn't fair.

The trafficking of the desperate, north to the U.S., was a well-established enterprise. The going rate could run anywhere from five hundred dollars to five thousand per head, depending upon how stable the vessel was and the likelihood of making it without drowning. The Cuban authorities were chartered with stopping the exodus at their shore, but as with so much in the world, compromises were made. Fuentes' take-home pay as a career officer was just short of five hundred dollars a month. But he was able to squirrel away up to several thousand more, subject to how many others had to be compensated along the way – in tonight's case, the patrol boat captain, who would distribute funds to the rest of his crew as he saw fit, and the harbor patrol commander, who had allowed an army officer use of his boat. When it was all paid out, half the money would be gone, leaving Fuentes with a tidy thousand-dollar profit to spend on his mistress, who, even in an impoverished society like Cuba, wasn't cheap to keep happy.

Fuentes watched the hull of the fishing boat disappear off the stern as the patrol boat made a wide turn and retraced its course into the harbor, and looked down at his watch. He could be back on land and pay everyone in an hour or less, leaving plenty of time with his delicate hothouse flower before he went home to his wife and four children, exhausted after another long, thankless shift in the service of his country.

Fuentes smiled to himself.

Whoever thought Cuba didn't understand capitalism hadn't been there.

CHAPTER 10

Santuario, Colombia

Two feral cats battled with each other at the end of a small street in the industrial area of town, their howls of pain and outrage the only sound other than the distant rumble of highway traffic as heavy trucks labored up the grade to the west. A pair of headlights bounced down the cobblestones and coasted to a stop in front of an old single-story warehouse. The decaying façade advertised tires repaired inexpensively and brakes resurfaced at a discount. Half the paint was peeled off the distressed surface from years of neglect, lending the building an air of abandonment, which was in fact the case.

A wide steel roll-up door faced the street, and a small metal pedestrian entrance stood with its door ajar beside it. In the shadows, Fernanda and Ramón watched as Viega stepped down from the passenger side of the Suburban and walked to the rear. He half-dragged a cuffed figure from the vehicle; the captive's close-cropped hair and vestments clearly identified him as one of the monastery monks.

When the pair arrived at the entrance, Ramón stepped aside. Viega pushed Franco through before stepping back, as though afraid if he crossed the threshold, he'd never be allowed to leave.

"He's all yours. Call me when you're through," Viega said, and hurried back to the SUV, not awaiting any response.

Ramón took Franco's arm and led him to a metal chair in the middle of the room, the only illumination a single bulb hanging from a frayed black wire that was suspended from a support beam overhead. Fernanda slammed the door shut and slid the bolt closed as Ramón forced the monk into the chair. When she approached him, his eyes were unafraid – a man at peace with himself, she thought.

"You've been lying to the police long enough. I need to know what you do, and I need to know it now. We've lost enough time," she announced as she pulled on a pair of latex gloves with a snap. Franco's eyes drifted to a toolbox sitting open on a wooden crate just out of the halo of light thrown by the lamp, and then they returned to hers, meeting her gaze unflinchingly.

"I have no idea what you're talking about," Franco said, his tone calm.

"You do, and you'll tell me. The man and woman escaped from the monastery. They had to have assistance. I think you helped them or know who did. If I'm wrong, I'll repeat my interrogation with every one of your brethren until I get it out of you. Do you understand?"

"I understand that you believe something that isn't true."

Fernanda sighed. "Let me tell you a story. When I was just a little girl, I had a brother. His name is unimportant. What *is* important is that he was a beautiful spirit – generous, kind, friendly. When he was nine, he began his service in our town's church, as an altar boy. A year later he was found hanging in the outhouse, where he'd rigged a noose out of wire and strangled himself by stepping off the toilet." Fernanda paused and studied Franco's face. "His last moments had to be excruciatingly painful, because his neck didn't break – the wire sliced through his flesh and he bled to death." She stepped nearer. "He killed himself because of the shame and self-hatred that consumed him, because of what was done to him by the town priest. Stories circulated after the good father was transferred elsewhere – other little boys with horrific accounts of their own – but by that time he had escaped the townspeople's revenge, spirited away by his superiors."

"I'm truly sorry for your loss, but what does that have to do with me?" Franco asked.

"I mention it because I want you to know that, unlike everyone else who has interrogated you, I'm not impressed by your position in the Church. If anything, it makes it easier for me to do what I must in order to drag the truth from you. Because, in a way, I'm doing it for my brother, not just for expedience."

"I want a lawyer."

Fernanda smiled, and the effect was blood-chilling. "You misunderstand your circumstance."

"I'm not saying another word until I have my lawyer."

"Oh, you will talk. You'll beg to talk, but only when I allow you to. First, I get my revenge for my brother. Only after I'm tired will I give you the opportunity to speak." Fernanda nodded, and Ramón slipped a knotted rag around Franco's head, forcing the knot into his mouth and tying the loose ends behind his head.

When Ramón was finished, Fernanda studied Franco with cool detachment and moved to the toolbox. "I'm afraid I didn't have time to gather all the instruments I would have liked. I originally conceived of your questioning as a perfect opportunity to use some of the more popular techniques from your organization's infamous inquisition period, but circumstances didn't deliver a rack or a Judas chair. Do you know what a Judas chair is?"

Franco's eyes widened.

"It was popular in obtaining confessions from the particularly stubborn. It's a chair with a sharp, pointed pyramid for a seat. The victim is seated on it, naked, with the point inserted into an orifice, and then as questioning progressed, lowered inch by inch. That sounded perfect for what I intended; but alas, there are none to be found nearby and we're in a bit of a rush."

Franco struggled against the bindings.

"Another popular technique was called the strappado. That's where the victim would be suspended from the rafters by his wrists shackled behind him. The muscles in his arms would rip from the weight, and then the ligaments in the shoulders, and then, as he was bounced by the interrogators, his shoulders would break. It sounds excruciatingly painful, doesn't it? Leave it to the Church to innovate convincing ways to extract information." She looked at Ramón. "Unfortunately, the overhead beams don't look like they'll support your weight – they're too old – and I'd hate to pull the building down on top of us. So I'll have to make do with more modern techniques, which I promise you are every bit as painful, if not more so."

She pulled on a green plastic apron and cinched it around her waist, and then held up a pair of cables with stripped copper wire ends. "The Inquisition didn't have the benefit of electricity. If it had, it could have dispensed with many of its tricks and gone straight to judicious application of voltage to sensitive areas of the body. I can assure you that it exceeds the worst you might experience with the old-school approaches. But don't take my word for it. You're about to discover firsthand that technology has made marvelous strides since the days of Torquemada."

Franco closed his eyes, realization dawning on him that this wasn't an act to frighten him into divulging what he knew.

An hour later Fernanda removed the apron and tossed it on the cement floor. Ramón stood by the door, his complexion ashen and his eyes averted. She noted Franco's slumped form and moved to the toolbox, where she withdrew a hand towel and cleaned her face before slipping off the gloves and dropping them onto the crate beside it.

"Your people will dispose of this?" she asked, nodding at Franco.

"Of course. His passing will be described by the coroner as the result of heart failure. Natural causes."

"Then let's go. We're already two days behind. Call Viega and arrange for us to have access to the area of the monastery where the tunnel starts. I want to be there in ten minutes."

"Will do."

"Do you know anything about the river he described?"

"Not really. But we'll be able to track it on my phone." He seemed to want to say something more, but instead dialed Viega and held the cell to his ear.

After a brief discussion, Ramón terminated the call and turned to her. "He'll arrange it. We're to be at the cable car station as soon as possible."

"He understands his men are not to touch the area?"

"I made it abundantly clear."

She took a final look at the dead monk and nodded. "At least now we're getting somewhere. We may be too late, but at least we're in the game again. We should have done this yesterday."

Ramón followed her stare to where Franco sat. "There's no question in your mind that he told you everything?"

"None at all. Nobody can withstand that kind of abuse and lie successfully." She pushed past him to the door and slid the bolt open. "Nobody."

When they arrived at the monastery, Viega was waiting for them at the upper cable-car station. Only a few cops were in evidence, all spectacularly disinterested in the new arrivals. Viega glanced at Fernanda as they walked toward the darkened building, the flashlight she'd brought swinging easily in her hand.

"I don't suppose we'll be seeing any more of the good father?" he asked.

"You have nothing to worry about. We'll handle the autopsy and quash any inquiry. You're effectively above suspicion," Ramón said.

"Well, turns out he was holding out on us, so your methods worked," Viega conceded.

They moved into the monastery's storage chamber, located the hidden access lever on the cabinet, and swung it open. Viega peered inside and retrieved his own penlight from his jacket pocket as Fernanda switched hers on. She took three steps into the passage and turned to Viega. "This is as far as you go, for now."

Viega looked insulted, but held his tongue. Ramón tilted his head in apology and followed Fernanda into the dank entry. They followed the sloping tunnel floor to the remains of the iron grid and were soon standing on the riverbank, moonlight silvering the rushing water. Ramón pointed downstream at the collection of wooden rowboats on the bank.

Fernanda nodded. "Looks like we've found their route. Fifty-to-one that they went downstream in one of those boats. Check with the local cops – there will be a boat missing. What's south of here?"

Ramón tapped his cell phone screen to life and studied a small map. "A few small bergs. The next real town is La Virginia."

"How far?"

"About twenty kilometers."

Fernanda eyed the boats first, and then Ramón. "Let's get back to Viega. We'll want the cops in La Virginia to help us with questioning the locals. If we're lucky, our little family will have left a trail. It may be cold by now, but it will be there. We just have to know where to look."

Ramón looked at his watch. "It'll be light in just a few more hours."

Fernanda gave him a hard stare. "Viega's going to have to wake the La Virginia police. We've lost enough time. At this point, every minute counts."

CHAPTER 11

Medellín, Colombia

Drago sat up in bed and pulled his shirt on. Alana was breathing softly beside him, the Rohypnol he'd dropped into her drink while she used the bathroom having worked its magic, but not before she delivered a workmanlike performance complete with impressive gymnastics and a faux screaming climax worthy of an Academy Award. She would be out for the duration, which suited him perfectly – he'd been listening for sounds of life next door, and it had been silent since their arrival.

After shutting the lights off so he wouldn't be visible from the street, Drago slipped on his pants and shoes, slung his bag over his shoulder, and moved to the window. He pushed the curtain aside and looked down at the gloomy backyard, the neighboring houses across the enclosed area completely dark. There was nobody outside, which he'd been sure would be the case at such a late hour – essential if his scheme to get into Renaldo's room without being detected was to work.

When he tried the latch, it was unlocked, which fit – there was no reason to lock a third-story window, and the cleaning staff would open them every morning to air out the rooms as they went about their business. With any luck, Renaldo's would also be unlocked. Which left creeping along the narrow molding to the next sill, sliding the window frame up, and pulling himself into the suite without waking either the cartel honcho or his whore.

Who would hopefully be out for the count by now.

If not, plan B was to neutralize them both, take Renaldo's phone, and hope that some germane information came across it before his corpse was discovered.

Drago studied the molding he'd have to traverse in order to reach the suite next door. It was no more than three inches deep and sculpted from concrete, which could be crumbly given the age of the building. He took three deep breaths, patted the butt of the sound-suppressed pistol in his belt, and eased himself into the night, feeling for the molding with his toes.

Once he was sure it wasn't going to collapse under his weight, he inched along the exterior, back to the wall, taking his time. For anyone else the experience would have been paralyzing, but for Drago it caused no more anxiety than crossing the street – he'd been in far more precarious circumstances, after all, and handled them with aplomb.

After thirty seconds, he reached the master suite window and was relieved to see a six-inch gap at the bottom, which would make entering child's play. The frame creaked softly as he lifted it, and once he had sufficient space, he pulled himself inside.

Drago was in the sitting area he remembered well from his stays. His quarry would be in the adjacent bedroom. The connecting door was half open, and Drago heard snoring over the muted jangle of a radio playing pop music at low volume. He crept toward it, eyes sweeping the space to ensure he didn't miss the man's cell phone on either of the two tables in the sitting room. He stopped at a dress jacket draped across the back of a chair and felt in it.

Nothing other than a package of cigarettes and a lighter.

Drago smirked in the darkness. It would have been too easy if the phone had been in the jacket. That wasn't how life worked – at least, not Drago's.

He cocked his head, listening for movement: the rustle of a sheet, a change in the sonorous drone of male snores. After several agonizing moments he was satisfied that the room's occupants were fast asleep, and he moved through the doorway, his steps soundless.

The bed was a jumble of forms, and it took Drago a moment to make out the single expected male and two smaller females, their nudity stark against the white sheets. He scanned the room and spotted the blinking red of an LED from the nightstand nearest the slumbering Renaldo. Cursing silently that he would have to get that close to the man, he crept toward the bed, which as he drew nearer, reeked of cheap floral perfume and sex.

Drago's fingers were closing on the cell when one of the girls stirred. He froze, not daring to breathe lest the slightest movement rouse her. She groaned softly and shifted on the bed, and then resumed sleeping. Drago's eyes darted to an empty bottle of rum on the dresser near the window and thanked Providence for the threesome's appetite for alcohol. If they'd been doing cocaine they would have been up all night, and he'd have had to come up with another approach.

Drago lifted the phone from the table and retraced his steps to the sitting room, where he quickly plugged the cable into the cell and uploaded the tracking software, which took twenty seconds. He checked to ensure his effort had been successful and rebooted the phone, wincing as it beeped softly when he powered it back on.

His return to the bedroom was anticlimactic, and he was in and out in moments. Drago stopped in the doorway and eyed the tableau of the inebriated drug lord and his companions, and then turned and took measured steps back to the sitting room window. His errand concluded, the only thing remaining to be done was to get back to his bed without plunging three stories to his death.

The return trip along the ledge posed no undue challenge, however, and thirty seconds later he was standing outside his window, eyes scanning the darkness.

Once in his room, he powered on his phone and activated the tracking application. It blinked at him in the dark and an icon showing no activity appeared on the screen, indicating it was working, waiting patiently for an incoming call or text. He scrolled to another icon, selected it, and found himself with a list of Renaldo's text messages.

Two hours later he'd finished his scan of the cartel capo's phone contents; but other than enough evidence to convict Renaldo ten times over, he had nothing. There were only references to looking for the targets, putting the word out, alerting immigration, but nothing that indicated the cartel had any idea where to find their quarry.

Drago swallowed the bitter disappointment and stripped off his clothes before climbing back into bed. He set his cell on the nightstand beside him and rolled toward Alana, who would be unconscious for at least another few hours before awakening with the hangover of her life. His phone would notify him whenever Renaldo received a call or a text message, so now there was little to do but wait. And he'd paid for the room all night, as well as Alana's able company…and there was nothing to be gained by allowing either to go to waste.

He closed his eyes, resigned to snatching a few hours of rest, and was asleep in minutes.

CHAPTER 12

La Virginia, Colombia

Fog hung over the valley as Ramón and Fernanda rolled into the downtown area of La Virgina and past the cathedral on the square, which was the focal point of the town's commercial center. The narrow streets were deserted as dawn broke, its amber rays lighting the sky through the ghostly haze.

"Not really a lot here, is there?" Fernanda asked as they rumbled over the uneven pavement.

"No. But the good news is that should make it easier to track our friends. Not much goes unnoticed in a town this size."

"Viega is already on the ground?"

"Yes. He roused the locals and they're knocking on doors. We're to meet him at the square." Ramón was interrupted by his cell phone chirping. He took the call, held a short conversation, and then hung up. "That was Viega. He's down near the river. Apparently a boat was found yesterday afternoon by a fisherman."

"Where?"

"About two kilometers south of town. An agricultural area. Portobelo. He's there right now with the police chief, interviewing the man. Do we want to join him?"

"Absolutely. I don't trust Viega to ask the way to the bathroom, much less parse descriptive nuances from a witness. He doesn't strike me as being particularly sharp at fieldwork."

Ramón shrugged. "That would make sense. Probably pilots a desk most of the time. The higher you climb in the force, the less you actually do."

"That's consistent the world over."

The drive to Portobelo took ten minutes, and as they crossed a two-lane bridge, Fernanda eyed the brown swirl of the river snaking from the mountains to the east.

"That's a much bigger river. Does the other feed into it?" she asked.

"Yes. The boat was found west of here."

Portobelo turned out to be a string of shanties scattered along a dirt road that paralleled the shore. Fields of crops on either side framed the tiny community of agricultural workers and fishermen. When they reached the end of the muddy track, they spotted Viega's SUV pulled under a tree and a police pickup truck parked beside it. Ramón eased onto the shoulder and shut off the engine.

They opened the doors and nearly choked as they were assailed by the stench of human waste in the muggy air, and Fernanda had to breathe through her mouth to avoid gagging. Ramón's nose twitched, and he scowled in distaste.

"They use the river for everything, obviously. Probably not a septic system in the entire place," he said, and then pointed at the riverbank. "There they are."

The fisherman turned out to be a youth of sixteen named Theo who had little to add to his discovery of the boat. Fernanda took him through a series of questions designed to trip him up, in case he'd found something in the craft and pocketed it, but she got nothing for her efforts but the blank stare of a marginal intellect. She was finishing up when the local police chief's radio erupted in a burst of static and an excited voice came on the air.

Viega approached her a moment later, his face haggard from lack of sleep. "They found someone in town who might have seen them," he reported. "A woman who sells meals to migrant workers near the park."

"Let's go talk to her," Fernanda said. "Tell the locals to cease and desist until I arrive. The more they speak to her, the more likely she is to omit details when I question her – it's common for those undergoing interrogation to simplify their stories on multiple passes. We don't want that. You can see how well it served us with this boy."

Viega nodded. "I'll convey your request."

Fernanda frowned at him. "It wasn't a request," she snapped.

Ramón and Viega exchanged a glance, and Ramón shrugged before trailing Fernanda back to the Suburban. He started the motor and put the big truck in gear and, as they were bouncing down the rutted track, looked over at her. "Might want to dial back the intensity a little. You'll find you get more cooperation with a little honey than with vinegar."

"Thanks for the advice, but we're out of time, and I don't care about anyone's bruised feelings."

Ramón swallowed hard and focused on the road, biting his tongue. The fog was burning off as they re-crossed the bridge, and when they reached the park, Viega and his entourage close behind, the air was clear and already warming.

Fernanda eyed the gathering of vehicles as they neared the square, mostly geriatric produce trucks parked in the shade. Ramón had barely coasted to a stop when she was out the door and marching to where two uniformed police were talking to an old woman with a tobacco complexion, her food cart already coated with a film of road dust, the caldrons on it steaming atop kerosene burners.

The taller of the pair of officers stared at her deadpan when she interrupted their discussion with a terse, "I'll take it from here." His eyes narrowed and he squared his shoulders, obviously rankling at being talked down to by a woman.

"And you are?" he snapped.

"The person taking over," Fernanda said.

The cop stiffened and was preparing a harsh response when Viega approached and cut him off. "Officer, I'm Captain Viega, and this is my associate. Thank you for a job well done. I trust you followed orders and didn't continue with the interrogation?"

The cop looked at his feet sheepishly, offering the only answer they were likely to get as he and his partner stepped away from the old woman. "She's all yours. Says she saw a strange woman here yesterday morning, and later, that she joined up with a man and a child."

Fernanda took a calming breath and smiled at the food vendor. "Tell me in your own words what you saw. Start at the beginning, slowly, and try to remember everything. We don't know what might be important, so it's critical that you search your memory for even the most insignificant details."

The woman nodded and began her account. She'd arrived at dawn, as she did each day, having awakened at four in the morning to prepare her food. She'd served three breakfasts and was worrying about how her business would go if it had started that slow when the woman appeared and bought food and started a discussion with one of the truck drivers. She'd thought that strange, and speculated that the woman was a prostitute desperate for drug money – until a few minutes later she and the white man had climbed into the truck with their child. The truck departed, and that's the last she'd seen of them.

Fernanda listened attentively, and when the old woman had finished, gently probed her with questions. In five minutes she was done and hurrying back to where Ramón was leaning against the SUV's fender.

"They got a ride with the truck driver. And he had Venezuelan plates." She looked off into the distance. "They're headed for Venezuela, if they aren't there already."

Ramón shook his head. "There's no way they could make it across the border. That's one of the areas where we have a lot of pull, and we circulated her photo and their description to all the border-crossing guards, along with a large financial incentive to anyone who catches them."

"I want you to put out the word to everyone in both crossing areas. Police, informers, whoever. At this point we need a wide net. I just hope we aren't too late."

"It takes a good fourteen hours to hit the closest crossing, which is Cúcuta. That's if everything went well. The likelihood is they got there yesterday evening. Traffic would be extremely light after dark, so they'd have been spotted if they'd tried to make it over."

Fernanda nodded. "I hope you're right. What about the other crossing point?"

"Maracaibo. Not nearly as heavily traveled, and another three hundred something kilometers north of Cúcuta. If that's where they're headed, they probably just got there a couple of hours ago, assuming the driver went all night, which is virtually impossible. Nobody in their right mind drives at night with the robbery situation being what it is."

"I want roadblocks there and Cúcuta."

Ramón smiled sadly. "There's a limit to what we can do. As we've discussed, that area is controlled by another group – a competitive cartel we're enemies with. In Cúcuta we're having to work in their backyard. It makes things more difficult. Not impossible, just difficult."

"Then you can't draw on your military contacts for roadblocks?"

"I'll ask, but don't count on it." He paused, thinking. "We have a decent number of informers in the region, so we should be able to relay the message about a reward to everyone in our network."

She exhaled impatiently. "Get the helicopter warmed up. I want to be there as soon as possible."

"It's about five hundred kilometers, but we'll have to cross the Andes. Figure…three hours?"

She fought to control her anger at the delay and nodded. "Then let's get in the air. You finally got the gear I asked for?"

"It's on the helicopter."

She pulled open the SUV door and climbed into the passenger seat. "Call the helicopter and verify they have sufficient fuel to make it nonstop to Cúcuta. I want to be airborne within minutes."

CHAPTER 13

Medellín, Colombia

Drago bolted awake as his phone trilled on the bedside table. He reached for it and thumbed the screen to life, and was instantly alert as he read the incoming text message. They'd found the girl. Or rather, they had a good idea that she was going to cross into Venezuela at any moment.

Alana stirred next to him and moaned softly. Unlike her prior evening's exclamations, this one was genuine and sounded pained. Drago ignored her and quickly donned his clothes as she rolled over and watched him in silence. When he was dressed, he fished a wad of pesos from his trouser pocket and peeled off several high-denomination notes. He placed them on the nightstand and offered a perfunctory smile that was as warm as an arctic wind.

"Thanks for a nice night," he said.

"You don't want...anything else?" she asked, her tone puzzled.

Drago allowed his eyes to rove over her flawless skin as she reclined on the sheets. He could believe that most were willing to ante up for another round if they stayed through till morning. But he didn't have the time.

"Maybe a rain check," he said. Neither of them believed a syllable of it.

She shrugged and closed her eyes. "You were the best."

He smiled to himself. *You have no idea, Alana, or whatever your real name is.* "So were you," he replied, and the obligatory lies dispatched, twisted the doorknob and stepped into the hall.

The bodyguard was still in his chair, snoozing. Drago took great pains to be uninterested in the man as he made his way to the stairs.

He'd gotten what he came for, and had no further interest in the cartel or its business. Although he did file away in the back of his mind that the data from the phone might be of considerable value to Renaldo at some later date. Either that, or it could be useful if he ever needed to negotiate with the cartel.

When he stepped onto the sidewalk, the city was coming awake, early morning pedestrians bustling to work around him as horns sounded from the larger boulevard two blocks away. He hurried to the main street and took a taxi to his apartment. Once there, he called a reliable charter service he'd used before and arranged for a private single-engine Cessna to fly him to Cúcuta, takeoff to occur within the hour.

He packed a small bag with all the tools of his trade he would need and, after dropping a thick stack of hundred-dollar bills and a fistful of gold coins inside, checked the time. Even with the usual delays that came with doing anything in Colombia, he would be in the air shortly. Judging by the stream of messages going back and forth on Renaldo's phone, the cartel was pulling out all the stops to find the woman and her family, and he hoped that if the trio were still in Cúcuta, the cartel would be successful.

Because he'd be right there when they were discovered if it took more than three hours, which it likely would. And then the most difficult assignment of his career would come to an end in a hail of gunfire as he returned the favor for his nocturnal swim and subsequent hospitalization in Chile. His hand instinctively moved to the back of his skull as he held the thought, the stitches a reminder of his brush with death. He had a mental image of the woman firing at him, and he nodded to himself as he surveyed the apartment for a final time.

He had a lot of catching up to do with her. If he had it his way, he would do so in private, one on one, perhaps as the brat looked on. He could make it last days.

The thought cheered him. If he played his cards right, anything could happen, even his ideal scenario of killing Matt and taking the woman captive.

Drago was humming as he made his way back to the ground level, visions of the woman, naked and bound in a cellar somewhere, dancing in his head. Perhaps he'd force her to kill her own daughter, presuming it was hers. That would be a good way to break the ice and get her complete attention.

By the time he'd flagged down another taxi, his nerves were humming with anticipation, and as the driver negotiated his way through traffic, Drago found that in spite of his fatigue and his performance with Alana, he was aroused at the thought of torturing the woman. He'd long ago learned not to question some of his reactions too closely, and instead sat back in the cab's bench seat and continued to follow the messages coming and going from Renaldo's phone.

There would be time enough once he'd fulfilled his contract to deal with the woman. That would be an unexpected perk.

He would take his pleasure where he could get it.

Right now he had to focus on being ready to pounce once the cartel had the charming little family in its crosshairs.

The plane was older than he would have liked, but after a walk around, he decided it was serviceable, if insanely expensive. He paid the pilot, tossed his bag on the rear seat, and slid into the copilot position as he checked the time. There were no tiresome security checkpoints to clear or demands for documentation, so he could come and go within Colombia unconcerned with his weapons cache being detected as long as he stuck to chartered flights. A few minutes later the Cessna was taxiing toward the far end of the runway, and after a run up on the engine revs, the little prop plane surged forward and lifted into the sky, leaving the cityscape of Medellín beneath its wings.

CHAPTER 14

Cúcuta, Colombia

A pall of smoke from wood fires and exhaust from poorly muffled vehicles hung over Cúcuta like a beige blanket as Jet emerged from the bathroom with dripping hair and moved to where Hannah lay sleeping on the bed. Matt looked up at Jet from his position beside the little girl with worry creasing his face. Jet held her hand against her daughter's cheek and shook her head.

"Time to find a doctor."

Matt nodded. "Agreed. She's not getting any better."

"Your turn for the bathroom."

"I only need a few minutes."

Jet eyed her daughter with concern. "I'll get her ready to go."

Matt was true to his word, and soon they had slipped out of the hotel unseen by the desk clerk and were at the clinic, where they encountered the first stumbling block of the day: a nearly packed waiting room filled with coughing, sniffling children and their parents. Jet dutifully completed the paperwork she was handed with invented data and asked the reception nurse how long she thought it would take to see a doctor.

"Oh, about an hour. Maybe less. We have two physicians working this morning. There's a lot of this bug going around."

"Is there another place where we can be seen quicker?" Jet tried as she fingered a wad of cash in her hand, hoping the woman might appear interested in an exchange of some pesos in order to move them up in line, but she wasn't biting.

"This is it. You can try your luck at the hospital or a private office, but most pediatricians won't even start work until ten or so."

Jet returned to where Matt had found seats and did her best to comfort Hannah, who was trying to put a brave face on, but having a hard time. When prompted, the little girl opened her mouth, and Jet confirmed that her throat was bright red, her tonsils on fire.

"Don't worry, sweetheart. The doctor will give you some medicine and you'll be better in no time," Jet said, hugging her close.

Minutes dragged by and the waiting room slowly cycled into the rear of the clinic where the doctors were doing their best to hurry the patients through. After forty-five minutes there were still six children ahead of them, and doing a quick calculation, Jet guessed that it would be at least that long again before Hannah was seen.

She turned to Matt and whispered, "I have to call Carl. And we're running low on money. I'm thinking I should try to sell one of the smallest diamonds to a jeweler here."

"You should be able to," Matt said. "It's a pretty large city, and a border town at that. It seems quite prosperous. Lot of new cars, so money's circulating."

"Can you stay with Hannah while I find an Internet café and a jeweler? It looks like it's going to be a while."

"Sure. No problem. You sure you don't want me to go?"

"No, if the police put out a bulletin for us, front and center will be a male Caucasian with a cast on his hand. I'd rather not risk anything this close to the finish line. With my complexion I kind of fit in here, but you stick out."

"Have I mentioned how attractive that complexion is?"

Jet kissed Hannah and rose. "Just make sure she's okay."

"You can take that to the bank."

Jet found her way outside, where the relatively low altitude conspired with the latitude to create a stifling environment. Now that the sun was ascending into the morning sky, the temperature was almost overwhelming, the heat waves rising off the parking lot asphalt distorting the perimeter trees as she walked toward the main street.

She passed a string of shops and cafés and found an office supply store that had two computers for rent, as well as a voiceover IP phone booth. After paying the clerk the minimum deposit, she dialed Carl's number and waited as it rang. When he answered, he sounded as grumpy as the prior day, if not grumpier.

"Hello?"

"This is Victoria."

"About time. I thought you'd call yesterday evening," he chided.

"I got tied up."

He paused for a beat. "I checked around. If you can get from Venezuela to Cuba, I can have new documentation for all three of you."

"What about some help traveling from Venezuela?"

"No love there. Five years ago I could have easily arranged it, but all my contacts have dried up, and nobody reliable is operating out of there because of the political situation. All the reputable smugglers avoid it like the plague. Too much risk of the military stepping in and grabbing your cargo. So I'm afraid you'll have to find your own way. Shouldn't be too bad if you're on the ground there. Same as anywhere. Find the crooks, cut a deal, watch your ass. Few people are trying to sneak into Cuba, so that part should be a piece of cake. Everyone's trying to get out, not in."

"You have anyone who can convert diamonds into cash?"

"What kind of weight are we talking?"

"Enough to pay you."

"I should be able to handle that. But I have a guy who knows stones like his children's smiles, so they have to be worth what you say, or no deal."

"No problem there."

"Then come to Cuba and we'll do some business." Carl paused. "You sure you need all three of you papered? The Victor I know would have...other options."

"We want a coherent set of docs. It's tough crossing international borders with a kid if everyone's got a different last name."

"Ah. Good point. I didn't think of that." Carl hesitated. "Where are you now?"

"En route," Jet said, unwilling to divulge any further information.

"I'll contact you once we have transportation to your lovely island."

"I'll be standing by. Nothing gets started until I see money. No offense, but a lot can happen en route, and I don't front for anyone. Even Victor."

"I understand. Once we get there, how long to get the documents?"

"Figure two full days. We need to take photos, and then it's all just a matter of walking it through. Hope you have no problem being Cuban. The passport department will issue genuine documents that will hold up under scrutiny. They're a hundred percent legit."

"I love Cuba. *Viva* Castro."

"I was hoping you'd feel that way."

"Excellent. I'll touch base once we're in Cuba."

Jet hung up and paid the overage for the call to the clerk, and then asked about jewelry stores. The woman behind the counter thought for a moment and recommended a shop four blocks away.

"Very expensive, but good quality, and sometimes they have a bargain," the woman said. "My uncle owns it. His name's Cruz. Tell him Maribela sent you, and he'll treat you right."

"Thanks."

Jet pushed through the double doors back out onto the street and, after surveying her surroundings and touching the pouch containing the diamonds, suspended on a leather lanyard around her neck, began the trek to where she hoped she could sell the smallest stone – a two-carat flawless emerald cut that would bring tens of thousands on the international market, and which she'd already resigned herself to bringing a fraction of its true value in Colombia.

CHAPTER 15

Cúcuta, Colombia

Fernanda stepped from the helicopter onto the tarmac of Camilo Daza International Airport and Ramón followed her, both ducking instinctively as the rotor blades beat the air overhead. They made their way to a late model green Jeep Grand Cherokee at the side of the private aviation section and waited while the copilot removed a black nylon rucksack from the helicopter cargo hold and carried it over. A short, heavily muscled man in a blue polo shirt and tan slacks stood by the car, holding the keys. Ramón, a baseball cap and sunglasses in place, shook hands and climbed behind the wheel as the copilot loaded the bag into the rear of the SUV.

Fernanda slid into the passenger seat, and then they were underway, pulling out of the airport and onto the frontage road. Ramón was visibly nervous, eyes darting to the mirrors and the surrounding cars. He'd reminded her several times on the flight that this was enemy territory, and that he, while not exactly a cinema star, was known to Mosises' rivals. If he were recognized, he would be gunned down without hesitation, just as any of the local cartel's men would be if they strayed onto Mosises' turf.

"Where is this hotel?" she asked.

"In the town center."

"How far from the border is it?"

"Maybe ten minutes. It's been forever since I was here. The town's grown a lot since the last time, so it could take longer with traffic."

"There's nothing closer?"

"Not really. It's only low-income housing as you near the border.

Short of sitting in a car at the river that separates the two countries, this is about as close as you can get."

"That's too far."

"If they try to get across, the guards will stop them. And I have a couple of local men watching the bridge and the trucks going across." He slowed as they neared an intersection. "Don't worry. We'll have time to get there."

"I wish I had a dollar for every time someone told me not to worry and it turned out to be wrong." She paused. "And this hotel is secure?"

"It should be. You're in no danger." He scowled at his reflection in the mirror. "It's me that has to worry."

"I'm with you, so that's not particularly reassuring."

"We'll check in separately."

As they entered the center of town, she was surprised at the amount of new construction underway – multilevel residential blocks, shopping malls, single-family houses. The hotel was a different story. The exterior looked like it dated from the fifties, and she lifted a skeptical eyebrow at Ramón. He seemed to sense her misgivings and gave her a tight smile.

"Don't worry. I've been told it's comfortable."

"Great." She eyed him. "Explain to me why they can't cross the border river in a boat, and why you're so certain it will have to be the bridge?"

Ramón laughed. "That river isn't deep enough to cross on a boat."

"Then what's to keep people from doing it on foot?"

"Armed patrols."

"On both sides?"

Ramón looked less sure. "I know they patrol it on the Colombian side, and Venezuela's sensitive about cocaine making it across, so I'd guess the same holds true there. It would be foolish to risk it."

"Desperate people do foolish things."

"But why would they be desperate? If I were them, I'd feel like I was in the clear now."

"They aren't stupid. They have no idea who's after them or why.

They can't know the scope of your organization. After the shoot-out at the monastery, they had to assume that everyone's an enemy, especially anyone in uniform, and that they're being actively hunted by the authorities." She cut the discussion short and opened her door. "I'll go check into my room."

The desk clerk was a young man in his twenties who seemed uninterested in Fernanda beyond her money. He slid a key across the reception counter and offered to have someone help her with her bag, which she declined. She'd asked for a room at the far end of the hotel, on the second story, and mounted the stairs cautiously.

In the room, she unzipped the duffle bag and considered the weapons inside. The sniper rifle she'd stashed near the monastery gleamed with a new sheen of oil – one of Ramón's men had retrieved it and cleaned it for her. She nudged it aside and found a pistol with three full magazines. Beneath it were suppressors for both weapons. At the bottom of the bag were half a dozen fragmentation grenades, night vision goggles, and the largest items: two LAW rockets in launching tubes.

She smiled as she patted the rockets. Overkill, as Ramón had remarked, perhaps; but she was through taking the surgical approach. If the woman made a run for it and tried to get over the bridge in a vehicle, one of the rockets would take out even a large truck and leave a smoking crater in its wake.

Part of her regretted that she hadn't thought to have Jaime secure one when they'd been watching the monastery cable car – if she'd hit it with a rocket, the woman would now be shish kabob, and Fernanda would be asleep in her bed in Rio, not operating on the two hours of sleep she'd managed to sneak on the helicopter.

Her cell phone rang a few minutes later, and she stared at it in a trance for a few seconds before answering.

"Hello?"

"It's Ramón. We got a call. They've been seen at a children's medical clinic in town. They're there right now."

Fernanda's pulse quickened. "What?"

"But there's a problem."

"What is it?"

"It's down the block from a police station. One of the cops spotted them going into the clinic."

"You're joking."

"I wish. What do you want to do? The cop said he'd keep an eye on the place, but he can't stay there watching the doors indefinitely, or his superiors will be suspicious. Apparently he didn't share his find with them. He wants the reward all to himself."

"Describe the clinic."

"I told you. It's a children's clinic – I don't know anything about it beyond that, but it can't be all that large."

Fernanda forced herself to remain calm. "Where is it? Do you have an address?"

"Oh. Right. It's about five minutes away. And yes, I do." He gave her the address.

"Hang on. I'm going to pull it up on satellite and see what the layout's like." She muted the call and punched the coordinates into her phone. An image popped up and she zoomed in. When she returned to the call, she was smiling. "I know how we're going to take them out."

"With the police right there?"

"Yes." She told him what she was thinking, and when she finished, he was silent. She waited, and when he finally spoke, his voice was low.

"Are you serious?"

"Do I sound like I'm making a joke? Are you driving, or should I get a cab?" She paused. "How do we know they're still there?"

"The cop said he'd call if they leave."

"Then we're down to the wire. Let's do this."

"I…this will have every soldier and policeman in the country looking for us after you're done."

"Tell someone who cares. Now come on. I've got work to do."

CHAPTER 16

The jewelry store security buzzer sounded, and Jet pushed the door open and entered the cool showroom. Chilled air tickled her skin as she walked across the marble floor to where two women about her age were waiting at the far end of the room. A security guard sat on a stool near the door, his revolver prominently jutting from his belt. The women stood behind brightly lit display cases, their hair and makeup impeccable. One of them took in Jet's clothes and offered a cold smile.

"Yes. May I help you?" the woman asked.

"I'm looking for Cruz."

"Mmm, yes. And what may I tell him it's regarding?"

"I want to sell a diamond."

Her eyes narrowed. "We don't buy used jewelry."

Jet met her gaze without expression. "That's good to know if I ever want to sell any. Tell Cruz that Maribela sent me."

The woman glanced at her companion. "I'm afraid he's busy at the moment."

Jet looked the woman up and down. "Look. I don't have a lot of time, and I have an offer to make to the owner of this store. Unless I'm mistaken, you're a salesperson, not the owner – which means you don't get to decide who speaks with him or doesn't. He does. So either tell Cruz that he has a customer, or you'll be cleaning toilets at the bus station instead of standing in the AC once he learns what you did."

Jet's tone visibly shook the woman, and she muttered, "Let me see when he can meet with you," before disappearing into the back. Jet studied the gems in the case, mostly emeralds with a few diamonds here and there, and looked up when the woman returned, accompanied by a slow-moving man in his sixties, his face blemished by liver spots, wisps of white hair combed over a tanned pate.

"You're a friend of Maribela's?" he asked.

"Yes. She said you would recognize a good opportunity when you saw one, and knew quality like nobody's business."

Cruz smiled, revealing a set of nicotine-stained teeth in receding gums. "What do you have?"

Jet gave the two women a pointed stare. "I'd rather discuss it in private."

Cruz studied her face and nodded. "I suppose there's no harm in that. You don't look like you bite." He motioned to her with a trembling hand. "This way."

Jet followed him back to an office, and they sat down at his steel desk. She fished the diamond she'd selected from her pocket and placed it on a rectangle of green felt in the center of the desktop. Cruz expertly locked a pair of jeweler's forceps on the stone in spite of his palsied fingers and moved it to a cheap microscope. He peered into it for a long time before setting the diamond down and looking up at Jet. "What do you want for it?"

"I know what wholesale is in New York or London."

"Yes, well, then, go to New York or London and best of luck to you."

"I figured we could use that as a starting point."

Cruz sat back in his chair. "Let me tell you something about diamonds. They're as common as flies. The only reason they have any value at all is because one family, De Beers, controls the entire market and trickles out stones at the rate of its choosing to maintain artificially high values. They're bullshit," he said softly.

"I know that. But regardless of how you or I feel about their intrinsic worth, the finer quality stones command a value that's relatively fixed. Just as gold or the dollar or fine art have no real value beyond what humans assign to them, so too with these little bits of carbon." She paused and tried a smile. "Since we both understand the fickle nature of the world, let's talk turkey. Wholesale on it is at least twenty-five grand."

"Like I said. We aren't in New York."

"No. We aren't. So it has to be discounted. I understand. The question is how much."

They haggled back and forth for five minutes, and when Jet left the shop, she had ten thousand dollars in her pocket. Less than the fifteen she'd hoped for, but she reminded herself that the loss was meaningless in the scheme of things – they needed money to buy their way to Cuba, nothing more, and ten thousand would more than cover that in a country like Venezuela, whose economy was a slow-motion train wreck with a population that treasured dollars.

She ignored the look of venom the saleswomen threw her on the way out and gave herself a moment to reacclimate to the heat after the chill of the air-conditioning. Thunder rumbled in the near distance, echoing off the buildings as the morning sky darkened. Jet noted the gathering clouds and walked toward the corner to head back to the clinic. As she did, she caught a glimpse of two young men keeping pace with her. Her inner alarms sounded, but outwardly she remained calm and oblivious, and when she stopped at a shop window to look at a pair of shoes, she appeared to be innocently window shopping, her eyes hidden by the sunglasses she'd slipped on as she'd left the store.

There was no mistaking it. The two men had slowed and were watching her.

~ ~ ~

Matt nodded at the attendant behind the reception desk and led Hannah to the exam room, following another nurse who'd called for them in a tired voice. She took Hannah's temperature and blood pressure, verified a few statistics on the paperwork Jet had filled out, and left the room. Five minutes went by and a kindly woman in her thirties entered, a stethoscope around her neck, heavy tortoiseshell-framed glasses on her round face.

After doing a short examination, she stepped away from Hannah and made a few notes as she reported to Matt. "She has an upper respiratory infection that looks like it started in her throat. You can see some white by her tonsils. I'll give her a shot of broad-spectrum antibiotic, and then you need to keep her on oral medication for five more days. Does she have any allergies?"

"No. Is she okay to travel?"

"The more rest she gets, the better, but it should pose no danger to her. Just keep her hydrated and don't miss any of the meds. And don't let her stop taking them once she improves – she needs to finish the full five days or runs the risk of relapsing, only this time with drug resistance."

"Of course."

"I'll be right back with the shot and a bottle of medicine. You'll only need ten pills, one in the morning, one in the evening. With food and a full glass of water."

Hannah watched with frightened eyes as the doctor left. Matt did his best to calm her, assuring her that the shot would only sting for a moment, and that he would see to it she got ice cream once they left the clinic. The mention of a treat calmed her down, although she was still agitated as they waited.

"Where Mama?" she asked in a small voice.

"She's going to be right back, honey. She just had to go call someone."

"Who?"

"A friend."

"Oh."

When the doctor returned, Hannah reluctantly rolled over and prepared for the indignity of a shot as Matt held her tiny hand, his eyes locked on hers.

~ ~ ~

Jet immediately suspected the woman at the store who'd been so objectionable of setting up a mugging. She'd probably texted a boyfriend to alert him that a pigeon would be leaving the shop flush with cash, ripe for plucking. Jet cursed the distraction from her primary objective, but understood that she'd have to deal with the threat. The only good news was that she wouldn't have to do much to lure them to a desolate spot – they'd think themselves lucky when she turned down an empty street, creating an opportunity to rob her.

She glanced at her watch and sighed. No point in delaying the inevitable, although if she could lose them, that would be cleaner. There was always the chance she'd attract the attention of a passing cop as she was taking them down, and that could quickly escalate into disaster.

Jet abruptly turned and took long strides. She made it to the corner in seconds. As she rounded it, she disappeared from their view, and sprinted down the street toward the clinic. The street was empty, the district one of offices, not retail shops, which worked to her advantage in covering ground, but against her as any sort of deterrent to her pursuers.

The pounding of running feet behind her told her everything she needed to know. The muggers weren't going to allow her to escape, so she would need to put them out of their misery somewhere private.

There.

She spotted a narrow pedestrian walkway on her left, leading a block down to a park, shadowed by trees. Not perfect, but it would do.

If she timed it right, she'd be out of sight for a few precious seconds – long enough to prepare herself to deal with the men without having to pull her pistol. Thunder roared overhead, but she didn't waver, now laser-focused on dispatching her assailants.

She stopped and turned to face the men as they came, her hands on her hips, like a headmistress waiting to scold two misbehaving students. Jet saw that they were barely out of their teens, but the flash of steel in their hands told her they meant business.

Jet altered her stance imperceptibly, relaxing the tension in her shoulders as she opted against pulling the gun from where it was hidden at the small of her back. The men slowed and approached with a swagger, overconfident, which was good. She removed her sunglasses and slipped them into her pocket, and then met the nearest youth's eyes.

"You don't want to do this. When you're on your way to the hospital, remember that I gave you fair warning," she said quietly.

Both men chuckled. "Bitch, give us the money or we'll gut you like a fish," the closest mugger snarled.

She shrugged and began closing the distance between them, a hint of a smile playing across her face as thunder boomed around them.

"Have it your way."

CHAPTER 17

Officer Emilio Lopez had been a proud member of the Cúcuta police force for nine years, during which time he'd distinguished himself by showing up to work sober most days, never having a brutality charge filed against him, and staying awake the majority of his shifts.

Cúcuta was a gateway for cocaine traffic to Venezuela, but a largely peaceful one, the territory well established as the turf of the Vicente Miguel organization, one of the most violent groups in the country. As such, none of its rivals dared challenge it in its home district, and a cautious peace had prevailed over the growing city for two decades, leaving it up to Officer Lopez to extort money from illegal vendors and prostitutes when he could – even a cop didn't dare confront the street dealers, all of whom were affiliated with the group. An enterprising man, he bolstered his illicit income by acting as an informant to Mosises' gang, offering regular reports on the Vicente Miguel cartel's operations, for which he was paid a pittance.

All of which meant that he made far less than his police brethren in larger towns like Medellín or Bogotá – a fact that embittered him no end. But today that was all about to change. Mosises had sent over a photograph of a woman he was on the hunt for, along with her companions: a white man with a broken hand, and a little girl.

When he'd caught a glimpse of a trio matching that description crossing the parking lot on their way to the clinic, he'd done a double take, and then had promptly telephoned his contact in Mosises' group and claimed the generous bounty for spotting them. He'd been told to watch the small building and report immediately if they left, which he agreed to do, although he couldn't be obvious about it – he had other duties to attend to, and didn't want to have to share his reward. So he'd kept an eye on the clinic as much as he could, only pausing to go inside the police station to answer questions or fill out reports.

He'd caught a glimpse of the woman leaving twenty minutes ago, but the man and the girl weren't with her, so she'd be back – probably going for breakfast or coffee. The wait to see a doctor was usually terrible in the mornings, he knew from experience.

Thunder rumbled from a line of leaden clouds gathering by the foothills and he cursed under his breath. The last thing he wanted to have to do was maintain a vigil on the clinic in the rain. So far he'd played off his loitering around the front of the station house as waiting for a robbery victim to arrive and file a complaint, but nobody would believe he was doing so in a downpour. His mind worked furiously on a plausible alternative explanation with which to satisfy his supervisor, who only minutes before had demanded how much more time he was going to waste waiting for his invented victim to arrive, but a long night of coconut rum and cigars with the boys had left Lopez's head somewhat fuzzy this morning, and he was drawing a blank.

Another peal of thunder, this one closer and louder, exploded from the sky, causing him to jump. The downpour would start any minute, he knew. The region's storms came on suddenly and raged for a few hours, and then faded just as quickly as they'd arrived, like the angry mood of a petulant child. The air felt heavy with moisture, and the distinctive smell of ozone and approaching rain drifted on the light breeze.

An SUV caught his eye as it pulled around the corner and rolled to a stop at the edge of the parking lot, its windows down. Lightning lit the nearby clouds, followed by a loud boom, and he looked over his shoulder at the gathering storm. A flash drew his attention back to the vehicle, and then his mouth dropped open as a woman stepped from the passenger side of the SUV with a rocket launcher and took careful aim. He stood frozen as a smoke trail streaked from the vehicle and through the front doors of the clinic.

The shockwave from the explosion rattled his teeth as he stood, stunned. Voices yelled from inside the police station, and then the woman fired another rocket from beside the vehicle, into the clinic's rear window. The detonation blew part of the roof into the air, and an orange fireball blasted skyward.

The Jeep roared away as Lopez fumbled his pistol into his hand, his movements seeming to him to be in slow motion. He fired at the vehicle as it screeched around the corner – mainly so he would have appeared to have done something, not because he thought he had a chance in hell of hitting it. Three officers, all with guns drawn, surged out of the station entrance as the heavens opened and rain began falling, lightly at first. Lopez stood frozen at the sight of the clinic ablaze, and then his captain was shaking him by the shoulders.

"What happened?" he demanded.

"I...a truck fired two missiles at the clinic," Lopez blurted.

"What? Description. What kind of truck?" the captain barked, and Lopez turned from the grim scene and began earning his finder's fee in earnest. He would describe an SUV, maybe a Dodge or a Ford, dark color, but they'd never find it – he'd see to that.

Any sense of guilt or responsibility for the slaughter quickly vanished as his own complicity dawned on him. Colluding with a cartel on a savage attack on a children's clinic would easily land him in jail for the rest of his short life if his role were discovered. He pushed the mental image of dead mothers and babies aside and began doing damage control – there was nothing he could do to help the kids now, and it wasn't like he'd known that Mosises' people would stage a stunt like this.

"It was an older Ford, I think. An Explorer. I don't think it had any plates."

~ ~ ~

Jet was only a few meters from the first mugger when the whump of an explosion reached her. The man was momentarily startled by the sound, and she used his hesitation to pivot kick the knife from his hand, sending it skittering across the pavement as she followed through with a pair of strikes to his chest that sent him tumbling backward.

A second explosion boomed, and Jet parried the remaining assailant's clumsy knife swipe and brought her elbow down on his forearm, snapping the radius and ulna with a crack. He howled in pain and released the weapon, his arm now useless, and she rabbit-punched him in the throat, dropping him like a bag of rocks.

The entire confrontation was over in seconds, leaving both men disabled, lying on the ground. Rain splattered around them, and after kicking their knives down the street, Jet bolted for the clinic – her stomach in a twisted knot as she ran through the drizzle, the sound of explosions impossible to mistake for thunder.

Jet covered the distance in under a minute. When she arrived at the parking lot, she stared at the clinic in horror, the structure belching black smoke from every opening. The rainstorm was intensifying, the cloudburst now coming down in sheets, but she sprinted for the smoldering building's gaping entry, oblivious to the downpour.

"Hannah! Hannah!" she cried as she neared the gutted structure, ignoring the deluge as her panic mounted. She slowed as she approached the demolished doors and swallowed hard when she spotted the charred remains of a child's arm in the wreckage. "Oh…God, no…"

"Mama!" Hannah's voice cut through the storm. For a moment Jet thought she was hallucinating, and she looked around wildly.

"Hannah?" Jet called, and was rewarded by Matt's voice from the rear of the building.

"We're back here."

Jet tore around the corner of the clinic. She pulled up short when she saw Matt holding Hannah in his arms, his bag hanging from his shoulder, water running down their faces. "You're alive!" she cried and ran to them, simultaneously laughing and crying with relief.

"Barely," Matt said. "We have to get out of here. This was a rocket attack. The first one blew through the front of the clinic. We were in the back with the doctor, and I barely got Hannah out the rear door before a second one hit the exam room."

"Rockets?" Jet repeated in disbelief. She peered around the area, the heavy rain limiting visibility, and turned to Matt. "Come on. I see our way out."

CHAPTER 18

Drago finished with the woman at the rental car desk in the Cúcuta airport terminal and followed her directions to a nearby bus stop, where a shuttle took him to the rental parking lot. He tossed his bag onto the passenger seat and glanced up at the clouds, the storm off the Andes rushing towards him. The final half hour of his flight in the prop plane had felt like an amusement park ride, the turbulent air over the mountains combining with the front making for an unpleasant approach to the border city.

A tree of lightning flashed nearby, answered a moment later by thunder. He slid behind the wheel and started the engine, and his phone vibrated. He scanned the messages that were being intercepted from Renaldo's phone and stopped at the latest one – an informer had spotted his quarry at a clinic ten minutes from the airport.

He pulled up a map on his cell screen and studied it. The quickest way would be to stay on the Boulevard Libertadores until he neared the major intersection on the western side of town, and then take surface streets that paralleled the river. Once the course was committed to memory, he dropped the transmission into gear and wheeled out of the lot, barely pausing to hand the attendant his voucher.

The sparse morning traffic grew heavier as he neared the town center, and he battled his impatience as the cars around him jockeyed for position, darting in and out of openings without warning, turn indicators considered a sign of weakness. As he approached the intersection where he would divert to the smaller streets, an orange flash lit the sky, followed closely by the flare of a second detonation, and then a column of inky smoke snaked into the overcast sky.

Drago stood on his horn as an overloaded truck crawled along, blocking his way, and then he pulled impatiently onto the shoulder and passed illegally. He narrowly avoided a concrete post and swerved back into the lane, cutting the lumbering conveyance off as he accelerated for the off-ramp. Rain began pelting the car, and he wrenched the wipers on. Ahead of him, he could see smoke rising like a signal, and he rode the rear bumper of the car in front of him until he could get around it. The driver made an obscene gesture at Drago as he roared past, which Drago ignored. He tried to contain the ominous feeling deep in his gut – he'd underestimated the extent to which Mosises' hit men would go to get the woman.

Drago had no problem with their tactics, only their competence. The Colombian cartels had a long history of brutal violence, but in spite of their reputations, were largely inept, using a sledgehammer where a scalpel would suffice. His fear was that they would make an attempt and fail, putting Matt and his whore back on alert, and that this time when the loving couple went to ground, they would stay gone. The thought of failure when he was this close made Drago physically ill, and he had to choke back bile as he drew near the clinic.

When he arrived, uniformed officers were swarming over the area, and it took him a few moments to realize there was a police station down the block. A grim-faced cop in a rain parka waved him past what remained of the clinic, smoke still bellowing from it in spite of the intensifying rain. He'd had more than enough combat experience to recognize the handiwork of rockets, and he wondered at the audacity of the attackers, given the proximity of the station.

This was typical of the sort of blunt-force trauma Drago had feared the cartel would employ: butcher dozens in an effort to kill a few, and hope their quarry died in the process of the complete destruction of the clinic.

He shook his head in disgust. Not at the loss of innocent lives; at the sloppiness. If he'd arrived only a few minutes earlier, he could have walked in, gunned his target down, dragged the woman and little girl out, and been gone before anyone realized what had happened. Now, his revenge against the woman who'd put him into the hospital was gone in a fiery blaze.

A gray sheet of rain pounded the roof of the car and he sighed to himself. "Well, that takes care of that, I suppose," he muttered, and followed a line of vehicles away from the area. "Rot in hell, you miserable bastard. You certainly caused me enough grief."

He debated sticking around but thought better of it. The cops would eventually begin looking for whoever carried out the attack, and would likely search questionable vehicles. He couldn't afford to be caught with his tools of the trade. In light of the destruction, the police would be looking for a scapegoat and would be all too ready to hang the crime on the first person they caught who seemed a reasonable fit.

Drago retraced his path toward the airport and pulled off at a shopping complex with an American chain restaurant, its yellow sign glowing like a beacon in the rain. His growling stomach announced that he could use some coffee and breakfast – he hadn't eaten since the prior night and had worked up a serious appetite with the lovely Alana. Now that Matt and his woman were ashes, he could afford to relax. Once he confirmed Matt's death with his agent, money would hit his bank, and then he'd be off to the islands with a new identity. Perhaps Malta. Someplace off the beaten path, where his friends in the CIA would never think to look for him.

He parked and slung his bag over his shoulder, and then dashed to the front entrance, the cloudburst pelting him with the intensity of a jilted lover as his shoes pounded on the wet pavement.

CHAPTER 19

Officer Lopez watched the fire trucks arrive and stepped away from his fellow policemen. He fished his cell phone from his shirt pocket and, after looking around to confirm that there was nobody close enough to overhear him, pressed redial and listened as the line rang. He'd debated not making the call, but had decided that if the three targets materialized at some point in the future and he hadn't called, he'd be dead meat. As usual for him, self-interest won the day.

When the phone picked up, he whispered urgently to Mosises' contact person. "You botched it. The rockets didn't get them."

The voice on the other end sounded surprised. "What?"

"They got away."

"How do you know?"

"I saw them take an ambulance."

"An...ambulance?" the contact sputtered in disbelief.

"That's correct. But now you have the entire police force, and soon, the military, in the mix. I can't believe you bombed the place."

The voice ignored his protest. "What can you tell me about the ambulance?"

"What do you mean, tell you? It's an ambulance. Blue and white."

"How long ago did it leave?"

"Maybe...five, ten minutes."

"Which is it? And why didn't you call immediately?"

"I have other things going on, what with World War Three down the block." Lopez shook his head in disgust. "It was probably closer to ten minutes. Happened right after the blasts. You'll be able to figure out the exact timing. That's all I have. I need to get back to the job. You left a hell of a mess to clean up."

~ ~ ~

Fernanda and Ramón were entering the airport grounds when Ramón's phone vibrated. He punched the line to life and listened, the color slowly draining from his face as he muttered an acknowledgement and disconnected. Ramón pulled to the side of the road and stared at his cell like it was a poisonous snake, and then slowly slid it into his pocket and turned to Fernanda.

"They escaped. Our informer just reported that he saw them steal an ambulance."

Fernanda's face could have been carved from wood. One eye twitched almost imperceptibly, and then both narrowed to slits.

"That's impossible," she hissed. "Nothing could have survived that."

"Maybe, but that's what he said, and he has no reason to lie."

"Damn it. If they were inside the building, they should be dead." Her voice grew dangerously quiet. "Your informer screwed us. There's no other explanation. Nobody walks away from a direct hit with two rockets. Nobody. Somehow they were tipped off."

"I doubt it. He wants his finder's fee as much as anyone." Ramón hesitated. "So now what do we do?"

"*Do?* We find them and kill them. That's what we *do*. Put a bulletin out to the cops that they've been spotted in a stolen ambulance and had something to do with the explosion. We don't need it to all hang together logically, just for the police to throw everything they have at finding them."

Ramón made another call and, after a muted discussion, hung up. "It's done."

"They're headed for the border. We need to get there immediately."

"There's no way they'll get across."

"They just walked away from the impossible. Of course they'll get across, you idiot."

Ramón looked like he'd been slapped. His mouth tightened into a thin white line and he glared at her. "You'd be well advised to calm down," he whispered, his voice glacial. "I don't care who you are. Do you understand?"

She inhaled noisily and softened her tone. "I'm sorry. That was uncalled for. I'm just…I need some sleep, and this comes as…an ugly disappointment. I didn't mean to take it out on you."

Ramón held her stare for a long beat and then turned away. "It will take us some time to make it to the river in this rain."

"Please get us there as quickly as possible." An idea occurred to her. "Maybe we can use the helicopter to patrol the border?"

Ramón shook his head. "Not in a million years. The police, the border guards, everyone will be on high alert after this. We'd be stopped inside of a minute, even assuming the pilots were willing to try in this storm and the tower gave us clearance for takeoff, which they probably wouldn't."

She stared through the window at the terminal on her right, and nodded slowly. "You're right, of course."

They had stopped and jettisoned the empty single-use rocket launchers in a dumpster at a construction site, so they had no fear of being discovered red-handed, but Fernanda had her rifle and associated gear in her rucksack, so there was some risk in returning to town. Still, Ramón had his orders, so he took the frontage road loop back toward Cúcuta and tried not to be furious with the Brazilian psychopath riding next to him. Her calm deliberation as she'd murdered God knows how many people had chilled him to his core, and he was no stranger to brutality. But this…this was a completely different level of indifference to slaughtering innocents than he was accustomed to.

He was shaken out of his thoughts by the pulsing flash of emergency lights on the boulevard. He slowed to let them pass, his breath catching in his throat, one hand instinctively moving to his windbreaker pocket, where he had his compact Glock pistol. Two fire trucks raced by, and he exhaled slowly, his eyes flitting to the rearview mirror before he returned his attention to the road and picked up the pace again.

The wipers thumped rhythmically as he eyed the GPS navigation system. Fernanda stewed silently beside him. If they got out of this intact, after carrying out a strike in a rival cartel's hometown, with the police and emergency services all on high alert, it would be a miracle. While he understood Fernanda's tenacity and even somewhat admired it, she was exhausted and subjecting them both to undue risk by demanding to go to the border rather than calling it quits and living to fight another day.

But Mosises had made it clear that she was to get whatever she wanted, and Ramón's role wasn't to second-guess the cartel boss.

Ramón rubbed his burning red eyes with a fatigued hand and turned onto one of the streets leading to the river that traced the Venezuelan border. This was madness, but he had no choice but to continue, regardless of the price. Jaime's death would be avenged, and Mosises had made it clear that failure was not an option.

He just hoped his luck would hold a little longer, and he'd make it out of Cúcuta alive.

CHAPTER 20

The ambulance slid sideways when it hit a deep pothole filled with rainwater and lost traction. Hannah screamed as the van yawed dangerously, for a few harrowing seconds out of control, and then Jet mashed her foot on the accelerator and the tires grabbed. Matt hugged Hannah to his chest as Jet peered through the downpour, the wipers inadequate for the job.

"You really believe we can make it across on foot?" Matt asked.

"I don't think we have much choice. Somehow, whoever's after us figured out where we were going. We need to get clear of Colombia once and for all." She took a corner too fast and the ambulance fishtailed before straightening out. "I'm betting that with this storm covering our tracks, we can make it. Nobody's going to be out in it if they can help it, and that includes underpaid Venezuelan border guards."

Matt nodded, clearly unconvinced. "And if you're wrong?"

Jet kept her eyes on the road. "I'm not." Then more gently, she asked, "You aren't hurt?"

"My ears are ringing like nobody's business, but we got out in the nick of time. I have a feeling we'll be a little hard of hearing for a day or two."

"I talked to Carl. He said he can't help us get to Cuba, but he can take care of things once we're there."

"Then we're on our own for now?"

Jet grunted. "Nothing new there. What did the doctor say about Hannah?"

"Infection. She'd just given her a shot and handed me some pills when the first rocket hit." Matt patted Hannah's leg. "She was very brave. Didn't cry or anything."

"So she's going to be fine?"

"That's what she said."

They drove in silence for several minutes, and Jet slowed to a more sensible speed as they put distance between themselves and the clinic. The rain abated to a drizzle as they neared the river, and after going through a large intersection with signs announcing that the border bridge was only three hundred meters away, she turned onto a narrow side street that led to a residential area with rows of low-income housing. Iron bars adorned all the windows of the drab single-story homes, the few cars littering the drives were old and corroding, and graffiti marred the perimeter walls.

Two police officers stood beneath a tree at the community entrance, sheltered from the worst of the rain. When they spied the ambulance, they waved at it frantically, and the shrill screech of a whistle pierced the quiet. Jet ignored them and gave the heavy vehicle more gas, leaving them behind as she tore down the street.

Three more turns and they arrived at a dead end. She slowed to a crawl and pointed to a brown slurry in the near distance, barely visible in the drizzle. "That's it. The river." Jet opened the door. "And the rain cooled things off some, which is a relief."

"We're still going to get wet. Not to mention we need to figure out how to cross the river. Assuming we can dodge the patrols."

She smiled, the tension receding from her expression. "Piece of cake. You ready to do this?"

Matt sighed. "I guess."

"Honey?"

Hannah looked at her with wide eyes and nodded mutely.

Jet's heart sank, but now wasn't the time for regrets over the hardships they were forced to endure. She couldn't help that unnamed adversaries had singled her out for destruction, and dwelling on how she felt about the situation wouldn't save their lives. Their survival depended on successfully making it across the river without being detected. With each passing minute the odds of doing so diminished, and wasting energy on recriminations over the unfairness of their situation wouldn't help. She needed to be strong for herself and for her daughter, so she wiped away the moisture welling in her eyes and stepped out of the ambulance.

Matt joined her, and she led them across the high grass to where the bank sloped down to the river. She pointed at a flat area to their left, where vehicles of all shapes and sizes were huddled on the gravel. "That must be some kind of flea market."

"Pretty optimistic given the weather."

"We might be able to use that. Get lost in the crowd as we make our way closer to the water."

Matt blinked away rain. "You were right about one thing. Nobody in their right mind would want to be out in this."

A voice called out from near the ambulance, and Jet picked up her pace. "Sounds like the police found the van."

"You think they'll shoot?" Matt asked as he trotted behind her.

"They won't be able to see us in a few more seconds, in this soup."

They ran in silence, the gravel crunching beneath their feet, and neared the circle of vehicles. Surprised faces stared from the interiors as they darted past, and then they were following the river north.

Matt eyed the muddy water dubiously. "Looks pretty deep from the storm runoff."

"We're only looking for one shallow area."

Shouts followed them from the circle of vehicles, and Jet began running harder again. "They don't give up easily."

"Look up ahead. The river widens out. We might be able to make it."

"I'm way ahead of you. If it's too deep, keep moving and I'll swim it until I can feel the bottom."

"That's a terrible idea," Matt said.

"You have a better one?"

He frowned. "Good luck."

Jet veered toward the river as another flurry of heavy rain pelted them, and splashed into the swollen rush of water. The level reached her knees, then her thighs, and then she was sucked under the surface as she neared the middle, where the current was strongest. Matt fought the instinct to run and try to help her, instead continuing at a flat-out run along the river's course. A stone gave beneath him and he cursed as his ankle twisted, but he ignored the pain and powered on, Hannah in his arms, his breathing ragged from the exertion.

Jet's head bobbed from the swirling rapids several yards beyond Matt and she sputtered. He resisted the overwhelming desire to call out for her, and instead continued forcing himself forward. True to her word, she was allowing the powerful current to carry her along. Near a wide bend she slowed and eventually struggled to her feet, the water only hip deep. She waved at Matt and he swung toward her and was in the river within moments. The pull was strong, but he was prepared for it and maintained his footing as Hannah closed her eyes tight in fear.

After a hurried crossing where he almost went down twice, the bottom rose and he found himself in shallows. Jet held out her hand as she scurried up the bank on the Venezuelan side, and he quickly followed her out. Once on dry land, they bolted for the brush line, angry cries from the far shore trailing them, but no bullets. They scrambled into the dense underbrush as thunder roared overhead, and Jet slowed, the tangle of branches tearing at her clothes and impeding her progress.

Matt trudged behind her until they emerged from the brush onto a muddy trail – a road, although not much of one. Jet turned to Matt as they moved to the shoulder and held out her arms. "I'll take her for a while."

Matt managed a tired half grin and passed Hannah to Jet. "You recovered from your swim?"

"A little muddy, but nothing the rain won't wash away."

"Think they'll try to follow us?"

"I seriously doubt it. This is a different country, and they don't have jurisdiction. I mean, anything's possible, but we're not going to wait around to find out." She shrugged at the empty surroundings. "And no sign of the military here. Probably all holed up until the storm passes."

"You want to stick to the road?"

"I think we have to. According to the satellite images I looked at, there should be some houses or farms up ahead, and then Ureña to the south. We're a little further north than where I was thinking we'd cross, but not that far off course."

"I hope you're right about the Venezuelans not caring about what was happening back in Colombia."

"I remember from the last time I traveled through Venezuela. The two countries aren't particularly friendly with each other, so their communications are probably lousy – and that's borne out by the truck driver's description. Besides, the Venezuelans don't have any beef with us." She slowed further. "You're limping."

"Just a light sprain. Nothing to worry about."

"You sure?"

"I don't think you can carry both of us."

Jet smiled as Hannah nuzzled her neck. "Let me know if you want me to try."

Half an hour later the storm had blown itself out, and as they made their way down the road toward the outskirts of Ureña, the sun emerged from the clouds. Soon the warmth became a humid stifle, and the road hardened as if by magic beneath their feet even as their clothes dried from the sun's glare. By the time they reached the center of the quiet little hamlet, they'd decided to chance a bus to the coast, where with any luck they'd be able to find a boat to Cuba, ending the trail once and for all at the shore of the Caribbean Sea.

CHAPTER 21

Cúcuta, Colombia

Drago couldn't believe his eyes when he read the message on his cell, forwarded from Renaldo's inbox. He read it twice, shaking his head in disgust at the news that the attack on the clinic had been unsuccessful and that the targets had liberated an ambulance and escaped. He stood in the middle of his breakfast and threw a few bills onto the table, and then pushed his way out of the restaurant and made for the rental car as warm rain fell around him.

How the cartel muscle had managed to destroy an entire clinic and miss the only people they were after was beyond him, but he'd seen similar idiocy before. None of which was much consolation – his fears had been realized, and his quarry was no doubt in full flight mode, alert to the slightest threat. Which put him at a serious disadvantage – because now, in addition to whatever morons the cartel had unleashed, he had to contend with a pair of very dangerous fugitives whom he knew from experience were as deadly as coral snakes.

Drago worked through the sluggish traffic toward the border, and was only slightly surprised when the flow slowed to a standstill as he neared the river bridge. He pulled to the side of the road near a park where a slew of vendors had taken refuge beneath the trees from the rain, and locked the door, his bag in hand. He had no idea where Matt and his little family had gone in the ambulance, but if it had been Drago, he'd have made for the border, following the instinct to get out of Colombia and away from rocket attacks.

He walked toward the bridge, ignoring the soaking he was receiving. Once over the river, Drago stopped and looked south.

Seeing nothing but rain, he crossed to the north side and squinted in the haze. *There.* By a collection of cars parked at the bank – a group of police arguing among themselves, judging by the waving arms and body language.

Drago returned to the Colombian side of the bridge and edged along the riverbank until he reached a group of cheap houses. He heard angry voices to his left and turned. Three cops were standing by an ambulance parked by a barren field. He didn't slow or break his stride, but he smiled to himself – he'd made the right call. His quarry was close by.

He continued north until he reached the circle of cars at the river flea market and overheard the policemen arguing over the wisdom of a hot pursuit into Venezuela as they awaited orders from headquarters. Drago didn't need to listen for the conclusion of the exchange. There was no way Colombian officials would green-light a foray into Venezuela, regardless of the reason. Nobody was going to risk an international incident to catch a pair of border runners with a child in tow, even if they were wanted for questioning – they hadn't been charged with anything, and until and unless they were, there were no grounds for reaching out to the Venezuelans.

The walk back to the car seemed to take twice as long, and when he made it back, he was dripping wet. The vehicles next to him were in the same spots as when he'd left, so nothing had moved in the fifteen minutes his foray had taken.

There was only one alternative he could see, and he disliked it intensely – he'd have to leave his weapons behind and cross into Venezuela on foot. He locked his bag in the trunk of his car and set off toward the bridge. He had no doubt that the Venezuelans would be on edge with the explosions on the Colombian side, not to mention that when your nation bordered the largest cocaine-producing country in the world, your customs staff was going to be jumpy on even the most relaxed days.

He could have spared himself the worry, because a ragged column of equally soaked Colombians was approaching from the far side of the bridge.

"What's going on?" he asked one of the group.

"Border's closed. Don't know what's happening."

"Colombians? Or the Venezuelans?"

"Colombian. There's police and military everywhere. Don't know what they're looking for, but it's probably going to be closed for hours."

Drago nodded in agreement even as his mind worked furiously. Naturally the Colombians would close the barn door. The instinct would be to seal the border to prevent whoever fired the rockets from escaping. That would be a fool's errand, but when governments reacted, it was usually more for appearances than as a result of any actual competence. Colombia was no different from the rest in that regard.

Which meant he'd have to come up with a better plan. And it certainly wouldn't involve trying to make it across a rainstorm-engorged river surrounded by inquisitive Colombian cops.

He returned to the car and secured his bag of goodies before heading back into town to talk to his pilot and see whether he could get into Venezuela under the radar. Barring that, he'd have to wait for the border to reopen, and hope that Renaldo's phone delivered some information more helpful than the chronicle of screwups it had graced him with so far.

CHAPTER 22

Ureña, Venezuela

After stopping at a three-story cinderblock hotel with the appearance of a marginally renovated prison painted a hue of orange unknown in nature, and getting directions to the highway stop where the bus north picked up passengers, Jet, Matt, and Hannah made their way to Carrera 1, the two-lane strip of battered pavement that wound through the mountains and connected to the main highway that ran to the Caribbean Sea.

A retired school bus hissed to a squeaking stop as they arrived, and four leather-skinned laborers disembarked. Jet confirmed with the driver that the bus was going all the way to the port city of Maracaibo, and then paid the fare in dollars, which were gladly received.

They trundled down the narrow central aisle and claimed a vacant bench seat adjacent to a pair of ancient women whose stern countenances poked from beneath frayed head scarves, their faces lined from lifetimes of hardship, eyes dull with age. The bus lurched forward with a grinding of gears, and in a few minutes Hannah fell into an uneasy sleep in Jet's lap, her head resting on her mother's chest.

The heat was abated by meager ventilation from the open windows, though the bus rarely exceeded walking speed as it labored up the long grade. The muggy stifle cooled with the higher altitude as they neared San Pedro Del Rio, on the far side of the range, and remained bearable for the rest of the journey. Once past the small town, they left the switchbacks and dead man's curves of the smaller hill road, merged onto a wider highway, and picked up speed.

The bus stopped for a ten-minute lunch in San Juan de Colón, and Jet was reassured to find Hannah's appetite returning. Matt bought enough food to feed a battalion and had the cook box it up for the ride, and soon they were bumping and swaying along again, making better progress as the highway flattened out.

The monotony of the trip was broken up only once, at a National Guard checkpoint at the *alcabala* bridge, when a trio of soldiers barely older than Matt's haircut boarded the bus, clutching machine guns and stared menacingly at the passengers. Fortunately, the driver appeared to know them, and after a few lighthearted remarks about the lack of pretty young girls aboard, the soldiers returned to their posts and the bus was on its way again.

Daylight was fading as they drew near their destination – the port of La Ensenada, the smaller cousin of the massive commercial harbor of Maracaibo. After considerable discussion, Jet had convinced Matt that their chances of finding a Cuba-bound cargo ship willing to carry three undocumented voyagers would be better in a less prominent hub, and they'd decided to find a hotel near the waterfront. Hannah could get some much-needed rest, and Jet would scour the ubiquitous bars that catered to seamen for a captain who wanted to earn some easy extra cash.

The driver grinned a dull yellow smile at Jet as he slowed to a stop and they stepped down to the street, and thanked her again for the dollars he'd converted for her. He had offered to change as many as she wanted into the local currency over lunch, and she'd taken him up on the offer, figuring that she'd attract less attention with bolivars instead of greenbacks. The driver waved at Hannah and roared away with grinding gears.

Matt surveyed the squalid surroundings and offered Jet a smile. "Charming. And we thought Colombia was grim?"

"We're not looking for a resort, just a flophouse for the night."

"Doesn't seem like the kind of place where there would be all that many hotels."

"That's okay. A lot of the time in Venezuela, as well as in Cuba, the locals augment their income by renting out a room to guests."

They walked along the main street toward the water, past a cemetery with crumbling headstones, a few wilted bouquets leaning against the markers. At the corner they stopped at a market. Jet bought water and juice, and as she paid, asked the young man working the counter about any guest houses in the area. He gave her directions to two near the waterfront, and they continued their trek as the sun disappeared behind the hills.

The first candidate got an automatic rejection from Jet due to its filthy yard and the pair of tough-looking shirtless men with mottled tattoos running the length of their arms who loitered on the porch. The second house was an improvement, although unmistakably fallen on hard times, an upper window replaced with plywood, the robin's egg blue paint peeling from its façade. Jet was leery until she met the owner, Cora, a jolly big-boned woman with an easy laugh and gleaming white teeth, who showed her around the property and ensured she was comfortable with her choice.

The room was clean and simply furnished, with the added bonus of a bathroom next door and no other guests in evidence. Matt and Jet took turns showering, Jet helping Hannah with the task, and then they feasted on the remnants of lunch, which proved to be delicious even after a day on the road. When they finished, Jet kissed Matt and took the stairs down to the main level.

Cora spotted her and frowned. "Best be careful, young lady. Things aren't as safe as they used to be. Plenty of men out of work, with too much time on their hands."

"Thanks. I'm sure I'll be fine. I'm just going out for a look around."

"That's a beautiful little girl you have. Be a shame for her to lose her mom."

"It would. So I'll make sure nothing happens."

"We close the doors at ten."

Jet glanced at her watch. That gave her a couple of hours. "Okay. I'll be back before then."

"Might want to stay away from the area by the docks. The places down there play to a rough crowd."

"I'll remember that. Thanks again."

Jet hurried the two blocks to the darkened waterfront, eyes methodically scanning the street. When she made it to the shore road, it was with relief. Not so much that she was afraid of being jumped as because she didn't want to invite more trouble – the altercation in Cúcuta was still fresh in her mind, and it would be disastrous to have to explain herself to the Venezuelan police, a corrupt and mean-spirited bunch, she knew from experience.

Music pulsed from three bars, barely more than shacks near the jetties, and she made straight for them, drawing confidence from the weight of the pistol at the small of her back. The first dive was almost empty, only a few plastic tables occupied by morose drunks sharing plastic bottles of rum. She hurried to the next and felt the attention of several dozen men as she entered; the only other females present were four of the saddest-looking hookers she'd ever seen.

Jet elbowed her way to the bar, ignoring the leers of the sailors, and fixed the bartender with a cool stare as she ordered a beer. He nodded wordlessly and rooted for a bottle in an ice chest behind the counter, and popped the cap before handing it to her. She sat on the rickety stool and waited for someone to make his pitch.

A sunburned man with a shaved head, wearing a dirty tank top that featured a four-wheel-drive truck on the back, approached her and set his beer down next to hers.

"You lost?" he asked in Spanish.

"No."

"Don't see many like you around here."

"Is that right?"

His eyes narrowed as he regarded her. "You working?"

"No. Looking for a boat."

He took a long pull on his beer and signaled to the bartender for another. "Yeah? What kind?"

"Why?"

"I know everybody in this dump. Name's Ricardo." He held out a hand, which Jet ignored.

"Any boats going to Cuba?" she asked.

He laughed, the sound a hoarse bark, and ferreted in his baggy jeans for a pack of cigarettes. He lit it and blew a cloud of smoke at the ceiling. "Why would you want to go there?"

"I'm adventurous," she said, and clinked her bottle against his.

"Yeah? Well, I might know a guy."

"That's nice to hear."

"I could introduce you, for a price."

Jet sighed and turned to face him, emerald eyes flashing in the dim light. "Tell you what. You introduce me and we work a deal, your buddy can pay you whatever the going rate is. That way I don't have to worry about you being full of shit, and everybody walks away happy if they get what they want."

"And what if he doesn't agree to help you?"

"Then the introduction was worthless."

Ricardo laughed again and drank deep from his beer. "Wow. You're really something, aren't you?"

"Why don't we let your guy decide that one?"

He finished his cigarette, polished off the rest of his second beer, and dropped the butt into the bottle. "You going to at least buy me a drink?"

She reluctantly pulled a small-denomination bill from her pocket and laid it on the bar, and then looked at Ricardo with overt skepticism. "Nobody's getting any younger, and I've got a curfew. Is he here, or are we going someplace else?"

Ricardo grinned, and she noted that he wasn't one to waste his time with niceties like dental hygiene. "Bar next door."

She stood, ignoring the way he slowly looked her up and down. "Lead the way. But a word of advice. Try anything funny and you'll be walking on sticks. Nothing personal, but I've had a really hard day, so my patience isn't what it normally is."

He laughed again, this time with less conviction. "Don't worry. I want the money more than anything else I could get from you."

"That's good to hear. Let's go."

CHAPTER 23

Maracaibo, Venezuela

Ario yawned and stretched his arms over his head as he stepped from the bus, pain flaring in his lower back after another fifteen-hour workday of driving. His life wasn't that bad, he told himself, working three shifts a week, four off, navigating the same stretch of road between San Antonio del Táchira, where his uncle put him up on his overnight stays, and Maracaibo, where he lived with his wife and five children. True, the pay was miserable, but the work was easy compared to what many had to contend with, and his biggest complaints were the numbness in his legs following a day on the road and his steadily increasing weight due to being sedentary.

He waved at another driver who was leaving the yard. The depot was largely empty late at night as the last of the day's buses arrived. Few were willing to risk overnight trips anymore since the country had fallen into disrepair and lawlessness, other than the daredevils on the main routes, with armed guards riding along to discourage robberies.

Ario signed in and dropped the keys into a lockbox. A mechanic would do a cursory once-over in the early morning, and then a different driver would head south as his counterpart drove north after overnighting in San Antonio del Táchira. Ario looked into the small dispatcher's office at where his friend Martin, a hirsute man with the world's worst toupée, was working the radio, which Ario knew largely meant reading pornographic magazines and surfing the web on the graveyard shift.

"Hey, tough guy. You made it again! I lost money on that bet," Martin joked by way of greeting.

"Yes, but there's always next shift. Anything happening?"

"We had another armed assault on the route from Caracas. Cleaned everyone out, but no casualties, by the grace of God."

"Would have been nice of God if he'd simply prevented the robbery in the first place, don't you think?"

"He works in mysterious ways, you blasphemer."

Ario caught sight of a fax on Martin's desk, a photograph and text printed on the single page. "What's that?"

"Oh. From the boss. They're on the lookout for this chick and her family," Martin said.

"Can I see it?"

"Pervert. Although she's hot, you can tell, even in the shit photo." Martin handed Ario the fax and resumed his game of computer solitaire. Ario was silent for several moments.

"What do they want them for?"

"Dunno. Didn't say. Just said there was a reward if anyone spotted them."

"Yeah? How big?"

Martin stopped what he was doing and challenged Ario. "Why are you so interested?"

"I think I gave them a ride today."

Martin's mouth dropped open. "You're kidding."

"No, really. Her, a kid, and a guy. A gringo. Just like it says here."

"Where did they get off?"

Ario thought for a moment. "Let's find out how big the reward is. The second I tell anyone where I dropped them, they no longer have to pay me."

"Pay *us*. I'll help you negotiate, but it's got to be us. Fifty-fifty."

"You're dreaming. Ninety-ten."

After a minute of back and forth, they agreed eighty-twenty was fair, based on Martin's superior negotiating skills. Ario was a simple man, whereas Martin had lived in Caracas, a big city, and as such was worldlier and could cut a better deal.

Martin dialed the number on the fax and a gravelly voice answered. "Yeah?"

"This is Martin Gonzalez, from the Emporio bus group."

"And?"

"You sent out a fax earlier today?"

The voice quickened. "That's right, we did."

"One of my group knows the woman you're looking for. She was on his bus."

"Are you certain?"

"Of course."

"Where?"

"Picked her, the gringo, and the kid up in Ureña."

"Where did she get off?"

Martin cleared his throat. "The fax mentions a reward. How much?"

"Depends on how solid the information is."

"It's solid."

The voice mentioned a number. Martin swallowed, trying not to show his surprise. "That's all?"

"Look, we both know it's a fortune. If you think you can do better, call someone else."

"No, no. That won't be necessary. How are you planning to pay it?"

"Cash. American dollars. We're good for it. Now where is she?"

"Not so fast. We'll tell you as soon as you hand over the money. Fair's fair."

There was a long pause. "You're playing a dangerous game," the voice warned.

"No offense intended, *patrón*. But we live in uncertain times. How soon can you meet?"

"Where are you?"

"Maracaibo."

"Let me check."

Martin heard a muffled conversation in the background, and then the voice in his ear again. "I can have someone there in about four hours. They have to gather the cash. Where exactly are you?"

Martin gave him the address. "There's security here at the depot, so nothing funny, all right? I'll be waiting for you."

"You'd be better served telling me where she is right now. There's some urgency to the situation."

"Then you better tell your guy to hurry."

Martine hung up and told Ario what had happened. Ario looked shocked.

"Twenty thousand dollars? What did she do, kill the President?"

"Who cares? You just made out like a bandit, my friend. The only downside is I have to put up with you stinking up my office for four more hours."

"I'll get some beer."

Martin grinned. "You know we aren't supposed to drink on the job."

"Who's going to know? It's not like they send inspectors. Besides, you're not flying a jet, you're answering the radio. Come on. Icy cold. My treat."

"You're a silver-tongued devil."

"Now upgraded to a platinum tongue, thanks to our mystery girl," Ario agreed, and they both smiled. Every so often life handed someone their big chance, and it was foolish not to grab it with both hands. Neither wanted to think about why anyone would pay that much to learn what bus stop the woman had gotten off at; it was none of their business. "I'll get the beer."

"Good man."

CHAPTER 24

La Ensenada, Venezuela

Ricardo led Jet to the adjacent bar, a ramshackle wooden building whose weathered sign featured a crude painting of a winking mermaid with breasts that blinked green lights in alternation, left right, left right, although not quite evenly timed.

Jet eyed the sea goddess and gave him a sidelong glance. "Nice," she said drily.

"It's a classy place."

"I can tell."

They entered and Ricardo looked around the room and then made his way through the sparsely populated tables to one near the rear of the room, where two older men with silver crew cuts sat smoking and drinking. The one with a bushy mustache shot daggers at Ricardo like he'd spilled a drink in his lap, and raised a single eyebrow.

Ricardo cleared his throat nervously. "Capitan Adrian, this is...a new friend. She's looking for passage to Cuba. God knows why. But I heard you were shipping out tomorrow, and I thought..." Ricardo trailed off, an expectant expression on his face.

"Oh, yeah?" Adrian said, and then nodded at his companion. The man rose and walked unsteadily to the bar. "Have a seat."

Jet did as instructed, and Ricardo fidgeted behind her. He lit a cigarette and eyed Adrian. "She said you'd take care of me out of whatever you work out."

The captain's gaze drifted to Ricardo's face. "Then I will. But I haven't even heard what she wants. Why don't you get yourself a drink on me and let me discuss business, all right?"

"I told you, she needs to get to Cuba–"

112

Adrian half stood, his jaw muscle clenching. "And I told you to take a load off over there."

The two men stared at each other for a tense beat, and Ricardo backed away. "Okay. I'll be at the bar."

Captain Adrian sat back down and tilted his head at the half-empty bottle. "You want a drink?"

Jet shook her head. "No, thanks. Ricardo tells me you're Cuba bound in the morning?"

"That's right."

"Any interest in carrying some passengers?"

Adrian's eyes studied her face. "How many?"

"Three. Me, my husband, and my kid."

"There are flights, you know."

"I like the sea."

"My boat's no luxury cruiser."

"I prefer a more genuine experience."

He nodded slowly. "You have papers?"

She shook her head and kept her expression flat. "I was robbed."

"But you have money?"

"They didn't get everything."

"That was lucky. Well, considering the risk involved in carrying undocumented passengers, it wouldn't be cheap."

"What range are you thinking?"

"Two thousand apiece. In advance. In dollars."

Jet was inclined to take the deal, but knew that stylistically it would be a mistake. She countered with three thousand for all of them, and they settled on five.

Her business concluded, she stood. Adrian took a long drag on his cigarette and stubbed it out in an overflowing ashtray. "Be at the dock by seven. We'll be fueling and loading the rest of the cargo, and taking off by eight. Bring cash. No excuses. If you miss us, we aren't going to wait for you." He pulled a pen from his pocket and scribbled a phone number on the back of a napkin. "Here's my cell if you have any questions."

"That's fine." She looked over her shoulder at Ricardo. "What about him? I don't want to get mugged on the way home."

"He's harmless. I'll take care of Ricky. But be careful. There are plenty of undesirables around, and you're a fine-looking woman."

"Thanks for the warning. Which ship is yours, and which dock?"

"The *Milan*. You can't miss her. Black hull, second dock from the refinery."

She nodded. "How long will the trip take?"

"Two full days and nights, assuming Mother Nature cooperates, to Cienfuegos, southwest of Havana. As many as three if it turns. But the weather reports call for relatively calm seas so far, so you're in luck."

She smiled at his words. "Yes, I feel lucky."

He returned his attention to his drink and waved a hand at Ricardo, the look of disdain returning to his face. Jet didn't stay around to hear their negotiation, and instead made for the door, aware that every minute she stayed, she risked attracting the wrong kind of attention.

CHAPTER 25

Frontino, Colombia

Mosises cracked an eye open as his cell phone rang on the nightstand. He checked the time as he rolled over to answer it: almost three in the morning. He saw the number and was instantly awake.

"Yes?"

"They're in La Ensenada. Up by Maracaibo, Venezuela. Or at least that's where they got off the bus."

"La Ensenada?" Mosises thought for a moment. "There's nothing there."

"There's a port. They're probably meeting a ship."

"Damn. Anything else?"

"No. Our contact in Maracaibo paid the reward. We've got to reimburse him, but that's nothing."

"Fine. I'll phone you back shortly. In the meantime, call the pilots and have them get going as soon as possible. I'll take care of Ramón and have him break the news to Fernanda."

Mosises hung up and called Ramón, who didn't answer until the fifth ring.

"Hello?"

"Get to the airport. You're headed to Venezuela. We know where they are." Mosises imparted the bus driver's information. They discussed strategy for a few minutes before disconnecting, and Mosises made two more calls, one of which was to Fernanda. She listened as he described the situation, and he could hear the frustration in her voice when he told her it would take three hours to reach the town by helicopter. She was adamant that she wanted to bring her weapons with her into Venezuela, and he agreed – there

115

would be no time to acquire specialized guns if their targets were on the move. His Venezuelan contact would smooth the way with customs and ensure they weren't disturbed on arrival. Mosises moved enough product through Maracaibo to know he could buy virtually anything from the staff at the airport, and it was just a matter of money – something he had in plentiful supply.

By the time he was done, he'd mobilized everyone he could think of. The murderers of his son would not escape again, he'd see to that. If they had still been in Colombia, they'd already be dead, but Venezuela was a special case, and he couldn't send an army after them like he wanted to. Still, Fernanda was deadly, and he had no doubt that she would take appropriate steps to locate and execute them.

Mosises stared at the wooden blades of the ceiling fan circling overhead in the gloom, and after five minutes of sleeplessness, sat up and moved to a cabinet at the far end of the room. He opened it and removed a bottle of twenty-year-old rum and poured three fingers into a tumbler, and then sat in a chair, staring out at the grounds where the moon grinned crookedly in the night sky, alone with the memories of his only son, now lost to him forever.

"They will pay, Jaime. They. Will. Pay," he whispered, and threw back half the glass, wincing at the burn in his throat as he swallowed. "You will be avenged if it's my last act on earth."

~ ~ ~

Maracaibo, Venezuela

Drago read his cell phone screen, and after a long pause, turned on the light in his hotel room. He'd taken a calculated risk that the little family would make for the nearest port, and he hadn't been far off. The text to Renaldo put them only ten kilometers south of him, in La Ensenada. His biggest problem now would be acquiring a gun – he'd left his weapons in Colombia, unwilling to risk detection when he flew into Venezuela.

He forced himself out of bed and stepped into his clothes. In every town, whatever the country, there was always a district where guns could be had for a price. Whether in Washington or São Paolo or Buenos Aires, the underworld worked the same: if you knew where to look, the streets were a twenty-four-hour shopping center for illicit goods.

Thirty minutes later he was sitting in an after-hours salsa club, outlining his needs to a young man wearing a flat-brimmed Yankees baseball cap, with tattoos emblazoned on his neck and a scar from a knife running down his right cheek. Two other toughs stood behind him, arms folded, watching him impassively like the posse from a bad rap video. The young thug sat back, a smirk on his face.

"Yo, man, that's some heavy shit you need. You planning to start a war or something?"

Drago smiled dangerously. "What's it to you?"

"You got the cash to handle it?"

"I know the going rate. Three grand should do the trick." Drago had requested a Glock 9mm and a submachine gun, with suppressors. The thug hadn't even blinked at the request. In a violent society with a mortality rate that was as high as many active war zones, Venezuela had more guns floating around than it did cars. It hadn't taken Drago long to find a willing conduit who claimed he could get him whatever he wanted. "And another five hundred for three spare magazines for each."

"That might be what it runs over on the other side of the hill, but here there's a premium, you understand? Five grand for the whole thing."

Drago knew he was overpaying, but time was money, and he was in a hurry.

"How long will it take?" he asked, his voice soft.

"Two hours, maybe a little more."

Drago considered it. "Done. Where do we meet?"

"Come back here. Place keeps going till dawn." The thug's eyes searched Drago's face. "You want a couple lines on the house, give you a little pick-me-up?"

"No, thanks. Just the guns."

"All right, then. See you back here at…six thirty?"

"Count on it. You want some cash in advance?"

The youngster shook his head. "Nah. You look like a man on a mission. I can tell you'll be here right on the nose. Am I right?"

Drago smiled again. "You have a bright future in business."

"That's how I roll, Pops."

CHAPTER 26

Port-au-Prince, Haiti

The best cell in a Haitian jail was as bad as the worst in a Turkish prison, Jon Renoir thought idly as he stared at the far wall, ignoring the seven other prisoners in the space. He'd been locked up for too long, his attorney unable to get a straight answer on what the specific charge was, and he had a sinking feeling that his arrest had been orchestrated by one of his rivals so he couldn't coordinate an effective defense when they moved into his territory.

The stagnant air reeked of stale sweat, urine, and filth. He shot a disgusted glance at the bucket in the corner that served as the community toilet, and then went on studying the other prisoners. They were unanimously emaciated and skittish, junkies who'd been picked up after stabbing someone or trying to mug the wrong person, or who had simply collapsed in the wrong place at the wrong time. What passed for the law in Haiti was both arbitrary and extreme, and often the arrested never made it out of jail alive – the accidental death rate for the incarcerated in Port-au-Prince had been the subject of numerous human rights organization protests, none of which had changed much of anything but which ditch the bodies were dumped in.

So far Renoir had been fortunate, and none of the inmates had attacked him. But he sensed it was just a matter of time – at least three of the prisoners were eyeing him like he was a drunk college girl at a frat party, and he had no doubt that whenever he drifted off to sleep, one of them would slit his throat in the blink of an eye. If his rivals were behind this, they would have ensured they'd placed professional killers in his cell, which in Haiti meant anyone willing to murder for a pack of cigarettes and a meal. Renoir had arranged enough hits to know the ropes, and he was under no illusion that he was intended to walk out of the building alive.

But Renoir was powerfully built and street savvy, which had served as sufficient deterrent so far. Each of his legs weighed as much as any of the other prisoners, and none of the captives seemed particularly suicidal, so as long as he could stay awake…

Which was getting harder to do. He'd refused offers of water from the guards, wary of being drugged, preferring dehydration to a final slumber at the hands of an assassin. The problem was that in the heat he was losing electrolytes as he sweated, and eventually he knew that he'd pass out.

He shook his head to clear it and caught one of the men studying him.

"Whatchou looking at, punkass?" Renoir growled.

"Nothin', boss," the man responded, his weasel eyes jaundiced a sickly yellow.

"Best mind your own business, you hear? Don't wanna get your fool neck broken, do you?"

"No, boss."

The popping of small-arms fire sounded from outside the high, narrow window. The prisoners froze – anyone living in Port-au-Prince was more than familiar with the gunfire. Answering volleys from pistols and shotguns boomed from within the jail, followed by the steady chatter of assault rifles on full auto. Shouting drifted from down the hall, and then the deafening explosion of a detonating grenade nearly blew out Renoir's eardrums.

"What the hell…?" one of the prisoners cried, and cringed as more gunfire erupted from inside the building.

A man's dying scream shrieked from the corridor, followed by another spate of shots. Renoir caught movement in his peripheral vision and spun quickly for a man of his size. The gleam of a blade in one of the prisoner's hands swung toward him and he blocked it, but too late, and he felt the warm rush of blood from his meaty side as the shank sliced deep just above his waist.

Renoir ignored the flash of agony and punched his assailant twice in the face, his football-sized fist moving at jackhammer speed. A spray of blood and teeth splattered the wall as the man slumped, but Renoir was on the attack and finished the assault by slamming the prisoner's head into the concrete wall, the crack of his skull splitting audible over the shots.

The dead attacker collapsed onto the floor, and Renoir glared at the rest of the prisoners as he held his side, his fingers slick with blood.

"Anyone else want to play? This boy need some company in hell," he snarled, challenging any other possible killers. The men looked away, and then the rattle of a submachine gun drew Renoir's attention to the flat steel cell-block door.

The shooting stopped and a key scraped against the lock. The bolt opened and the door swung wide, and then three men with AK-47s entered, bandannas hiding the lower part of their faces. The lead gunman's eyes met Renoir's.

The crime boss grinned. "About time you showed up. One of these cockroaches cut me."

A fourth gunman entered, carrying a ring of keys filched from a dead guard, and approached the barred door. After several unsuccessful tries, the lock sprang with a snap and the door creaked open. Renoir stepped through it and turned to the men who'd been giving him the evil eye and pointed to them. "Shoot them," Renoir said, and the lead gunman blew the men's heads off as the other inmates ducked for cover.

Renoir nodded in satisfaction and followed the gunmen out of the cell block. None of the other prisoners moved until they heard engines growl from the window and the sound of big vehicles pull off. Without a word they rushed to the open door and made their way into the holding area, where dead police officers lay in contorted positions on the bloody floor. Three of the men scrambled for guns lying by the bodies, their cash value significant on the streets of Port-au-Prince, while the others bolted for the exit, the keening of approaching sirens all the warning they needed.

By the time reinforcements arrived, Renoir's group was long gone, as were the men who'd shared the cell with him. U.N. peacekeeping soldiers stepped gingerly through the corpses, weapons at the ready, but more than aware that the threat was past, the jail empty. Police filed in from other stations over the next ten minutes, but by the time they arrived, all that remained to be done was the loading of body bags and the scheduling of a news conference filled with empty promises to bring the perpetrators to justice.

CHAPTER 27

Maracaibo, Venezuela

The sun was rising over the water when Drago returned to the after-hours club. The only vehicles on the street were a garbage truck emptying overflowing dumpsters and an army Jeep with four masked soldiers brandishing assault rifles. Drago waited until the Jeep had passed and knocked on the door. Moments later it opened, and a bouncer with a face like a ham nodded to him and stepped aside.

Drago entered the club, the walls painted matte black with psychedelic posters mounted in chromed frames, and moved past the few remaining tables of die-hard partiers finishing their drinks and cigarettes. He approached the door that led to the back room, where one of the gun dealer's henchmen stood, his jacket barely concealing the shoulder-holstered pistol wedged beneath his meaty arm.

Drago nodded to him. The bodyguard grunted a greeting and twisted the doorknob. Drago squeezed past him and stepped into the office, where the young dealer was sitting behind his desk, his smirk firmly in place. Bodyguard number two stood behind him with his hand on the pistol in his belt.

"Yo, youngblood, take a load off," he said to Drago.

Drago sat opposite him, his face impassive, waiting. The dealer pushed a mirror with a line of white powder on it to the side, reached onto the floor next to his chair, and hoisted a nylon bag onto the desktop. He unzipped it, removed a pistol and a MAC-10, and set both down in front of Drago, who eyed the machine pistol skeptically.

"What the hell is that?"

"Best I could get in the time you got, big man," the dealer said, laying a single small suppressor on the table beside the guns.

"I'd be lucky to hit a car at ten feet with that piece of crap. MAC-10s are for drive-bys, not serious work."

"Ain't all that bad."

"You can't get me a real gun?"

"Take it or leave it, Dad."

Drago fieldstripped the pistol and examined it, then pieced it back together. He did the same with the MAC-10 and shook his head in disgust. "Does this thing even fire?"

"It do indeed."

"It looks like it's straight off a B movie set."

The dealer shrugged. "You wanted a chatter gun. That's what it is."

Drago shook his head and withdrew a wad of dollars wrapped with a rubber band. He tossed it to the dealer. "Highway robbery. What about a suppressor for the MAC?"

His host smirked again and began counting the cash as Drago inspected the magazines in the bag. "Couldn't get one," he replied, thumbing through the bills with practiced ease. He was looking up from the money when Drago slapped a magazine into the MAC-10, chambered a round, and sprayed the dealer and the bodyguard with slugs. The dealer's shirt sprouted a collage of red blossoms and the bodyguard slammed into the wall, his weapon half-drawn, now useless to him. Drago waited a beat and then emptied the machine pistol through the wooden entry door.

The MAC-10 snapped empty and Drago moved to the bag. Even with ringing ears he could hear a woman's scream from the club floor. He slipped another magazine into the MAC-10 and tossed the Glock into the bag with the remaining magazines. Drago paused and eyed the dealer, who was struggling for breath behind the desk, the wounds in his chest burbling blood with each inhalation.

"You were right. It'll do," Drago said, and after pocketing the money, made for the ruined exit.

When he stepped over the second bodyguard's corpse and into the club's main room, it was cleared of customers. He walked to the entrance, where the sun was shining through the partially open door, and after peering out at the sidewalk, stowed the MAC-10 in the bag and exited onto the street, his movements calm and unhurried as he walked through the run-down district, to all the world just another pedestrian on his way to work.

Drago checked the time and rounded a corner. When he was out of sight of the club, he increased his pace. At a larger thoroughfare, he flagged down a taxi and slid into the rear seat.

"How long will it take to get to La Ensenada?" he asked the driver.

"Oh, maybe fifteen minutes. Depends on traffic, you know?"

Drago nodded. "If you can get me there in ten, there's a big tip in it for you."

The driver put the car in gear and considered Drago in the rearview mirror. "In a hurry, huh?"

"You have no idea."

CHAPTER 28

La Ensenada, Venezuela

Fernanda exhaled impatiently as Ramón piloted a Nissan sedan into the impoverished town. A group of children shambled along the dusty street on their way to school, uniforms ragged and worn, their faces already hard from an unforgiving life with little future.

As they neared the waterfront, she sat forward, her nerves tingling. She could sense it: the woman and her family were here, trying to escape Fernanda's wrath. But they wouldn't stand a chance. She knew that finding them wherever they were holed up would take too long, but a better idea came to her after studying the harbor and the surrounding buildings.

The Nissan reached the shore road, and Ramón looked to Fernanda for direction. She pointed to her right. "Do a lap. Let's see what's at the docks."

Ramón cruised along slowly, and Fernanda eyed the various ships tied to the concrete jetties. When he reached the wall that separated a massive oil refinery from the rest of the harbor, she gave the ships a final appraisal and checked her cell phone.

"Make a left here," she said, and Ramón obliged. The sun's rays washed across the dashboard and they shielded their eyes. Fernanda pointed at a beige spire jutting skyward. "There it is."

Ramón rolled to a stop in front of the church doors and Fernanda got out of the car, rucksack in hand. "Wait over on the far end of the strand and call me if you see them."

"You sure this is the best way to handle it?" he asked.

"Absolutely. There's too much ground to cover for us to watch all the boats. But from the bell tower I'll be able to monitor the entire area, and when I see them, I can pick them off before they know what hit them."

"Okay. Same with you. Ring me if you spot them."

Fernanda nodded and turned to the church, impatient and anxious. Even now she could be missing the woman as she neared one of the cargo ships. Ramón was a convenience, but she was tiring of him, although his presence was a necessary evil. Without Mosises' help, she'd have never been able to pinpoint her quarry to the obscure port, much less get to Venezuela so quickly. But she wouldn't call Ramón until after she'd put a bullet through the woman's skull. She'd had enough of the cartel's ineptness, and had seen all she needed to with Jaime's botched assault on the monastery and the bad lead on the clinic to involve Ramón until after the shooting was over.

From now on she'd do things her way.

She eased one of the tall double doors open and entered the church. A young priest walked toward her from the altar area, and she smiled disarmingly as he approached.

"Welcome to God's house, my child. Let me know if there's anything I can–" he began.

Fernanda's lightning blow to his throat caught him completely by surprise, instantly crushing his larynx and choking him. He collapsed on the stone floor and flailed like a beached fish as Fernanda watched him wordlessly. After several minutes his complexion turned blue from cyanosis, and he lay still. She dragged him to the confessional booth and propped him up inside, drew the red velvet curtain, and then made for the rear of the church and the stairs that led to the bell tower.

When she was beside the altar, she listened for any movement, but heard nothing. The priest, as she expected, had been alone, preparing the church for any stragglers in need of spiritual guidance. The sign out front promised a mass every evening at six, and at ten and six on Sundays, so she had all day before she had to worry about anyone getting suspicious about the good father's absence.

The stairs were off the vestry. She took them two at a time, anxious to get into position.

The wharf was just beginning to stir when she reached the top of the tower. Two amorous pigeons flapped away, startled by her arrival, and she smiled bitterly. *Enjoy it, my feathered friends, because you never know how long it's going to last.* Igor's face popped into her mind and she blinked it away. She needed to stay focused, not daydream about lost love. She would mourn Igor in her own time – once he'd been avenged, and not before.

Fernanda inched toward the gap and looked out at the shimmering blue of Maracaibo Lake, which fed into the Caribbean Sea north of the city. The morning sun gilded the surface as she scanned the cargo vessels. Seamen and dock laborers were just arriving to work, the activity muted at the early hour. Near the refinery, two men wrestled a thick fuel hose to a medium-sized cargo ship as the captain watched from the deck, but there was no sign of the woman or her family.

Fernanda unzipped her bag, withdrew her sniper rifle, and set the suppressor and two magazines beside her before peering through the scope. She calculated the range and figured that the docks were no more than four hundred meters away – a manageable shot for a professional, especially with no real wind and high humidity.

Fernanda adjusted the scope and then sat back and affixed the suppressor, twisting it onto the machined threads carefully. When she was done, she slipped a magazine into the rifle and loaded a cartridge, and then went back to scanning the boats, the stock resting on the thick lip of the bell tower, the barrel all but invisible – not that she had any concerns about detection. She was positive that the last thing in the world the woman would be expecting was to be picked off on her way to a boat in Nowhere, Venezuela. She probably assumed that she'd gotten away clean, which would have been the case had it not been for Fernanda's involvement.

Fernanda settled in for a wait, the gun comfortable in her hands. The men onboard the ships were clearly visible in the scope, the resolution so high it seemed as though she could reach out and touch them.

Now it was a matter of patience, and she could outwait the best of them.

As her quarry was going to discover as their last living realization.

CHAPTER 29

La Ensenada, Venezuela

The taxi carrying Drago stopped at the waterfront, and he paid the driver the promised bonus. He took in the empty square as he climbed from the cab. The taxi rumbled away over the distressed pavement, and Drago moved to a small park across the street from the quay and sheltered himself from the morning sun beneath a grove of trees. Not much was moving on the docks, which didn't surprise him, and should work in his favor. The town was small enough that there could only be one reason for Matt and the woman to have come there instead of continuing to Maracaibo, and that was to find a boat.

They would be smart enough to figure out that any major harbor would likely be on alert – but a second-string port like La Ensenada would be at the bottom of most lists, which made it perfect. It's what he would have done. And they were pros, so their instincts would be similar.

Now he just needed to find them.

He considered the layout of the wharf and asked himself how he would have done it. He was sure they'd already found a willing vessel, given their motivation. While it was possible they were already aboard, it was unlikely, in case there was an unexpected search by the authorities – a fairly common occurrence in ports near Colombia. No, they'd wait until the last possible second and then board just before the boat departed.

He fished his binoculars from his bag and killed time by scanning

130

the ships — as sorry a collection of rust buckets as he'd ever seen. A vendor pushed a cart across the parking lot toward the first jetty, ringing a chime to alert the workers, but other than that and a few scraggly seagulls marching along the concrete embankment, the area was deserted.

After ten minutes, he grew bored and studied the surrounding buildings, the ache in his head reminding him of his sleep deficit. The town was a shithole, even by third world standards, with its noxious lake water and all the structures in disrepair. He tried to imagine what it must be like to live in a purgatory like La Ensenada and shook his head.

Something flashed on the edge of his vision, and he turned the spyglasses toward it. He saw a multistory home, a few warehouses, a church... Whatever it was caught the sun again and glinted.

In the bell tower.

He cursed. He'd gotten it wrong. His quarry hadn't assumed they were in the clear at all. They were conducting surveillance on the port, watching for watchers. Watching for him.

And he was exposed. Although...his appearance was different enough that it was possible they wouldn't recognize him, especially under his stained baseball cap and sunglasses. The woman had only seen him in the dark, at the river, for a moment. Matt was a different story, but depending on which of them was up there working the morning shift...

He dropped the binoculars back into his bag and stood. Now committed to making a move, he crossed the road at a measured pace, taking care to do so while walking away from the port so all a watcher would see was the back of his head. As Drago approached the sidewalk, he turned and skirted the buildings until he arrived at a street that led toward the church. He hadn't felt the sensation of being in the crosshairs, so he was confident that he hadn't been spotted. That, and he was still breathing, which he was sure he wouldn't be if the woman or Matt had placed him.

At the next intersection he took another small street, and within a minute had the church in sight, closing on it from the rear, out of the field of view of the bell tower. Once near the building, he felt in his bag for the pistol and slipped it into his waistband. It wasn't easily concealable with the suppressor on, so he'd have to risk his shots being heard – a small enough concession for being able to exact his vengeance. Slipping away after shooting them would simply be more difficult. Then again, Drago had built a reputation for specializing in the impossible, and dodging some small-town cops would pose little challenge for him.

Drago moved to the rear entry to the church, but the door was locked. He glanced around and, after confirming he was unobserved, broke the pane of glass in the door with his elbow and reached in to unlock the deadbolt. The door offered no resistance and he pushed into the vestry, which was in keeping with the rest of the town, Spartan and bleak.

Once inside, his ears strained for sounds of life, but he didn't hear anything. He made his way toward the bell tower stairs and, as he moved, pulled the MAC-10 from the bag and felt for a magazine. His fingers grazed one of the distinctive long shapes, and he retrieved it and slid it into the handle before locking the bolt back and ready, taking care to do so as quietly as possible.

The stairway was narrow, the ancient wood planks worn smooth from generations of the faithful. Drago mounted the steps with silent caution, aware that any slip at this point would warn his quarry. He winced with each creak of the old timbers, seemingly deafening to him, but in reality almost inaudible. When he neared the landing at the top, he quieted his heart rate, preparing for the kill as he fingered the machine-pistol trigger in anticipation.

~ ~ ~

Fernanda shifted in place, her knees sore from the hard surface, and did another slow sweep of the docks. A second crew of dockworkers had arrived and moved to a ship behind the one being fueled, and she eyed each figure to ensure that none of them were the woman or Matt, disguised.

Movement at the edge of the parking lot drew her attention, and she swung the rifle toward two figures striding toward the jetty. She peered through the scope at the back of the pair's heads, and realized with a start that it wasn't two people at all – it was three: two adults wearing caps and dark glasses, one of them carrying a child.

Fernanda steadied the rifle as she drew a measured breath, and then a soft scrape from the stairway behind her startled her. She whirled toward it with the rifle as the doorway exploded with muzzle flashes.

Pain shrieked through her chest, but she managed to squeeze off a shot, and then her vision starbursted and she was blinded by agony. She coughed once, a band of pressure suddenly squeezing her ribcage like a vise, and then she tumbled forward, dead before her head hit the cement with a dull thud.

Drago's lips twitched in victory as he closed the distance between himself and the woman. He toed the rifle away from her lifeless hand and kneeled beside her, taking care not to spoil his pants in the thick pool of blood, and turned her over so he could see her face.

And froze.

Even with part of her cheek blown off, he realized his error. This wasn't the right woman. She looked similar to the other, but the cast of the eyes was different, less Asian, and her face was a little fuller, the jawline different.

"Damn," he muttered, trying to process what had just occurred. If this wasn't her, then…it was another pro, no doubt hired by the cartel.

Which meant the woman was still out there – and now alerted by the gunfire.

His stare drifted to the bell tower aperture, and he snatched the binoculars from his bag and scanned the waterfront. Everyone on the docks was pointing at the church, which wasn't unexpected. But what was were the two figures now running for the black-hulled cargo ship at the far jetty.

"You," he hissed under his breath. He lowered the glasses and reached for the rifle, and cursed again when he saw the ruined scope shattered by one of his rounds. The low-powered guns he had were barely adequate for close-in work, and there was no chance of hitting anyone at what looked to be at least three hundred meters and growing by the second, even if he emptied his weapons in their direction, hoping to get lucky.

He raised the glasses again and watched as the pair mounted the ship's gangplank, and then he scanned down the hull to the stern to see the name.

The *Milan*. Flagged in Liberia.

The tower seemed to sway, and he groped at a vertical beam for support. Fury coursed through him at his blunder. Not only had he shot the wrong person, but his quarry was within easy reach and he was impotent to stop them. The spell faded after a few moments, and he wiped his brow.

Drago looked around the bell tower, regaining his bearings, and made for the stairs. There was nothing to be achieved by remaining any longer, other than having to shoot it out with the police. But if he was fast enough, he might be able to make it to the ship and finish them once and for all.

All he'd need to do would be to evade any cops, bluff his way aboard the boat, and manage to execute two skilled operatives, who were probably armed and waiting for him to make a move – all the while praying that he didn't have another little episode in the process.

Normally optimistic, he admitted to himself that his odds of achieving that were somewhere between slim and none, which left him with two choices: either continue to the boat and embark on what would almost certainly be a suicide mission, or lie in wait for it wherever it was headed.

Framed that way, there was no choice. He'd need to get out of La Ensenada while he still could, before a manhunt was launched and the town was closed off as the police searched for the church shooter. If he stayed, he was guaranteed to be caught and, even with his pull, would likely die in a Venezuelan prison – his client would disown him, and he'd be left to rot.

That was unacceptable.

He'd be waiting wherever the boat was headed.
And when it arrived, he'd finish the job.
With extreme prejudice.

CHAPTER 30

Jet and Matt ducked when they heard the chatter of gunfire from the church and immediately sprinted for the *Milan*, zigzagging to create more difficult targets. When they reached the gangplank, a rough-looking seaman with a knit cap pulled low over his brow was staring at the church, the pair of dockworkers manning the fuel line oblivious to their arrival, standing nearby with open mouths. The deckhand barely seemed to register them until Jet spoke.

"We're Captain Adrian's passengers."

The seaman looked confused, as though he hadn't understood her. Jet tried again. "Where's Captain Adrian?"

"Oh, he's up on deck. By the superstructure."

"Can we board?"

The crewman was looking over her shoulder at the bell tower, his attention again drawn by the shooting. "Huh? Oh, yeah, you're passengers. He told me you'd be coming."

Jet led Matt, who was carrying Hannah, up the gangplank. Once on deck they approached Captain Adrian, who was staring at the church. His eyes darted to them for a moment and then back to the skyline.

"Did that shooting have anything to do with you?" he demanded.

"It's possible. We need to get under way. Now."

He shook his head. "It doesn't work that way. We're fueling. It will take another hour to fill the tanks."

"Tell them to disconnect the hose. We're leaving," Jet said, steel in her tone. "Don't make me escalate this. You aren't my enemy, but I'm not going to sit at the dock and wait for whoever was shooting to come for us. Do you understand?"

Adrian's eyes narrowed. "Who the hell do you think you're talking to? This is my ship, and I want you off of it, now. Go figure out your problems on your own. I didn't sign up for this."

She pulled her shirt up so he could see the butt of her pistol. "Captain Adrian, tell your men to untie the boat and disconnect the fuel line, or you'll do it at gunpoint. I don't want to hurt you, but I will to save my daughter's life. Do you understand?" Jet's green eyes locked on his. He held her glare and nodded slowly.

"You're making a huge mistake," he warned.

"Maybe, but I'm not sticking around to see who's shooting. And neither are you."

Adrian grunted and then called out to his men. "Remove the fuel line and make ready. We're getting under way. I'll be in the bridge."

The seamen and dockworkers on the jetty looked confused. Adrian turned back to Jet and Matt. "You know that hijacking a boat is about as serious an offense as there is, right? Carries the death penalty in a lot of places. I think Venezuela's one of them."

"Every second we're at this dock might be a death sentence. Start the engines and we'll discuss it on the way out to the ocean," Matt said.

Adrian regarded him and shook his head. "You'll never get away with this."

Jet shrugged. "We will if you keep your mouth shut. I'll double the fee. Ten thousand. Cash. The only ones who'll know you took some convincing will be us."

She could see greed flash across his face. If they were putting out to sea anyway, all he had to do was forget their little tiff and he'd make out like a bandit.

"What are you running from?" he asked quietly.

"I crossed the wrong people. They hold a grudge. But there are limits to how far they'll go to get us," she said, only half believing her words. "And I don't think they saw us come aboard."

"How can you be sure?"

"Do you see any gunshot wounds?"

"Then what was the shooting about?"

"I don't know. But I don't want to wait around to find out."

Adrian scowled as he considered the offer. "No more threats, is that clear? And keep your gun out of sight. There are no weapons allowed on a cargo ship like this. You could get us all thrown in a Cuban jail if you're not careful."

"You'll never see it again."

"Ten thousand. Before we get under way."

"Let's go up to the bridge. You can count it once we're away from the dock."

Adrian nodded and held a small radio to his lips. "Get the engines started."

The radio crackled. "Yes, sir. Powering up."

Adrian dropped the radio back into his pocket and gave Jet and Matt a hard stare before turning and marching to the superstructure, his footsteps thudding angrily on the steel deck. Jet and Matt trailed him, and as they neared the watertight door, Matt leaned into her, his voice quiet.

"You think he bought it?"

"I think he wants ten thousand dollars of untraceable money. That makes it easier for him to convince himself."

"What if we're wrong and he radios for help? We can still be intercepted."

"We'll stay with him at all times. In shifts. Won't let him pass any messages to his crewmen without us seeing them, no whispered discussions. We can do this, Matt. It won't be easy, but it's our best shot."

Matt nodded and studied the bell tower. "What do you make of the shooting?"

"I don't know. Could be unrelated. But right now, I don't feel lucky. Do you?"

She didn't wait for him to answer, and instead increased her pace to keep the captain in sight, her expression determined as Matt had ever seen.

When they reached the bridge, Adrian watched his men cast off the lines and ordered his helmsman to get underway. The helmsman did so without fanfare, and soon they were steaming toward the Caribbean.

Adrian eyed the gauges and shook his head. "We may not have enough fuel to get to Cienfuegos," he grumbled.

Jet sidled up beside him and handed him a fat wad of currency. "Perhaps this will soften the blow?"

Adrian pocketed the money before the helmsman saw it and smiled grimly. "I'm serious. Depending on the seas and the wind, it will be touch and go."

"Well, we're committed now, so do whatever you need to do so we make it. Maybe back off on speed?"

"I'll do that, but the truth is you can only conserve so much, and then it's in Mother Nature's hands."

Jet nodded. "Isn't everything?" She stepped away from Adrian. "Where should we put our things? My little girl needs to get some rest. She's not feeling well."

"I can show you to your cabin," Adrian said, and turned to the helmsman. "You've got the wheel."

The helmsman grunted an acknowledgement. Adrian took a final look at the fuel gauge and motioned to Matt and Jet. "Follow me. It's not the Hilton, but I have a feeling you won't have any complaints."

CHAPTER 31

Ramón spotted figures at the far end of the wharf, making their way to the parking lot, and he sat up, trying to see them better. He was fumbling with his spyglasses when he heard gunfire from the church and stiffened. It was unlike a professional of Fernanda's stature to be shooting indiscriminately. Then he remembered her weapons cache, and his brow furrowed as he swung the glasses toward the bell tower. She didn't have an automatic weapon like the one he'd heard. Just the sniper rifle, which fired single shots, and her pistol.

The shooting had been non-suppressed. Her guns were suppressed.

Ramón concentrated on the lot again. The figures had reached the jetties, but he couldn't make them out from the laborers milling about — it was too confused, and now everyone was moving too erratically to be able to spot an anomaly.

He took a final look at the church and started the car. Whoever had been shooting, there was one person it couldn't have been — Fernanda. He slowed at the thought. If not her…then could it have been the man or the woman? But how?

Ramón braked and pulled over two blocks from the church, where he could watch the entrance without being obvious. *Think.* What should he do? If Fernanda was in trouble, what could he accomplish? Any damage was already done…and he could be walking into an ambush.

Better to wait and see what happens next. He was in uncharted territory, and he didn't feel like risking his neck to discover what had gone wrong.

Minutes ticked by, and two beaten police trucks screeched to a halt in front of the church, their beds full of officers with bulletproof vests and brandishing assault rifles. The trucks emptied out and the cops set up a perimeter, and four of them pushed through the front doors of the church, guns at the ready.

He watched as the remaining police maintained their positions, rifles pointed at the building like it was going to attack them. More time crawled by, and two of the officers returned from inside the church, shaking their heads. A discussion among the group ensued, and then the officer who appeared to be calling the shots got on the radio while the rest shuffled around nervously.

One of the cargo ships moved ponderously from the dock, its superstructure barely visible over the rooftops between him and the water, drawing Ramón's attention. Its smokestack spewed a plume of black diesel smoke skyward as its huge engines rumbled across the waterfront. Ramón stiffened as the last two officers came through the church doors and one of them pointed inside. Ramón could tell from the man's body language that he was agitated, and he slid down in his seat, wondering how he could get out of there without being seen. Whatever had happened inside was obviously bad, and it would be only a matter of time before the police got their act together and began searching the area.

And when a Colombian cartel member was found with a gun within footsteps of the scene of the crime, it was a safe bet he would be treated like public enemy number one.

Ramón rolled down his window, put the transmission in gear, and eased around the corner. The officers didn't even glance in his direction. He exhaled a sigh of relief. He'd stash the gun and wait for things to calm down, and then once it was safe, try to learn what had happened. There was no other prudent course he could see, and he was sure Mosises would agree when he reported in.

For now, he had to focus on not drawing attention to himself, and find somewhere to hide his weapon.

He retrieved his cell phone and thumbed a text message as he drove, outlining the situation. A response blinked on the screen a minute later, instructing him to stay on site and do what he could. Ramón snorted to himself as he surveyed a pile of rubble near the far end of the waterfront street. It would do as a hiding place for the gun, but even as he eyed the heap, a sinking feeling spread through his gut. They'd been right behind their quarry, and then everything had gone upside down on them. He wondered if that was how it had gone down at the monastery. One second Jaime and his best men had been ready to pounce...and the next they were dead.

Ramón coasted to a stop beside the debris. He couldn't allow his imagination to get the better of him. He didn't know what had happened at the church, and would wait until he learned more before making any decisions. In the meantime, he would do as Mosises instructed and stay in position, watching the docks and waiting for the woman to show herself.

Then, it would be an altogether different game.

With the police on alert, she and her gringo friend would have a much harder time slipping onto a boat. So the situation could work in their favor if Ramón kept his head.

Still, the thought that a professional as lethal as Fernanda could have somehow been ambushed didn't portend good things.

Ramón ditched the pistol beneath a rotting plank at the edge of the trash pile and returned to the car. In spite of his better judgment, he obeyed Mosises' instructions and drove to the lot and parked, showing only normal interest in the ambulances and police vehicles on their way to the church. A restaurant was open across the street from the docks, and he found an empty table inside by the picture window and ordered coffee and a pastry, resigned to being there for the duration, judging by the number of emergency vehicles headed to the bell tower.

Four hours dragged by with nobody but workers and seamen milling around the waterfront. A contingent of soldiers, who looked baffled by why they had been stationed there, guarded the approach, along with four uniformed policemen. Ramón, floating in coffee and jittery from the caffeine, decided to change his view by strolling to a seafood shack a block away and ordering lunch. He was finishing a surprisingly good filet of local rockfish when his phone rang. It was Mosises' Venezuelan contact.

"I have someone on the ground in La Ensenada who filled me in on the situation at the church. He's a member of the police force investigating the murders."

"Murders? Plural?"

"Correct. A priest and a woman."

Ramón nodded. "So the woman is dead."

"I'm afraid so. Shot a dozen times."

"That's all they have?"

"Yes. They found her rifle, so they know she was planning on shooting someone or something from the tower. Beyond that, it's a mystery. One that, knowing how things work here, will never be solved."

"Have you spoken to our mutual acquaintance?"

"Yes. He's up to speed."

Ramón hung up and eyed the wharf. There was no point in stalling the inevitable, even if he wanted to. He texted Mosises, who responded after a ten-minute lag. His message was short and to the point: *Question the dockworkers and see if anyone saw anything. Find out what ships left and whether any took on passengers.*

Ramón frowned as he considered the order. How was he supposed to do that with police and military everywhere? He debated his alternatives and was about to send a message back, saying it was impossible, when an idea struck him. If he posed as an inspector of some sort, investigating the shooting, and avoided the uniforms, who were largely lounging out of the sun near a stand that sold drinks and cigarettes, he could probably bluff his way through. Few would demand to see identification if he carried himself with enough authority. At worst, if found out, he could claim to be a private investigator following up on an unrelated case involving Colombian runaways.

It was thin, but there was no reason it wouldn't hold up.

Ramón sent a message to Mosises, outlining his idea, and the response came in seconds: *Do it.*

He paid the check, walked to the first jetty, and began questioning the workers, who were largely not very bright and who hadn't seen anything. When he reached the second dock, he struck paydirt as the sun dropped into the horizon. A short, wiry man with deep wrinkles that hinted at nights with rum and chemical fortification nodded as Ramón began his questions.

"Only boats that left today were the *Milan*, this morning, and the *Sea Star*, about an hour ago," he said.

"Did they take on any passengers that you know of?"

"We were fueling the *Milan*, and right after the shooting, some people went aboard. What was odd is that the captain cut off the fueling early. We've been scratching our heads about that all day. I mean, he could have made a mistake on how much he needed, but that would be a first."

Ramón raised an eyebrow. "Really? Do you remember anything about the people?"

"Just that they seemed like a nice family. Of course, everyone was more interested in the shooting at that point. I mean, it had just happened. Sounded like a war broke out or something."

"A family?"

"Right. Mother, daughter, husband."

Ramón didn't react, not wanting to arouse suspicion in the seaman's eyes. "That's kind of odd, isn't it? Why would anyone want to be a passenger on a cargo ship?"

The worker shrugged. "Takes all kinds. But she was a looker. I remember that."

"And the man?"

A head shake. "Sorry. Don't remember."

Ramón nodded. "The *Milan*, huh? Any idea where they were headed?"

"Yeah. Same as usual. Cuba. They do a run every week." The man's eyes narrowed. "Why do you want to know?"

"Just trying to be thorough. What was the shooting like? Did you see anything?" Ramón asked, changing the subject to more lurid fare.

"No. It all happened so fast. But it was like firecrackers going off, you know? Pop pop pop."

"Fast like that, huh?"

"Yes. A machine gun. I know from my army days. You don't soon forget the sound."

"You said the family showed up after? How long after?"

"Oh, like, maybe thirty seconds. Almost immediately."

"Are you sure?" Ramón said, failing to hide his surprise. He would have bet money that the answer would have been five or so minutes, to allow the woman to get out of the church and reach the docks.

"Yeah. Everyone was still looking over at the church. It had just happened."

"Ah, I see."

Ramón continued his questions for another minute, but got nothing more. He left the dockworker to his duties, his mind racing. They were on the ship.

But if the mystery woman hadn't killed Fernanda, who had?

The thought that they were missing an important piece to the puzzle lingered like the aroma of decaying fish as he texted his findings to Mosises and awaited further instructions, which wound up taking an hour to reach him. When Ramón received the message, his eyes widened.

Mosises was out for blood, all right.

CHAPTER 32

Maracaibo, Venezuela

Drago sat on the veranda of his hotel, staring out at the Caribbean. The islands at the mouth of the lake rose from the water like sentries. His hair was still damp from a shower, and he had a glass of passable rum in hand, his bare feet up on the railing, the warm evening breeze pleasant.

The run from La Ensenada had been harrowing, and he'd narrowly avoided being stopped at a roadblock only seconds after passing a pair of police cars that had screeched to a halt on the road north, blocking the flow of vehicles out of town. Of course they'd been too late, but the response had been faster than he'd thought it would be – in Colombia he would have had hours from the first cops arriving on the scene. Apparently the Venezuelans were more competent than the police in his adopted home. Worth remembering, lest he underestimate them.

He'd spent the morning working his way from La Ensenada on rural roads that ran along the shore of the lake, skirting the main highway in case there were any more roadblocks – there probably wouldn't be, but he wasn't feeling like pushing his luck after gunning down the wrong woman. He still couldn't believe how similar the two looked, but it was unlike him to make mistakes, and that had been a massive one.

Drago had disassembled the MAC-10 and tossed the pieces into a lake at a deserted beach halfway between the two cities, sea birds picking at the sand in search of food the only witnesses. Once he was rid of the weapon, he felt better – now there was no way to tie him to the shooting.

All that remained was for his agent to get back to him.

He'd called in with the name of the ship and requested a rundown on it – everything he could discover. A crew list, the captain's history, ownership, and most importantly, the itinerary. Once he knew where it was headed, he would be at the port when it arrived and make short work of his targets.

The couple no doubt believed they'd left any problems behind in Venezuela, their departure undocumented on a tramp cargo vessel, even after the gunfire. They had no way of knowing it was connected to them, even if they had suspicions. Nobody had shot at them, and the likely explanation was a turf battle or a drug deal gone wrong in a country where gunfights were a daily occurrence. Like Mexico's border towns, Venezuela had been taken over by criminal gangs that battled one another as well as the army and the police, and the port cities were the most hotly contested areas due to the value of the goods moving through them.

He had no question that the pair would be on alert, but they would likely relax with time, once on land, when nobody came after them. Then, when they least expected it, he would strike.

Drago allowed himself the daydream of extracting his vengeance, picturing the terrified eyes of the woman as he inflicted the unspeakable upon her and her little girl, with Matt nearby, dead or dying. He smiled at his arousal, an affirmation that he was not only still alive but vital, and took a pull on his cocktail.

His phone rang inside the hotel room. He rose, found the cell on the bed, and stabbed it to life.

"I've sent you everything I could get," the agent said, without preliminaries. "The ship's bound for Cienfuegos, Cuba. Liberia registry. Owned by a consortium out of Caracas. Does a circuit between the ports, carrying cargo both directions."

"Where's Cienfuegos?"

"Southern part of the country."

"Not by Guantanamo, is it?" Drago asked softly, wondering if there was more in play than he was aware of. The U.S. had an infamous presence there. Could this Matt be involved in more than diamond theft?

"No, in the center, closer to Havana."

"Hmm. You'll forgive my ignorance of Cuban geography."

"I imagine you'll be a quick study." The agent paused. "But a piece of good news. The ship carries a locator chip. Its track can be followed in real time."

"Really?"

"Yes. I included all the information you'll need to do so."

"When does it arrive in Cuba?"

"Day after tomorrow. Scheduled for early afternoon. You've got time."

"That's fortunate. I suppose you know my next request."

"I'm already on it. The usual weapons, I presume?"

Drago smiled to himself. "You're a gem."

"All in the interests of closing out the contract. The client is growing increasingly impatient with each passing day."

"The target has proved more resourceful than anyone believed." Drago didn't mention his blunder with the woman.

The agent hesitated. "Are you quite sure you're up to this?"

Drago's exasperated exhalation was audible. "Is this back on the table again? I made it clear I can fulfill the contract." He paused. "Is it you or the client who is questioning my abilities?"

The agent's voice tightened. "The client isn't questioning anything but the timing."

"Fine. I'm tip-top. The contract is simply more complicated than we first assumed. It has nothing to do with my condition."

"Very good. Check your inbox...and good luck. I'll get back to you about equipment in Cuba. I trust you can get there on your own?"

"Yes. I'll let you know if I need help with that."

Drago disconnected and forced himself to a calm state. He wasn't accustomed to anyone doubting his competence, and the inference from his agent was that he was slipping. It cut particularly deep because of the mistake with the woman. Would he have made a similar error before his hospitalization? And the headaches and dizziness – was he really fully functional, or was he deluding himself? Had he lost his edge? And if so, was he so impaired that his ability to carry out the contract was at risk?

Self-doubt was like a slow poison, insidious and destructive and, in his business, deadly. Skepticism and pragmatism were strengths, but wondering about whether you were losing it went nowhere good.

He moved to his bag, extracted his notebook computer, and downloaded the files the agent had sent him. The tracking software for the ship's position was easy to grasp, and within minutes he was watching a pulsing icon in the Gulf of Venezuela, making its way toward Punta Espada.

Drago pulled up a satellite image and did a fast recon of the nearby coast to see if there were any ports where he might be able to hire a fast boat to intercept the cargo vessel, but quickly dismissed the idea. There was nothing of note there, and even if there had been, the couple would be watching for signs of pursuit – he didn't doubt for a moment that they'd be on edge until well away from Venezuela.

He zoomed in on Cuba, located Cienfuegos, and spent an hour researching the port city. A hundred and forty miles from Havana, it was easily driving distance, which would help if the weapons he'd requested were in the capital, which seemed the most likely scenario.

Drago next turned to the details of the ship and, when he was finished, sat back on the bed and nodded.

"You won't get away this time, you bastards," he muttered, feeling an area of his skull that was still tender. Pain radiated from it and he immediately dropped his hand, annoyed at the sensation it could still cause. He pulled the bottle of aspirin from his pocket and dry-swallowed two with a wince, which then slowly transformed into a grim smile. "This time you go into the meat grinder, and you don't come out as anything but sausage."

A portion of his mind realized that the voicing of his thoughts was a sign of mental instability, but the rum singing in his stomach pushed the doubts aside. He'd crush the target like a bug and then take a long break to recover. There was nothing to worry about.

"Nothing at all," he whispered. He caught a glimpse of himself in the mirror, hair askew, eyes wild, and threw back his head and laughed. "The first sign of being crazy is being unaware that you might be crazy. So I've got that going for me," he said, and then tossed the notebook aside and went for another splash of rum, his willingness to consider his faults exhausted by the alcohol.

CHAPTER 33

Jet watched the pod of porpoises that had appeared at dawn, cresting from the azure sea, their sleek gray forms high-velocity aquatic projectiles as they celebrated a new day's arrival. The ship had plowed north all day and through the night, the engines droning beneath their feet as she and Matt had traded off shifts to ensure no compromising communications were sent. She'd relieved him two hours earlier and was wide awake, having snatched six hours of solid sleep with Hannah by her side in the cabin below.

Adrian sat beside her as he eyed the radar, the vessel on automatic pilot. He took a long sip of strong, dark coffee and moved to a printout awaiting his review.

"This isn't good. There's a front moving south. Reports are fifteen- to twenty-foot head seas and thirty-knot winds," he said.

"What does that mean for us?"

"Depends on how bad it gets. But it reduces our chances of making it to Cuba to about fifty-fifty." He frowned. "I told you we should have taken on more fuel."

"Can we slow further? Maybe we can dodge the worst of it?"

"We're already down to sixteen knots. We'd normally be doing twenty-two. A further reduction won't accomplish much. We're at about our optimal cruise speed right now. It's always a compromise between time and fuel. Faster, we can turn the cargo in fewer days, which makes it worth burning more. But in terms of efficiency, there's not going to be a lot of difference between, say, eleven and sixteen, due to the weight we're carrying. A headwind will erase any gains."

"When will you know more?"

"I'll watch as the day progresses. We should start seeing it get uglier by around noon, and we'll be in the midst of it by sundown."

"Are there any ports along the way where you could get fuel?"

"Haiti or Jamaica. But they both have their issues. Let's see how we do today. I'll have a better idea of whether we're in real trouble by early evening."

She looked away from the gauges. "I'm sorry we put you in this position."

"Hey, I raised two kids of my own. I can understand why you did what you did, but it doesn't change anything. And my job will be on the line if I run out of fuel and don't have a hell of an excuse. Not to mention I'll be the laughingstock of the fleet." He shook his head. "How's the cabin working out?"

Jet shrugged. "As advertised."

"And your daughter?"

"She's improving. An infection. But she's taking her pills. You know how that goes."

He smiled, and then his face grew serious. "I've been thinking about the shooting. If it was directed at you, how did they miss all three of you?"

"I don't know. That part doesn't make any sense."

"It's possible that you weren't the targets, you know. Probable, actually. I've been monitoring the news out of Maracaibo. They said it was a drug deal gone wrong. We see our fair share of those."

"Explains why we're still alive, I guess," she said, doubt in every syllable.

"Doesn't change anything in terms of our odds of making it, but I figured you'd want to know."

Her tone softened. "I appreciate it."

"No problem."

She sniffed at the aroma rising from his mug. "Can I talk you out of a cup of that coffee?"

"Of course."

She followed him back to where the pot was steaming, and he

removed a cup from a cabinet and poured her a healthy slug. She took it from him and sampled it, and then made a face.

"Wow. You don't fool around, do you?"

"No. Wouldn't want to fall asleep at the helm and run into Florida." He eyed her as she took another sip. "Would you really have used your gun?"

"I'd do anything to protect my daughter."

He nodded. "I figured."

"Smart man."

"Not that smart if I let you force me to take this barge out with only half fuel."

"As I recall, I didn't give you much choice."

He eyed her dubiously. "If I'd have really wanted to stop you that much, I could have. I was in the navy for years."

Jet let him have it. There was no point in explaining that he would have had two broken arms if he'd tried anything.

She decided to change subjects. "You said you have two kids? Boys or girls?"

He laughed. "They're all grown up now. Two girls. The twenty-seven-year-old is married to a guy who owns a restaurant in Caracas and has three of her own; the twenty-five-year-old is living in Miami. She's the sensible one. An accountant."

"Single?"

"Yes. Life's different up there." He gave her a sidelong glance and checked the radar again. "You remind me a little of her. Very independent. Does whatever she wants."

"And your grandchildren?"

"All boys. Five, three, and one."

"You must be very proud."

"It's the best thing in the world. I can spoil them, and then their mother takes them and I go home. No diapers to contend with, no disciplining, just the good times. How old's your little girl? Three?"

"Almost."

"She's adorable. You're very lucky. You should cherish this age. They grow up too soon."

"Believe me, I do. You have no idea what I've gone through to keep us together."

"Well, I hope you find some peace. A child needs a certain stability to flourish."

Guilt stabbed through Jet. Poor Hannah had seen little enough consistency in her short life: snatched at birth, thrown into an adopted family, pulled out of that situation and then moving from place to place, kidnapped, endangered, always one short step from disaster…

In the darkest part of the night, she wondered sometimes whether she'd done the right thing, taking her from the couple in Nebraska. The answer was always the same: Hannah deserved her real mother, not someone chosen by David without her knowledge. Once things settled down and they lost their pursuers, they would find a quiet home somewhere far away, somewhere safe, and Hannah would grow up, hopefully happy, to have a better life than her mother had gotten stuck with.

Jet's mind wandered to Matt. Maybe at some point Hannah would have a little brother or sister. It wasn't impossible. Jet was still young, and Matt would be a wonderful father. The offspring would definitely be attractive…

She looked fixedly at Adrian. "Yes, they do need stability. And believe me, I'm working on it. I love my daughter more than life itself. I'd do anything for her."

"I know the feeling," Adrian agreed, and tapped the fuel gauge. "Let's hope we make it. Seems like you've had enough drama for one trip."

She thought about the debacle in Chile, the hijacking of the container ship, the gunfight at the monastery, the flight from Colombia, and nodded in agreement.

"More than enough."

CHAPTER 34

Frontino, Colombia

A black Chevrolet Suburban growled up the circular drive of Mosises' estate, gravel crunching under its tires, the windows tinted so dark they were opaque. Mosises watched as it rolled to a stop in front of the entrance, and scowled as Ramón got out.

"Welcome," Mosises said. "Come in. Felix is here as well."

Ramón followed Mosises into the expansive home with its floors of polished Honduran mahogany and imported French furniture. They made their way to the rear veranda, where Felix was seated at one of the circular tables, a cup of coffee before him, dark wood fans spinning beneath the overhang, struggling to temper the morning sun's heat.

"Sit. Coffee?" Mosises asked, and without waiting for an answer, snapped his fingers. A steward standing by the dining room entrance nodded as Mosises called out to him. "A cup."

Ramón took a seat next to Felix and shook hands with him. When the coffee arrived, Mosises took his customary chair, his back to the wall, looking out at the manicured grounds, and retrieved a half-smoked cigar from a crystal ashtray.

"So they're headed to Cuba," he said, his voice soft.

"That's correct," Ramón confirmed. "We've been able to track the ship. They'll be there tomorrow afternoon."

"What happened with the Brazilian? Fernanda?"

"It's still unclear. I originally thought that perhaps the other woman had killed her, but the timing doesn't work, so apparently there's another party involved we don't know about."

"That's troubling," Mosises said. "Our job is to know everything."

"Well, we know where they're going to land," Felix said, speaking for the first time.

Mosises nodded. "Yes. And I want both of you to arrange an appropriate greeting. There's a flight to Havana out of Bogotá this afternoon. You will be on it."

"Very good. And weapons?"

"Our associate in Cuba has all the guns you could ask for," Mosises said. Cuba was an important staging area for cocaine shipments, as was Venezuela. Besides which, the local tourist trade, which amounted to millions of foreigners to Cuba every year, many on sex holidays with the plentiful young prostitutes that were a mainstay of the impoverished island, consumed hundreds of kilos each year, paying street prices instead of the lower-profit wholesale Mosises realized from shipments elsewhere. "I've already spoken with him. He will provide whatever you want."

"How is everything here?" Ramón asked. "Any…problems?"

"Nothing I can't handle," Mosises snapped. The truth was that there had already been two instances of pushback from suppliers probing for weakness, hoping to negotiate better terms in Jaime's absence. Mosises had dealt with both swiftly and ruthlessly, slaughtering the entire families of the two upstarts. But he couldn't afford to be distracted, as he had been by the search for the woman, and he was relieved that chapter was coming to a close. "Deal with them, and then come home to help me with the business. I'm too old for this. I need young blood to carry on."

"What about Renaldo?" Felix asked.

Mosises took a long pull on the cigar and studied him thoughtfully. "None of your business. He has his place. You have yours. We shall see how that solidifies based on how you handle your errand in Cuba."

Ramón signaled to the servant for a refill to cover the small smirk that flitted across his face at Mosises' smackdown of Felix. He should have known better than to question Mosises' plans. Ramón hoped he would continue making foolish mistakes like that – it would assure that Ramón replaced Jaime as the acting head of the cartel instead of

Felix. Judgment was every bit as crucial as ruthlessness in the day-to-day operations, and Ramón knew that Mosises was filing away information for later consideration, even from seemingly insignificant interactions like this one.

"Any preference in how the targets meet their end?" Ramón asked.

The server arrived with the coffee pot and refilled his cup. Mosises remained silent until the man was out of earshot. His face was impassive, but both Ramón and Felix could sense the tension radiating off him.

"As painfully as possible. Film it. I want to be able to watch their deaths."

Ramón nodded. It was as he expected.

"You can rely on us," Ramón said, but his tone said that he didn't mean *us*, he meant *me*.

The distinction wasn't lost on Mosises. "I'll hold you to that. Now take the helicopter and go to Bogotá."

Felix and Ramón stood, their audience at an end, and filed out of the house to the waiting Suburban. Felix turned to Ramón as he opened the passenger door, his face dark. "You think you're pretty slick with the old man, don't you?" he hissed.

Ramón's face betrayed nothing. "What are you talking about?"

"We're going to have to settle things once we're done in Cuba. I won't go quietly," Felix warned.

"Go where? What's gotten into you?"

Felix stepped away. "I'll take my own car to the airport," he said, and stalked off.

Ramón smiled as he climbed into the SUV. Felix, his half-brother, was a hothead, which could work in Ramón's favor. If he could be kept off balance, he would make more mistakes, and they would be noted by Mosises.

And then, regardless of Felix's intentions, the old man would decide where and how he went, not Ramón. And to Ramón would go impossible-to-comprehend rewards: money and power so great it dwarfed that of many world leaders. Condos in Florida, mansions in the Caribbean, villas in Europe, dream yachts equipped with hot and cold running nymphs…

Ramón didn't intend to let all that pass him by. Mosises had made it clear that he was next in line for the mantle. Nothing would stop him, Felix included. Blood might be thicker than water, but when it came to business, blood was also the ultimate currency, and if more needed to be spilled to solidify Ramón's position, so be it.

"No, Felix, I believe you won't go quietly. But we shall see. It's never over until it's over," Ramón whispered as he watched Felix's agitated shoulders move to the BMW parked by the six-car garage.

Ramón checked his watch and turned to the driver. "The airport. And make it snappy."

CHAPTER 35

Havana, Cuba

Horns honked along the famous Havana *malecón* that paralleled the waterfront as cars slowed for the explosions of spray driven by waves crashing against the rocks, flooding the road with the regularity of a metronome. Drago's taxi was a new model Honda with surprisingly icy air-conditioning, and its suspension largely cushioned the uneven pavement on the inbound road from the airport.

He'd caught the morning flight from Venezuela to Havana, which was only half full, mostly with businessmen who kept to themselves, for which he was grateful. He contented himself with dozing the entire trip, ignoring the man in the seat next to him, who seemed happy with the arrangement. After a rocky landing at the airport, which more resembled a penitentiary than an international hub, he cleared customs on his Colombian passport and moved to the taxi stand, where he was delighted to find a fleet of newish vehicles, not the 1950s relics he'd expected.

"First time in Havana?" the driver asked as they passed the Meliá hotel, an area landmark built by American gangsters in the 1950s and now owned by a Spanish hotel chain.

"Yes."

"Business or pleasure?"

"A little of both," Drago responded honestly. He'd dreamt of the woman again last night, only in his dream she was not only his captive, but naked, her skin glistening with a sheen of perspiration as he went about his work. Drago viewed his fixation as a sign, an omen, of the reward awaiting him after the most difficult assignment in his career, which was saying something.

"Ah, then you come to the right place. The city's got everything you could want, and then some. But you got to be careful, especially at night. Shit can get crazy, you know?"

"Sure. I'll have to watch my step."

They coasted to a stop in front of the Parque Central hotel, and Drago paid the driver. The man pocketed the generous tip, waved, and drove away, sending a kit of pigeons soaring into the air over the park across the street, which was filled with young people enjoying the late morning sun. Drago watched the vehicle round the corner and then continued to a strip of shops adjacent to the square, where he placed a call. Five minutes later a squat man wearing a panama hat, a white button-up short-sleeved shirt, and navy blue slacks approached him.

"Do you have the time?" he asked.

Drago nodded, eyeing the three cigars in the character's breast pocket. "Yes. A cigar fan, are you?"

The man looked around and grunted. "This way," he said, his voice low, and moved down the sidewalk at an unexpected clip given his age and his short legs. Drago tailed him for two blocks and then followed him into a run-down building, where they climbed a set of questionable stairs before entering a suite of offices, plaster peeling off the walls and ceiling, a standing fan blowing warm air through the open window.

"Sit. Please," the man said. "You made it without issues?"

"Yes. The trip was fine."

"Wonderful," he said, and sat behind a desk that looked like it had been there since the Spanish had built the harbor fort. "You can call me Oscar. I have your items as well as a car." Oscar unlocked his desk drawer, reached inside, and extracted a ballistic nylon bag. His eyes twinkled as he held it aloft and then set it on the desktop with a clunk.

Drago withdrew and inspected the weapon, a Russian-manufactured Makarov 9mm pistol with a sound suppressor and four of the latest-issue twelve-round magazines filled with ammunition. It was in reasonable shape, worn, but serviceable, and he reassembled it with practiced hands.

"This will do. And the rifle?"

"Ah, yes," the little man said, rising and moving toward a gray metal locker in the corner of the room. "We couldn't secure your first request, but I think you'll find what we did get to be acceptable."

Drago frowned and his tone turned annoyed. "I thought I was clear that there were to be no substitutions."

"It's either this or no rifle. I took it upon myself to procure it – if you don't want it, no problem." Oscar opened the locker and removed a gun bag, and then returned to the desk and placed it atop the scarred top like a prize.

Drago unzipped the bag and removed the rifle, which appeared nearly new. Oscar smiled appreciatively as he eyed it.

"It's an Alejandro sniper rifle. Made here in Cuba. Fires a Soviet-style 7.62x54mm round. Magazine holds eight shots. Bolt action, PSO-1 scope, accurate to a thousand meters," Oscar said. "Depending on the shooter, of course."

Drago slid the bolt open and smelled oil. "Of course."

"This one is sighted for five hundred meters. The rounds will penetrate any bulletproof vest at that range. If that's of interest."

Drago had heard of the weapon, but had never seen one. He dismantled it and liked what he saw – the machining was precise, and the feel was of high quality. He looked up at Oscar and nodded once. "I suppose I'll take it. Don't have much choice, do I?" Drago paused. "And the ballistics computer and laser range finder?"

"Oh. That proved to be impossible to find. I am sorry. With the Americans limiting what we have access to, some things simply don't exist on the island. I tried my best, but nobody had one."

Drago's eyes narrowed to slits. "Better hope I don't wind up needing it. A missed shot because of the lack of one would be…most unfortunate."

"I understand. But it's not because I didn't scour all my sources. There are simply none available."

Drago slipped the rifle back into the bag and reached into his jacket. He withdrew an envelope and tossed it to the arms merchant.

"There's thirteen thousand, as agreed. I'll want two back since you don't have the computer."

After quickly counting the wad of bills, Oscar handed some back to Drago. "I'll show you to the car. But first, we must package your items so they don't draw unwanted attention." He stood and moved to a pile of cartons, and selected a rectangular one. Two minutes later they were back on the street, Drago with the box under his arm, the rifle inside, the little Cuban at his side carrying his bag.

The car was a ten-year-old Fiat. Drago gave it a once-over and took the keys.

Oscar adjusted his hat with a plump hand, tilting it at a rakish angle, and smiled. "Stolen yesterday, new plates this morning. Fake registration in the glove box along with a map. Return it when you're through. If you must leave it somewhere, just tell me where. You have my contact information."

With that, Oscar handed Drago the pistol bag, spun on his heel, and walked away, their business concluded.

Drago stowed the weapons in the trunk and then slid behind the wheel and started the car, which sputtered uncertainly before settling into a rough idle.

The map proved invaluable in navigating the city's byzantine streets, and he was on the Autopista Nacional highway to Cienfuegos in thirty minutes. The green of jungle streaked past as he drove southeast, one of only a few vehicles other than heavy trucks and the ever-present army vehicles that seemed to dominate every other corner.

He'd decided to arrive in Cienfuegos early, reconnoiter the waterfront, and spend the night in a local hotel rather than remain in Havana. He passed a billboard featuring a giant Che Guevara with a fist clenched in revolutionary salute, and he smiled to himself at a country that had been frozen in time, the island's communist revolution kept alive almost sixty years after the fact, its failure to achieve anything of note ignored in favor of the rhetoric spouted by its leadership at every turn. He knew the irony was that the fathers of the uprising had been the offspring of the wealthy, bored and filled with intellectual ideas garnered at privileged universities, who had led their countrymen in a revolt that had changed little for the average Cuban other than the master they slaved for.

"Poor bastards," he muttered, and stopped on the last syllable.

He wasn't going to talk to himself anymore. Drago had decided that last night. This little slip, more an exclamation than the beginning of a one-sided discussion, meant nothing.

He was holding it together. No question. And he'd be finished with his task tomorrow when the ship arrived in the afternoon. At which point he could filibuster for days in the privacy of his hotel room if it made him happy.

But not until then. For now, it was all business.

Except for his idle vision of the woman.

That was something more.

His bonus for a job well done.

CHAPTER 36

Southwest of Port-au-Prince, Haiti

The wind howled across the superstructure as the *Milan* plowed through fifteen-foot seas. The evening sky had darkened with twilight's approach, and the wind was living up to the thirty-knot promises of the weather report. Captain Adrian stood beside the helmsman as the heavy ship labored northwest, Jet at his side.

He looked down at the fuel indicator and grunted. "That's it. We're not going to make it. We'll have to change course and head for Haiti to take on more fuel." Adrian turned to the helmsman. "Set a course for Port-au-Prince. We're about equidistant between Haiti and Santiago de Cuba, but we won't be fighting the headwind and the swell nearly as much heading east."

"How long will it take to get to Haiti?" Jet asked.

"Should be there by late morning, at the latest." Adrian tapped the fuel gauge again and shook his head.

Jet stepped closer. "What is it?"

"It's these gauges. They're not that precise."

"And?"

"I believe we have enough fuel to make it to Haiti, but I'm not a hundred percent certain."

"But shouldn't the wind direction help us?"

"Yes, just as it hurt us all day. But only to a point. It'll be touch and go."

The helmsman entered in the new coordinates, and the autopilot slowly adjusted the steering until the seas were on the port stern. The bucking movement of the ship diminished to a slight roll. Adrian considered the radar screen.

"Not much around this strait. All the cruise activity is closer to Jamaica."

"So nobody you can borrow, say, a few thousand gallons of fuel from?"

"Afraid that's not how it works."

The wind abated sometime after midnight. The engines droned beneath their feet as Jet and Adrian remained awake, fortified by caffeine, and in Adrian's case, cigarette after cigarette.

Matt was relieving Jet on the bridge at five a.m. when an alarm sounded and a red light blinked to life near the throttles. Adrian leapt from his chair and moved to the helm, and then swore a string of colorful oaths before shaking his head at Jet.

"The starboard engine flamed out. Won't be long before the port does the same." He reached for the radio and, after checking their position, depressed the transmit button and sent a Mayday. When he was done, he waited, and a minute later a Creole-accented voice crackled over the speaker.

"*Milan*, this is the Port-au-Prince Coast Guard. What is your precise location? Over."

The second engine sputtered out and the ship was eerily silent other than the sound of the alarms. Adrian twisted them off and spoke into the microphone.

"Port-au-Prince, this is the *Milan*. We are approximately sixty kilometers from the bay. Almost due west." He gave the latitude and longitude. "We're dead in the water. Over."

"What is the nature of your emergency? Over."

"We're out of fuel. One of the tanks must have a leak. Over." The embellishment was the only plausible explanation for why a veteran captain would run dry.

"Roger. We will deploy a vedette and a tug to escort you to port. The tug can be there in about four hours. The vedette in three. Please stay in radio contact. We'll alert you once we have you on radar. Over."

"Very well. Thanks. Over."

Adrian's face looked drawn when he set the microphone back in place and looked to Jet and Matt. "You heard him. Three hours until they'll be alongside."

"I can't believe we made it this close and ran out," she said.

"This is why," he said, pointing to the fuel dial. "The gauge still shows above empty. I told you they weren't precise."

"What do we do now?" Matt asked.

Adrian sighed. "Try to get a few hours of sleep if you can. It's going to be a long night."

"They'll tow us into port, and then we get fuel and we're good to go?" Jet asked.

"It's not quite that easy. The company doesn't have an account with the Haitians, so we'll have to pay cash or wait for a wire transfer to clear before they let us leave. And there will be the cost of the tow. That won't be cheap."

"How much do you think it'll be?" she asked.

"I'd think five thousand dollars' worth of diesel would more than get us to Cuba, plus the tow, which could easily run double that."

Jet did a quick calculation. She didn't have anywhere near that much cash left.

Adrian walked away from the helm and Jet followed him. Adrian murmured to her in a soft voice when they reached the window. "I talked to the helmsman. He's been with me for six years, so he'll go along with the fuel-tank leak and won't say anything. But it would be best if you made yourself scarce. I need to brief the crew, and then go tear a seam open on the main tank so it can be repaired once we're in port. That way I don't get fired for incompetence, although at some point someone might notice the bill for this week's run in La Ensenada was half what it should have been."

"What will you do if they figure it out?"

He smiled and lit another cigarette. "I'll blame the Venezuelans. They shorted us, maybe ran out and didn't tell us. The company will believe me. I have no reason to lie. That, coupled with a small leak…it's not the best possible story, but it hangs together."

"I'm sorry."

"Stop apologizing."

Matt approached and took Jet's hand. "Hannah's asleep in our cabin, but you should get down there. I'll hang out up here."

Jet nodded. Matt would keep an eye on Adrian while she got some rest.

Adrian looked ready to protest, but Matt's expression made him reconsider. Matt softened it with a small grin. "Don't worry. I'll be as quiet as a church mouse."

Adrian spun and returned to the wheel, and Jet squeezed Matt's hand before stepping toward the stairs. "Thanks."

"Get some rest. I'll come get you if there's any reason to."

"How's Hannah? Fever almost gone?"

"Yes. The pills worked."

"At least that went according to plan." She looked through the window a final time at the pitch-black sea and shook her head.

"About time something did."

The coast guard boat reached them just before nine a.m., when the seas had flattened and the wind had died down. The bump of the hulls meeting as the vessel lashed itself to the *Milan* woke Jet, and she reluctantly rose and made her way to the bridge with a sleepy Hannah to watch the rescue at sea play out.

CHAPTER 37

When Jet reached the bridge, three Haitian officers were standing by the helm, talking in low tones with Captain Adrian. One of the Haitians, a bulldog of a man, looked over at her without breaking the discussion. The hair on Jet's arms stood up as she overheard the conversation.

"No, we only need a tow. We're stable here," Adrian insisted in accented English.

"You are carrying passengers?" the bulldog demanded.

Adrian hesitated. "Yes. It's not unusual."

"Of course not. But I'll need to see passports for everyone aboard. Crew, passengers, the lot."

Adrian nodded. "That's not a problem. But why?"

"If you're going to enter Haiti, it's standard procedure. We don't want illegals coming in."

"I'll tell the crew."

Twenty minutes later, everyone was assembled on the bridge. The Haitians checked the crewmen's papers and then came to Matt and Jet. Jet smiled shyly at the humorless officer and handed over their passports. He flipped them open and then handed them back.

"Very good. And the girl?"

"I can't find it. I looked everywhere."

His face clouded. "I'm afraid that's not good enough. Everyone is required to have travel documents, even children. It's a violation of international law to travel without them."

"I understand that. It's just that I can't find it. Maybe by the time we make it to port?"

The Haitian's brow furrowed and he turned from her. "Wait here.

I'll check." He radioed to the vedette, speaking in French. "Call headquarters. Ask Lamont what to do. We have three passengers, one of them a child, and she doesn't have her passport."

Three minutes later a different voice came over the radio and barked in rapid-fire French. "This is Lamont. If the girl doesn't have papers, bring all three of them in, and we'll see what we can get out of them in exchange for a visa. Do they look like they have money?"

The officer stole a look at Jet and Matt. "Probably."

"Bring them in. Sounds like an easy payday. We'll throw them in the brig until the courts open tomorrow and they can face a magistrate. It's Paulime on Mondays, and he'll be generous sharing the fine he levies."

Jet's face didn't change. She wasn't going to let on that she spoke French, and the Haitian obviously hadn't considered the possibility. But she realized in an instant they were in deep trouble. Haiti had a reputation as being slightly safer than Somalia, which meant it was run by thieves and crime lords. And because Hannah's passport had been lost at some point in their travels, the islanders saw an opportunity to extort whatever they could from her parents. The problem being that when they were taken in, they'd be put into a holding cell, and there was no doubt they'd be searched. And she had almost three million in diamonds hanging around her neck in the little pouch. The stones would vanish while they were in custody, she was quite sure. If anything, it would provide a powerful reason for them to die while incarcerated, because the dead rarely complain about missing fortunes.

She waited as though she had no idea what was to come next, and then seemed to have an idea. "You know, there's one place I didn't look. If it's that important, I'll take another pass at our luggage. I'm sure it's in there somewhere."

The officer looked annoyed, but didn't say no. She could see the heady vision of a slice of the fine evaporate in his expression when he turned to one of his men. "Would you escort her to her room so she can search her bags again?"

Jet handed Hannah off to Matt and made her way down the stairs to the stateroom deck and entered the small room. She made a big show of looking through the built-in desk and the chest of drawers, and shook her head. "No, it's not here. Damn."

"Then back to the bridge."

"Okay. I need to use the bathroom. I'll only be a second."

The man nodded, and she ducked into the head and removed the pouch. She opened the cabinet beneath the sink and peered into the space, and then wedged the leather bag between the sink and the wood support frame, out of sight, next to where she'd hidden the pistol. It was unlikely that anyone would perform a thorough search of a bathroom cabinet in their absence, and even if they did, they'd have to shift the plywood to find anything. It wasn't perfect, but it was the best she could think of.

She flushed the toilet, rinsed her hands, and then opened the door. "Thanks."

"Let's go."

Back on the bridge, Matt was doing his best to keep his temper as the officer explained in English that if the child's passport wasn't located, they would have to take them in and they'd have to appear before a magistrate. They stopped their discussion when Jet arrived.

"Well?" Matt asked.

She shook her head. "I don't know where it went. Maybe it fell out of the bag in Venezuela? Or was stolen? There are pickpockets everywhere, and a passport..."

The lead officer scowled. "I'm afraid you will need to come with us. The regulations are clear."

"Why can't we stay with the boat? We can't swim to shore, and you can position a guard or something when we arrive to ensure we don't disembark. It's not as though we want to enter Haiti," Jet tried.

"I appreciate you telling me how to do my job, but I'm afraid it's not my decision. My superior said to bring you in. The matter is out of my hands. A judge will determine how to handle things – they will want to ensure you aren't kidnapping the little girl."

"Are you mad? She looks just like me. She's my daughter."

"Yes, well, that's not for me to determine."

"This is outrageous," Matt said. "We demand to be taken to the embassy."

"Please. You come for a boat ride. You see the magistrate tomorrow morning. It's a formality."

"She needs her medicine. She's been sick," Jet said. "Matt, would you get it for me?"

The officer shook his head. "I can't allow you to delay us any further. It is a long run back to shore."

"But the doctor said—"

"Madame, it is of no concern to me what your doctor said. You're traveling with an undocumented minor. You will be taken into custody, as my boss ordered, and appear before the court when it opens tomorrow."

"Why not today?" Matt demanded.

"It's Sunday. So your embassy is also closed."

Jet tried a final time. "Please. It'll just take a minute to get her pills."

The officer's face darkened. "Enough. Ensign, escort the passengers to the boat. See to it that they're made comfortable in the holding area," he snapped, turning to one of his men. "I'll be along shortly."

Jet looked to Adrian. "I remember your cell number. I'll call when I can. Don't leave without us."

"By the time a wire transfer arrives, it will be Monday, so don't worry," Adrian said, his face grim.

They made their way down the gangplank to the coast guard vessel, its white hull paint worn away in multiple spots, the red and blue insignia not much better, and were shown to an enclosed room built into the steel bow of the forty-foot vessel. The adjacent head reeked, and Jet's sinking feeling increased. She sat down with Hannah and whispered to her, "Breathe through your mouth, sweetie. This will be over soon."

Matt moved to the porthole and pried it open, and the odor abated somewhat. "I don't have to tell you this is bad, do I?" he murmured.

"No. I get it."

"You stash everything?" he whispered as he sat down beside her.

"Of course."

She told him about the overheard discussion between the Haitians, and his jaw clenched.

"What a bunch of crooks," he grumbled.

"We took a risk, and we lost this round. They'll clip us for some easy money tomorrow and we'll be free to go. That's just how things work."

"It never seems to stop, does it?"

She didn't answer. There was no need.

CHAPTER 38

Havana, Cuba

Ramón and Felix sat in uneasy silence as Ramón drove toward Cienfuegos in their rental sedan, the morning glare blinding them as they headed east. They'd arrived the day before and had met with Mosises' contact in Havana for weapons before checking in to what passed for a top-shelf hotel for the night. Neither of them had ever been to Cuba, and Felix clearly wasn't impressed.

"It's a shithole," he pronounced as they neared the port city, passing through the outlying slums. "I thought Havana was bad, but it's Paris compared to this."

Felix had stayed out late in the hotel bar after Ramón had taken his leave of the place, finishing his glass of after-dinner Añejo rum and declining the charming invitation of a blue-eyed blonde of German extraction working the area, who couldn't have been over eighteen. He would have time enough to celebrate once they'd successfully concluded their business, and he left it to Felix to paint the town red, opting instead for a decent night's sleep.

That decision had been a wise one, and Ramón secretly enjoyed the look of pain on Felix's face every time they hit a rough patch of pavement.

"Oh, I don't know. It's got a certain island charm," Ramón countered, strictly to be perverse.

"If you find shanties and mosquito-borne diseases charming, you came to the right place."

The slum transitioned into drab multistory low-income housing projects rising from the surrounding jungle like brick monoliths. Every few kilometers they passed billboards exhorting the citizenry to produce more so everyone could enjoy prosperity, or featuring a revolutionary slogan declaring that Cuba would never surrender to imperialists or colonialists.

"They really believe this crap?" Felix growled. "It's like we stepped into a time machine." He eyed a passing military transport vehicle with dozens of soldiers aboard, broiling in the swelter as the sun beat down on them. "And there's a ton of military around."

"Cienfuegos is a big port. I'm not surprised."

A row of red and white smokestacks in the distance belched clouds of gray into the sky, contributing to the toxic haze hanging over the city. Felix shook his head. "We're in hell."

"Cheer up. The boat will arrive this afternoon, and then we can get out of here."

Ramón's frown deepened. "How do you want to do it?"

"You heard Mosises. He wants it slow and painful. I'd just as soon shoot them when we see them, but he's the boss. So we'll follow them to wherever, wait until we see an opportunity, and then off them. You can film it while I do the work. That would fit your style."

"We're both going to get a piece of this. You're not getting all the credit."

Ramón gave him a sidelong glance. "Got a headache? You look a little green."

"It's sitting in this car that's making me sick. That, and the company."

"Have I ever told you that you have a winning personality?"

"Just drive."

They drew near the port and cruised along the waterfront to the commercial dock area, where several older ships were tied along the wharf, being offloaded by ancient cranes. This was the dock the *Milan* was scheduled to arrive at, and they surveyed the surroundings with skepticism.

"Not a lot of cars, are there?" Ramón said.

"No. It's going to be tough not to stand out."

"We'll park over by the little drink shack. We can see the dock from the tables."

"That?" Felix snorted. "Hello, food poisoning."

"You're a ray of sunshine today, aren't you?"

Ramón found a spot with some shade from the trees ringing the lot and parked. They took in the desolate stretch of boiling asphalt, the only other vehicles rusting from years of salt condensation eating through their paint.

"At least we're not going to have a problem seeing them. Maybe I'll take a nap while we wait for our ship to come in," Felix said.

"What happened to earning part of the credit?"

"I said taking, not earning." He eyed the shack and the young woman standing, bored, behind the counter. "Wonder if they sell beer there?"

"Most assuredly. Probably icy cold. But we're on the clock."

Felix swung the door open and stepped out into the glare. "They're not going to be here for hours. I've got a hangover. A few beers will have burned off by the time they arrive."

"Not a great idea."

"Mind your own business."

Across the lot, Drago pulled back into the shadows of an abandoned concrete building, binoculars clamped to his eyes. He'd been expecting someone else to show up, and wasn't surprised, after his experience with the woman in the bell tower, when they did.

But these two weren't professionals. They were thugs. About as much tradecraft as a streetwalker. Completely unlike someone who would have a sniper rifle in an obscure Venezuelan church.

He suspected they were part of Mosises' cartel. They looked the part and displayed the finesse of Colombian bully boys.

Drago lowered the glasses and shook his head in disapproval as one of the men approached the drink vendor and bought a bottle of beer. This pair took amateur to a new level. Matt and the woman would smell them before they got off the boat.

Which meant he'd have to neutralize them before the ship arrived.

He blotted sweat off his forehead with his sleeve and grinned without being aware he was doing so.

"Not a problem," he muttered. "Not a problem at all."

CHAPTER 39

Port-au-Prince, Haiti

The patrol boat neared the coast guard dock and two crewmen hopped from the deck with lines to tie it off. The pilot killed the engines and the vessel quieted.

In the bow chamber, Jet waited with Hannah clutched to her breast as footsteps approached and the door opened.

"We're here. Everybody out," the Haitian said, stepping away from the door.

Jet carried Hannah onto the rear deck and squinted against the sun as she surveyed the skyline. Dilapidated government buildings ringed an open area with trash blown across it, and beyond the compound, various crumbling edifices littered the shore. A few islanders rode bicycles along the waterfront, their clothes barely more than rags.

The officer neared them with an evil grin. "Welcome to Haiti. God's miracle."

"Where are you taking us?"

"The jail is over there," he said, pointing to one of the squat concrete bunkers.

"Jail? We haven't committed any crime," Matt protested.

"Well, sadly, we don't have anywhere else we can hold you, so you'll have to make the best of it."

"This is...why are you doing this?" Jet demanded. "You can put us up at a hotel and post a guard. Or wait until the ship arrives and keep us onboard."

"Again, I appreciate your helpful suggestions on how I should conduct official business, but I don't have the option. So it's a cell for the night." His smile widened. "At least there's a women's jail and a men's. Could be real trouble if I stuck you in with the boys." His leer was genuine. "Lot of them might get the wrong idea."

"At least put us in one cell, separate from everyone. My daughter's sick, and she's just a baby. There's no good reason to put us with criminals," Jet said.

"You're in luck. There's nobody in the women's cell right now, so nobody's going to bother you. But there might be as night falls, so I can't put your husband in with you. That, and it's against regulations. There's a reason it's called the women's section," the Haitian said.

Jet looked to Matt, who shrugged. "Don't worry about me. I'll be fine. Although I intend to file a complaint over this treatment. We both have passports, so this is completely unwarranted."

"We have our rules, and you're in our country now. We didn't invite you," the officer said, his voice taking on a dangerous tone.

"We were on a boat that ran into trouble. It's not like we're here voluntarily," Matt countered.

"Save it for the magistrate. I'm sure he'll get it all sorted out. You'll see him in the morning." The officer nodded to two of his men, who moved to either side of Jet and Matt. "This way."

The interior of the jail was worse than the outside and reeked of bleach and body odor. Two whippet-thin men in shorts and sweat-stained T-shirts sat on a bench in front of a counter, their wrists chained to metal eyelets. Both had been in a fight, judging by their faces, which were swollen and crusted with dried blood.

The officer stood with Matt as a female guard processed Jet and Hannah into custody and then led them back into the bowels of the building. As Jet had expected, the officer did a cursory search and confiscated her watch and wad of dollars, and was visibly annoyed when Jet demanded an itemized receipt so the cash didn't disappear or shrink overnight. The woman looked to the officer for guidance, and he grudgingly nodded as two other cops materialized from the back – the presence of witnesses kept at least that part of the process honest.

The cell was painted a flat gray and was covered with names etched or burned into the paint. The guard held the door open for Jet and Hannah, and then locked it behind them with a dull clunk that echoed off the walls. A stainless steel toilet with no seat occupied one corner, but was broken, judging by the smell, and Hannah's nose crinkled in distaste as they sat on the floor as far from it as possible.

Two long horizontal barred openings ran below the ceiling, providing meager ventilation in the ugly space. Jet offered Hannah a smile of comfort, but it was no good, and she burst into tears. Jet hugged her to her chest as she sobbed, and it took every ounce of fortitude Jet had not to join her as her eyes welled.

Matt's processing was faster, but his luck wasn't as good. He was put into one of the three men's cells, all overflowing with islanders, their expressions varying from despair to rage and hatred. Matt ignored the catcalls and insults as he was escorted down the corridor, and was relieved to see that there were only two men in his cell. His optimism vanished when he got a better look at them – both appeared to be at the end of their ropes, barely conscious on the hard cement floor and reeking of alcohol. One was sleeping with his head next to a pool of vomit, oblivious to the cloud of black flies buzzing around it.

Matt turned to the guard as the man slammed the door shut. "You've got to be kidding."

"Welcome to the Port-au-Prince Ritz. Let us know if you need anything."

"How about a bucket of water to rinse that mess away, for starters?" Matt said, inclining his head at the vomit.

"I'll put in your request with room service." The guard paused theatrically. "Oh. Wait. They're not working today." The man gave Matt a gap-toothed grin. "It's Sunday. I forgot."

"Come on. Just a bucket of water."

"Let me check with the concierge. Oh. That's right. We don't have one."

The guard sauntered away, leaving Matt standing at the bars, watching him go. The stench of unwashed bodies and their various excretions was overpowering, but he'd been in worse predicaments and wouldn't let this faze him. A bead of perspiration trickled down his face from his hairline and he shook it off, willing the anger that threatened to explode from him away. This was bad, but he was alive, in reasonable condition, and it was only for a few hours, which could go by quickly or take forever, depending entirely on his outlook.

The heat enshrouded him like a blanket, adding to the oppressiveness of the cell, and he resolved to make the best of a terrible situation and use the time to rest.

He slid down the wall near the bars and closed his eyes, forcing his mind away from the dire scene in the jail. The shrieks and howls and yells receded as he drifted to the calm place he'd inhabited for hours on end while in the jungles of Laos, aware of his surroundings but distant enough so that his body seemed separate. The connecting door to the cellblock slammed behind the guard and Matt shifted on the hard cement floor, doing his best to ignore the chaos and misery around him, and resigned himself to a long wait.

CHAPTER 40

Cienfuegos, Cuba

The afternoon heat had reached its zenith, the interior of the car uncomfortable even with the air-conditioning blowing full blast, when Ramón's phone vibrated in his pocket. He checked the caller ID and sat up straighter as he answered.

"Yes?"

"You need to fly to Haiti," Mosises snapped. "Our contact there is trying to arrange for a charter flight from Havana."

"Haiti? Why?"

"Renaldo checked online this morning using the website that tracks ship-locator chips, and the damned thing was off the Haitian coast, dead in the water. He called our man on the ground in Port-au-Prince, and he confirmed through his sources that the boat ran out of fuel. It's being towed into port as we speak."

"Port-au-Prince..." Ramón repeated.

"Yes."

"What about weapons?"

Mosises laughed drily. "It won't be an issue. Leave what you got in Cuba. You don't want to risk a problem at customs."

"Can we fly out of Cienfuegos?"

"No. The airport doesn't have any charters, and there are no flights to Haiti from there. As it is, we'll probably have to pay through the nose to find someone on short notice like this, and there's the air traffic clearance to obtain, but it's not that long a flight. Like I said, our man is working on it. He should have something ready later."

"What do they speak in Haiti?" Ramón asked.

"A little English. Mostly French." Mosises hesitated. "I've got our Haitian contact trying to get more information on the ship. I'll call you when I know something."

"Okay. We're on our way back to Havana," Ramón said, smiling. Felix didn't speak English, whereas Ramón did – yet another advantage for him once they reached Haiti.

"Text me when you get there."

Ramón hung up and filled Felix in on the conversation.

"So we drove all the way here for nothing?" Felix demanded.

"Take it up with the old man if you want. They didn't know until this morning."

"I can't believe they weren't checking its progress every couple of hours."

"Renaldo's in charge of that, and he wasn't about to lose sleep to track a boat. You know Mosises doesn't even have Internet. It took him years just to get up to speed on phone messaging."

Ramón shifted into gear and rolled toward the driveway. "We should have enough gas to get back to Havana. At least that will save time."

"I knew I should have slept through this."

"I'd have you drive, but you smell like a brewery."

The sedan pulled onto the street and tore off, tires chirping as Ramón gave it gas. In the shadows of the abandoned building Drago watched it go, wondering what had happened. He hadn't checked the feed from Renaldo's phone all morning, but now fished his cell from his bag and activated it.

Two minutes later he was packing his gear.

Was anything about this operation going to go according to plan? He'd never been involved in anything so unpredictable before. From Argentina to Chile to Panama to Colombia to Venezuela to Cuba, and now...Haiti?

He called his agent as he trotted to the car. "I need any information you can get me on flights from Cuba to Port-au-Prince."

True to form, his agent didn't sound surprised or inquisitive. "What's your timing?"

"Stat."

"Stay on the line."

Drago heard computer keys clicking in the background and then his agent's voice returned. "There's a commercial flight on a puddle jumper out of Havana at eight tomorrow morning. That appears to be the only thing."

Drago did a quick mental calculation. "What about a private plane?"

"In Cuba? I'll check, but that's a long shot. It's not like there's a big charter fleet."

"Book the puddle jumper for me, but keep on trying to find a private flight." He gave his agent the name on the passport he was carrying.

More typing. "Confirmed."

"What do you know about Port-au-Prince?"

"Very little. I'll do some research. Call me back in an hour."

"Will do."

Drago twisted the ignition key and the Fiat wheezed to life. Disequilibrium made the landscape blur for a moment, and he took a deep breath, willing it away. The dizziness faded and he closed his eyes, waiting for it to completely pass.

The phone in his pocket pinged, signaling that Renaldo had sent a text. Now immediately interested in the cartel honcho's communications, he read the message.

Which was from a number in Haiti.

The coast guard took three people off the boat that sound like yours. Man, woman, and child. They're in the port jail. I will meet your men when they arrive and provide whatever they need. In the meantime, I will see if I can insert someone into the jail. Have your boss call me as soon as possible to discuss. Jon

Drago grinned. So they had been taken into custody, were behind bars, and wouldn't be going anywhere.

He had some breathing room.

The downside being that yet another amateur was going to make a try for them and no doubt screw it up. The cartel simply couldn't learn the simple lesson that if you wanted something done right, you needed to hire someone competent.

Of course, that hadn't worked out so well for them at the bell tower, but if Drago hadn't been there, the hitter would have, without a doubt, flipped the little family's switches in a matter of moments.

Drago rolled onto the highway, Che's stern countenance glowering at his departure from a black and white billboard in his rearview mirror, assuring everyone that fighting to the death was the only option.

~ ~ ~

Mosises dialed Jon Renoir's number and waited for him to pick up. When he did, music was blaring in the background.

"*Allo?*"

"Jon. Turn down the music. I can barely hear myself think."

"Of course, Mosises. One moment."

The song cut off and the Haitian's voice returned. "Better?"

"Yes."

"Your man Renaldo relayed my message?"

"He did. What did you wish to discuss?"

"The passengers were taken into the jail. I'd like to know what it's worth to you to have them dealt with while they're inside."

Mosises paused. "I would be very grateful. On a personal basis, and a professional one."

"How would you make that gratitude known to me?"

As Mosises thought, Renoir was angling for a better cut of the cocaine they trafficked in Haiti, as well as that transshipped from the island to the U.S.

"Perhaps a more generous slice of our pie. But there are limits to what this favor is worth."

"Of course. I'd never take advantage of you. Would you say another one percent is fair?"

Mosises ran the numbers in his head. That amounted to a king's ransom. He tried to keep the irritation out of his voice when he replied. "I'm afraid you have an inflated view of our profits. The industry has changed, and there are so many intermediaries now it's a fraction of the old days."

Renoir laughed. He remembered those years well enough. "So what are you offering?"

"I'm sending two men to handle it. You're meeting them."

"Yes, and I will provide whatever support I can. But it would be more of a sure thing if I had my side take care of your problem. There's nowhere to run in a cell."

Mosises considered it. If he said no, Renoir's assistance might be less enthusiastic, and Ramón and Felix's efforts hampered. The threat was unspoken, but both men knew how the game was played.

"I can offer a quarter percent for one year." Mosises paused. "That's a lot of money, Jon. We both know it."

"*Bon.* I won't insult you by going back and forth. A half percent and we have a deal."

They settled on a third of a percent, and Renoir signed off with an assurance that everything would be attended to, and that his men would find themselves with nothing to do but enjoy the Haitian weather. Mosises disconnected and frowned. Nothing about this had been easy, and his son had given his life as proof. If the Haitian could end it now, he would have gladly given two percent, but business was business, and he would have lost face with Renoir if he'd overpaid for a simple matter. As it was, he would see if Renoir could perform; if not, Mosises was out nothing. If Renoir was successful, then it was worth whatever Mosises paid, and more, to see Jaime's killers crushed like the cockroaches they were.

Mosises ground the smoldering cigar butt he'd been chomping on underfoot and left it for the servants to clean up, suddenly tired, and feeling every minute of his sixty-two years.

CHAPTER 41

Port-au-Prince, Haiti

The shuffle of soles against the jail floor stirred Matt out of his fugue state. He slowly opened his eyes and found himself regarding two islanders standing outside the barred door, both of them young and wiry, with expressions that were as mean as striped snakes. The shift had changed as night had fallen, and the two new guards showed no interest in Matt as one unlocked the door and the other stood well clear of the men, his hand on his gun.

"Now, you boys behave or we'll come in and crack some skulls, you hear?" the smaller guard said.

Both prisoners mumbled assent and entered the cell. "Jesus God," the first one exclaimed, eyeing the man slumbering in his own vomit. "That's foul."

Matt stood. "Can we get a bucket of water to wash this down with? It's really bad," he asked the guards.

The guards looked at each other, then at the prone man, and shrugged. "We'll see."

The newcomers sat down on the floor opposite Matt and closed their eyes. The two original prisoners were still out, but the one who hadn't thrown up moaned occasionally and rolled over. Whatever they'd been drinking, Matt thought, must have been stronger than rocket fuel. He hoped that the guards would take pity on them and bring some water, but he wasn't optimistic. He hoped that Jet was having an easier time of it.

Matt didn't need a watch to know that it was getting late. His inner clock said somewhere around midnight, and he didn't open his eyes when the bare bulbs lining the corridor were extinguished, leaving only one at each end still glowing. The other cells had quieted as the inmates got what rest they could, and the block was largely quiet, other than the sounds of men snoring and occasionally retching or passing gas.

The comatose groaner rolled over yet again, and this time struggled to pull himself toward the wall so he could sit against it. His filth-encrusted tank top rustled against the floor, and Matt cracked one eye open to see if he'd make it.

Which is when he saw the shank in one of the two newcomers' hands as the other pulled his own knife from his pocket. The two islanders exchanged a furtive look and then rose quietly. Matt remained still, waiting for them to approach. He knew it would be difficult to stab a man who was sitting on the floor due to the lower position, and that they'd be hard-pressed to do so simultaneously. They had no idea he knew they were coming for him, and in the gloom, hadn't seen the slit of his eyes watching them.

Matt waited until the lead islander was only three feet away and then sweep-kicked his legs out from under him. He caught the attacker by surprise, and the man hit the concrete hard, knocking the wind from him. Matt was already rolling, and shot to a standing position as the second islander rushed him.

The sound of Matt's cast slamming against the man's jaw, breaking it like dry kindling, was followed by a tortured scream of agony as the islander fell. Matt followed through with a kick to the head, knocking him out cold. The shank dropped from the killer's numb fingers, and Matt knocked it away and then dodged the first islander's clumsy attempt to stab him in the calf.

Matt silently wished he'd been wearing boots when he kicked the man in the side and heard ribs break. The man howled in pained rage, and Matt answered it with another blow, this time to the attacker's knife hand. His foot landed solidly on the prisoner's forearm and the shank skittered across the concrete. The islander screamed a curse and then Matt finished it, delivering a drop kick to the man's genitals with all the power he could muster.

The steel corridor barrier slid open and the two guards came running, clubs in hand. When they arrived, they found Matt sitting placidly in his original position, eyes closed.

"What the hell…" the first guard said, his voice trailing off when he saw the makeshift weapons by the door.

"You. Get up and face the wall. Now," the second guard ordered.

"Your boys here had an accident," Matt said, his voice calm. "They slipped and fell when they were coming at me with the knives you let them in with," he said, clearly and distinctly, so all the other prisoners could hear him. "Do you usually allow prisoners into cells with lethal weapons?"

"Face the wall," the second guard barked, but the first one was still staring at the shanks.

"Ben," he said in French, "how did they get the knives? Didn't you search them?"

"Obviously not well enough." Ben moved behind Matt as he stood facing the grimy cement.

"I didn't do anything but defend myself," Matt said, and then everything went black and he crumpled to the ground as a spike of pain lanced through the back of his skull.

Ben stood over him, his truncheon in his hand, and nodded. "That'll take some of the fight out of you, tough guy."

The other guard shook his head. "Ben…"

"Pick up those knives and give me a hand dragging this pair out of here. I don't want to leave them in the cell so he can kill them."

"Don't you think if he'd wanted to kill them, they'd be dead?"

"Shut your trap and help, you," Ben snarled, and then caught a glimpse of the conscious prisoner watching them in silence. Ben moved toward him with an ugly expression. "Talk to anyone about what you seen, I find you, you hear?"

The man nodded. "Don't want no trouble."

"So what happened?" Ben demanded.

"I don't know. I didn't see."

"That's right. You don't know nothing, you don't. You best stay out of things don't concern you. Man has to choose his battles, you understand, you?"

The prisoner nodded slowly again, any fight draining from his face. "I do."

Five minutes later the two injured prisoners were being watched over in the hallway by the guards as they waited for the doctor to arrive. Neither was in any condition to go back into a cell, and the guards knew it. Nobody looked in on Matt, who lay face down on the floor, a thin stream of blood coagulating on his face from where the truncheon had split his head open, his eyes closed, spared the indignity of his position by the numbness of oblivion.

CHAPTER 42

Port-au-Prince, Haiti

The props of the twin engine King Air slowed as it coasted to a halt at the outer edge of the tarmac in front of the Guy Malary Terminal – the small plane area at Port-au-Prince International Airport. The pilot cut the power and the ground crew chocked the wheels.

Ramón and Felix stepped from the plane and stretched. The flight had taken three hours, and they'd been forced to wait until four a.m. to depart due to Cuban air traffic control. But now they were in Haiti, and they surveyed their surroundings with fatigue.

Felix yawned and rubbed the dusting of stubble shadowing his face. "Did I complain about Cuba being a shithole? This must be the septic tank it drains into. What's that stench?" he said, sniffing the air with a frown.

"Smells like raw sewage to me. Should we cross this off your list of favorite vacation spots?" Ramón asked, needling him.

They were interrupted by two uniformed officials walking toward them across the tarmac, one clutching a clipboard in his hand, the other fiddling with the pistol in his belt holster. The pilot and copilot hopped down from the plane and opened the storage hatch, and handed Felix and Ramón their overnight bags.

"This way, you," the clipboard bearer said. His French-accented English was difficult for Ramón to understand, but he got the gist of it and directed Felix to follow the man into the shade of the terminal awning.

A third official stood by a collapsible plastic table with rusting legs and motioned for them to put their bags on it. They complied, and he did a quick search and then nodded. Next stop was passport control, which was a rickety stand with a bored fat man behind it, more interested in scratching himself than their papers.

When they were through with the formalities, a tall local in a cream-colored shirt, burgundy shorts, and muddy sandals stepped forward and called to them in broken Spanish.

"*Señores,* welcome to Haiti. Take your bags for you?" he offered, holding out a hand.

Ramón and Felix shook their heads. The islander shrugged and led them through the tiny building to a waiting SUV illegally parked in the red zone out front, a traffic policeman smiling at them as they neared. Their escort gave the cop a high five and he moved off to other chores, leaving them to climb into the vehicle and make their way to the street.

"We're going to go see Papa Jon," the man said. "I'm Clyde. Me, I can get you anything you want, I can."

"Where are we going?" Felix asked as the ruined structures disintegrated further into shacks.

"Jon has a kind of office in Cité Soleil. It's not fancy but gets the job done." Clyde cackled. "That it do."

Ten minutes of driving and they arrived at a prefab corrugated metal structure with at least twenty gunmen standing around it, AK-47s the clear weapon of choice. Clyde led them into the building and motioned to a desk at one end. Both walls were lined with crates, and a mini-split air conditioner in the corner blasted Arctic chill into the roasting air.

Renoir rose from behind the desk and offered his toothy grin, a smile that resembled nothing so much as a barracuda's. "Gentlemen. Welcome. Have a seat and let me bring you up to date," he said in passable Spanish.

They sat in front of the desk, Felix's eyes locked on the chromed Desert Eagle resting casually by an ancient phone.

"How was your flight?" Renoir asked. "What can I get you to drink? Water? Juice? Beer?"

"Nothing," Ramón said, shaking his head.

"Okay, then. Here's the situation. Last night, two of my boys got taken down by your man when they tried to slit his throat in jail. I don't know how, but they're beaten up pretty good, they are."

"You sent a pair of hit men in, and they couldn't get the job done?"

"Something happened. I'm trying to find out what. Needless to say, they won't be working for me much longer."

"Was the man hurt at all?"

"Took a blow to the head. But he'll be fine. Has a minor concussion and a bump."

"Then the effort served no purpose," Ramón said quietly. "What about the woman and the little girl?"

Renoir sat back in his chair and rocked gently. "That's a different matter. We couldn't get anyone in last night, but I'm working on it for today. The problem is she's scheduled to appear before the magistrate at ten, so we're running out of time."

Ramón thought for a moment and then nodded. "Do you know this magistrate?"

Renoir grinned again. "It's a small island. Everybody's related to somebody who knows somebody."

"It would be best if they were released immediately."

"What?"

"That would be the best scenario. We can be waiting for her and the man when they're back on the street." Ramón paused. "We'll need weapons. Preferably submachine guns. And pistols."

"You planning to do this close in, eh?" Renoir asked.

"I don't know. I want to go over to the court and look at the area. But a long-distance kill is out of the question. Mosises wants to make a point with this one."

"Fine by me. But there's a problem."

Ramón's stare stayed on Renoir's face. "Yes?"

"The man's being charged for getting in a fight."

"Then he's going to be held longer?"

"Looks that way to me. Way these things work is the magistrate is going to fine him big time."

Felix leaned forward. "That could work in our favor."

"How?" Renoir asked.

"Divide and conquer. We can strike when she leaves, and kill him later, at our leisure."

"You want me to have another try at him while he's locked up?" Renoir offered.

"No, we'll take it from here. All we require is weapons. And transportation."

"Easy. You met Clyde. He'll be happy to drive you around."

"And if we need our own vehicles? Cars, motorcycles? We'd prefer to be on our own for this."

Renoir spread his hands, palms upturned. "What is it you say? *Mi casa, tu casa.* But I have to warn you. Haiti is crazy dangerous, and without Clyde, it could be you run into all kinds a trouble. You're safe here in Cité Soleil, but once you leave, you're on your own."

Ramón nodded. "I understand. Get us guns while we're looking over the courthouse, and we'll know more later what vehicles we need."

"No problem on the guns. You just let me know what you want, and they'll be here like magic."

Ramón stood, and Felix followed his cue. "Then let's not waste any time. A pair of 9mm pistols with an extra magazine each, and two submachine guns should be sufficient for starters. Clyde will call when we see the layout."

"They'll be here in an hour. Will FN P90s be okay substitutes for the submachine guns? We've got some of those."

"Perfect. Nice and small."

"Then they're all yours."

"Good. And now, if you'll excuse us…."

"I'll talk to some people – maybe they can get to the magistrate and have the girls released. Might cost, though. You okay if I've got to grease the wheels?"

Ramón nodded. "Do what you need to do."

"We'll be back shortly. We can talk again then," Felix said.

Clyde was waiting for them outside, where the temperature was already climbing from baking to unbearable. He didn't seem to notice, standing to one side, smoking a cigarette and joking with two of the gunmen, who were barely out of their teens.

"Yes, *Señores*. Where we off to?"

"We want to see the courthouse."

He took a final drag on the cigarette and blew two long plumes from his nose. "Okay, boss, I gonna have you there in no time, I will."

CHAPTER 43

Jet looked up as heavy boots approached her cell. The night had passed in snatches of fitful sleep, the buzzing of mosquitoes and flies incessant, the appalling aromas nauseating. They had been brought water and some moldy bread at eight by a truculent female guard, and hadn't seen anyone since.

Two uniformed women stood with the coast guard officer, who glowered around the cell before stepping back to let them open the door. The first guard fiddled with the keys while the officer tried a humorless smile. "It's your big day. Magistrate's already in court." He looked at Hannah. "How's she doing?"

"Let's get this over with," Jet said, keeping her tone neutral, but seething with barely concealed rage at their treatment. The officer tilted his head at the guards and led them down the hallway. "Can we at least clean up so we look presentable?" Jet asked as they neared the door.

"Don't worry. We don't stand on formality much around here. You look just fine."

"What about my money?"

"You'll get everything back when you're released. You haven't been yet."

"But I'll need the money to pay any fine."

"Tell that to the magistrate."

They walked together to the courthouse a hundred meters away and entered the courtroom, which looked more like an abandoned classroom than a hall of justice. About a dozen islanders slumped on wooden benches, watching the proceedings with desultory expressions, the air thick with humidity.

The magistrate was an older Haitian clad in an elaborate robe who dispensed with the cases after a cursory pronouncement, which was usually met with stifled groans from the assembly. Jet glanced around the room and turned to the officer, who was sitting down the bench from her. "Where's my husband?"

The officer ignored her. She weighed repeating the question, but after a warning frown from the magistrate, decided against it.

When the case was called, the guard prodded her and she stood. The magistrate read a document and looked at her curiously before pounding the gavel once.

"Five hundred dollars for the little girl's entry visa. Fifty for the expense of tending to you for the night," he said, his English almost unaccented and clearly fluent.

Jet choked back the outrage at his final words and sighed in relief. "Thank you, Your Honor. My money is being held by the clerk in the jail next door. It will need to be released to me in order to pay."

"That's fine. I hereby authorize it."

"What about my husband?"

"That's a different matter entirely. He was in a fight last night and badly injured two of his cell mates. I can't release him – the injured parties have recourse against him, and the regulations are clear. I'd advise you to find an attorney to counsel you in this matter. I'm afraid I have to remand him to the main prison for holding, with no bail, as he's a flight risk."

"What? He was in a fight? He must have been attacked."

The magistrate shrugged. "The report says he sustained a head injury in the fight, so I wouldn't dally in securing representation. While we try to care for all our imprisoned, sadly, we lack the resources to do so in every case." He looked down his nose at her from the bench. "The main prison isn't a pleasant place, so best not to delay. These matters can usually be speedily resolved."

So that was where the extortion came in. She wondered what their fine would have been if Matt hadn't been attacked. Probably higher for him, because they needed at least one of them to be able to get money transferred so they could pay the other's fine.

"Your Honor, I'd like to see him, since he's injured," she tried.

"Yes, I'm sure you would, but that's not an option." He banged the gavel again with finality. "Next case, State vs. Montpellier."

The guard grabbed her arm, and she took a deep breath to dampen her urge to break the woman's hand. It would do nobody any good, and she didn't want to further endanger her daughter. They needed to get her pills as soon as possible so they could finish the antibiotic course in the hopes that the one-day delay hadn't caused the infection to recur. And she needed to find out how much it was going to cost to free Matt – today, if possible.

Her mind was racing as they headed back to the jail. He'd been attacked, no question, and it didn't surprise her that he'd taken his assailants down. That he'd been hurt was the unexpected part, but there was no point dwelling on it. She had to get him out. If the prison was worse than the jail, she couldn't imagine it, and didn't want him subjected to any further abuse, especially while injured.

Jet's items and cash were returned to her, and she counted every bill before walking over to the courthouse, still with her escorts and Hannah, to pay her fines. Once free, she hurried to the exit with her daughter without another word to anyone. She needed to find a lawyer immediately, but had no idea where to start. Her best hope was that a good hotel might have contact information for someone reputable. And she and Hannah definitely could use a shower.

A line of taxis waited at the curb. She looked them over skeptically. The lead car was a thirty-year-old Toyota Camry, the second an Isuzu pickup truck with a shell, its exterior festooned with a rainbow of neon-painted colors. A middle-aged islander dropped his cigarette into the gutter and approached her.

"Taxi?" he asked in French.

"Yes. I want to go to the best hotel in Port-au-Prince."

"That would be The Inn at Villa Antibes."

"Fine. Let's go."

Jet opened the Camry door and stopped at a stain on the cloth seats. "What's that?"

"Oh. Sorry. The last fare was a mother with three kids. One of them had an accident."

"I think we'll take another cab. No offense."

The driver shook his head. "No, no, you can sit up front with me. No problem. Let me move my junk."

Jet was unconvinced. "I'm sorry, but—"

The driver already had the passenger door open and was throwing his bag and book onto the soaked rear seat. "There. See?"

She sighed. The man probably didn't see many fares every day and seemed desperate to give them a ride. Against her better judgment, she relented. "Fine." She gave Hannah a small hug. "Come on, honey. We can both fit in the seat."

Once they were on their way, Jet saw the driver's cell phone in his pocket and she remembered to call Captain Adrian. She asked to use it with the promise of a substantial tip, and he almost crashed in his eagerness to hand it to her. She dialed Adrian's number and was relieved when he answered.

"Hello?"

"Is the boat all fueled up and ready to go?"

"Who is…oh. You. We're at the dock, and no, we haven't taken on fuel yet. Still waiting for money to arrive from headquarters."

"Did you get into trouble?"

"They weren't happy, but I'm not losing my job, either, so in the end it's fine."

"Don't leave without us."

"I can't go anywhere right now even if I wanted to."

"I'll be by later to get my stuff. I need my daughter's meds."

"Can't miss the ship at the dock. Biggest one in the harbor."

She hesitated. "Adrian, I wanted to say again how sorry I am."

"*Que sera, sera.* You owe me a drink."

"You? Drink?"

"I'll see you when I see you."

She was interrupted when a motorcycle pulled alongside the driver's side of the taxi, its loud exhaust drawing her attention. The rider withdrew a compact submachine gun and pointed it at the car.

Jet ducked down and screamed a warning at the driver, and then gunshots exploded, shattering the window in a spray of broken safety glass.

CHAPTER 44

Drago stood in line at customs with the rest of the passengers from the Havana flight, his agent having been unsuccessful in securing a charter the prior day. The queue shuffled forward slowly, the immigration staff unmotivated in the heat to do much of anything faster than tortoise speed. When it was Drago's turn, the uniformed woman paged through his passport, stamped it without comment, and handed it back to him. He smiled fake gratitude at her and checked his watch for the tenth time since landing – every minute he was held up was another that his quarry could escape again, and he was determined not to allow that to happen.

His agent had contacted another client, a mercenary who had done work in Haiti, who'd put him in touch with a local arms merchant. There was a Beretta 9mm pistol waiting for him to pick up for the giveaway price of twelve hundred dollars. Drago hurried to the taxi stand and gave the driver the address, his patience eroding as the temperature climbed.

The cab dropped him off in front of a restaurant near the harbor. The exterior was painted Day-Glo colors and advertised "Family Style Island Fare" in English, French, and Spanish. The front door was locked, but opened a crack after he knocked. A boy no older than ten looked him over.

"Who you?" he asked in English.

"I'm here for Bobo."

"Yeah? Why dat?"

"He has something for me. I'm Daniel," Drago said, using his current alias.

200

"Dad? Daniel here!" the boy yelled into the darkened interior of the restaurant. Footsteps approached and an older version of the boy filled the door.

"Come on, then. Got your package in the back, I do."

Five minutes later Drago departed, the Beretta in his belt, its butt covered by his loose shirt, as a taxi Bobo had called for him rolled up the dusty street. Drago marveled at the amount of refuse a poor country could produce – judging by the mounds of it clogging both sides of the road, trash collection day took place annually, if that.

The jail was half a mile away but took forever to get to due to the congested streets, what with every manner of broken-down bicycle and barely running vehicle blocking the way. When they arrived, he paid the driver and jumped out, relieved to be rid of the broiling interior, the car's climate control having expired around the time Drago was born.

Drago walked along the path to the jail and veered off at the last moment to an area at the side where two guards were smoking. He tapped out a cigarette from a pack he'd bought in Cuba, mostly out of curiosity to see whether Cuban tobacco really made a difference in the taste, and asked the men for a light. One of the guards leaned forward with a lit match, and Drago took an appreciative puff and nodded.

"Thanks."

He made small talk with the men in English, asking about restaurants and safety, and offered them some of his cigarettes, which they gratefully accepted. Eventually he steered the conversation to their jobs and the inmates.

"I heard some people were pulled off a boat and brought in yesterday."

"Yeah? Where you hear that?"

"I'm an attorney," Drago said, as though that answered the question.

"Oh. Yeah, they was here."

"Was?"

"Two of 'em was released this morning. Third's gone to tha main jail, he did."

"Which one was released? Man or woman?"

"Oh, the woman. Her and the kid."

"Well, that saves a ton of work for me," Drago said. "Any idea where they went?"

"No, boss. Gone is gone, you know?"

He nodded. "I do. Want another cigarette for the road?"

"Sure."

Drago took slow steps back to the street, slowing to fake interest in the display of pirated movies a toothless hag had fanned out atop the world's filthiest blanket. His worst fears had been realized – the woman had managed to elude him again. Not so Matt, but he was behind bars, safe for the time being from Drago.

"Tree movies for da price a one, today only," the vendor tried in English, after an offer in French was met by Drago's puzzled stare.

"That's tempting. Say, where are the big ships here? The cargo boats?"

She pointed off to her right. "Dey on da harbor, course."

"Of course."

"You gonna buy something?" Her face took on a conspiratorial expression. "Maybe you like a lil company? Friendly boy or girl? Clean, they are."

"I'll get back to you," he said, and moved off in the direction she'd indicated, walking slowly in the oppressive heat.

The *Milan* wasn't hard to locate, and Drake did a quick lap of the area around the docks, which were as bleak and filthy as everything else he'd come in contact with since setting foot on the island. What passed for a fishing fleet was moored behind the vessel, and the dirt expanse that fronted the water was empty except for the ever-present trash, a few feral cats rummaging through rotting fish skeletons, and a single-room diner at the far end, servicing the wharf.

Lacking anywhere else to watch the boat from, he made his way to the diner and sat outside in the shade with a sweating bottle of soda. Other than a few dockworkers shambling along carrying tools, the area was deserted. A lone pelican that looked on its last legs made a slow circling approach. Drago watched as it folded its wings and plunged into the water and then emerged a moment later swallowing its prize. The circle of life and death complete, he thought, and then sat up straighter when an older man wearing a captain's hat climbed down from the *Milan* and approached the diner.

Drago nodded to him, one expat to another, and waited as he went inside and ordered a drink. Drago bided his time, knowing the heat inside would drive the man out soon enough, and didn't have to wait long before he reappeared with a beer in one hand and a cigarette in the other.

"Want a light?" Drago asked in English, and the man nodded. Drago obliged with the lighter he'd purchased from the shopkeeper, and the man sat at a table nearby. "Hot enough for you?" Drago asked, sipping his Coke.

"Scorcher," the man agreed.

"You crew on that rig?"

"Captain."

"Oh. Don't see many like that around here. Lose a bet?"

"Problems. Had to find a port. This was closest."

"Well, hope it gets fixed soon."

"That makes two of us."

"Where were you headed?"

"Cuba."

"Really? I've never been. What's it like?"

"Ten times cleaner than this."

"That's not saying much, is it?" Drago rose and held out his hand. "Name's Daniel."

"Adrian. What are you doing here?"

"Writing an article on Haiti. Usual suffering human-interest stuff."

"Oh. Sure."

Drago lit one of his own cigarettes and nodded at the *Milan*. "How many crew does a boat like yours use?"

"Dozen to twenty, usually. Sometimes more. Depends."

"That doesn't seem like a lot."

"The big container ships and tankers use even fewer. Doesn't make sense that the larger they are, the less crew's required, but there you go. A lot of stuff is automated these days."

"That's interesting. And passengers?"

Adrian hesitated. "Usually only cargo. Bananas. Dry goods. That sort of thing."

"Oh. Another guy, maybe one of your crew, said you had passengers this trip. This ordeal has to be rough for them."

Adrian didn't say anything for a long beat. "One of my crew told you that? What did he look like?"

"I thought he was crew. Kind of short. Dark skin. Don't remember his name."

The captain finished his beer. "Couldn't have been one of mine. Nobody's been off the ship." He sniffed and pushed his chair back. "Funny you've never been to Cuba. I'd recognize a Cohiba cigarette anywhere. Very distinctive aroma. Didn't realize they exported them."

"Yeah, there's a shop in town that sells all kinds. Probably get them cheap because we're so close here."

"Could be." Adrian straightened and tossed his bottle into the trash.

"Captain Adrian, right?"

"That's right."

"Captain, I've got a pistol leveled at you under this shirt. I really don't want to blow a hole in you big enough to put my fist through, which the hollow-point slugs it's loaded with will, but if you don't do exactly as I say, I'll have no choice. Do you understand?" Drago lifted his shirt so Adrian could see the gun.

Adrian's face went pale. "I don't have much money on me."

"That's okay. I do. But that's not what I'm after."

"What do you want?"

"I want you to take a walk along the water with me."

Adrian looked confused. "Why?"

"Because I want to talk to you, and I don't want anyone to overhear us," Drago said, standing.

"Who's going to overhear?" Adrian protested.

Drago ignored the question. "Walk in front of me. South. I'll be right behind you. Try anything and you'll get a bullet in the kidneys. Which is a horrible way to check out. You don't want that."

Adrian complied, and Drago allowed him to put about ten feet between them. "Where are we going?" Adrian asked.

"Keep walking."

They did, past the *Milan*, and Drago spotted the floating wreckage he'd selected for his interrogation.

"There's a fishing boat on your right. The green one. Climb aboard."

"That thing? It looks like it's ready to sink."

"Beauty's in the eye. Just do it."

Adrian snorted. "You're serious? Why can't we talk up here?"

"Because I said so."

CHAPTER 45

The taxi driver groaned and clutched his side, where four bullets had hit him as they stitched through the side of the car. Jet rammed her hand down on his right leg, mashing the accelerator to the floor, and the car surged forward. She grabbed the steering wheel and narrowly missed an overloaded truck coming from the opposite direction, and then swerved, trying to hit the gunman as he drew alongside.

The move surprised him and he nearly lost control as he fought to avoid being struck. He almost collided with a cart selling fruit as he swung into the other lane, and had to pocket his gun to work the clutch.

Another motorcycle drew parallel with the passenger side and she swerved again, twisting the wheel hard to the right, and it dropped back. Hannah screamed as they headed straight for the rear of a van, and Jet let up on the driver's leg and guided the slowing car around it, scraping one side in a shower of sparks as metal tore at metal.

The driver stiffened, coughed blood down his shirtfront, and groaned out his final breath. Jet pushed his leg aside and reached for his door handle as the car slowed further. Her fingers found the lever as the motorcycle on her left revved toward her, and she threw the door open and pushed the dead driver out of the car with all her might.

The bike had to dodge the body as it rolled to a stop, which gave Jet enough time to slam the door closed and accelerate as she stomped on the gas and downshifted the automatic transmission to get more torque. The car lunged ahead, and she jerked the wheel as the second motorcycle neared, shrieking sideways onto a narrow street before upshifting and straightening out.

Glass blasted from behind her head as a round struck the rear window, and she weaved back and forth in an effort to keep the bikes from pulling alongside. "Lie down on the floor," she told Hannah, who nodded and slid down. "Stay down there with your eyes closed until I tell you it's okay to sit back up, okay?"

She was interrupted by the first motorcycle drawing even with her again, and she tromped down on the brake and gave the steering wheel a brutal turn. The bike hit the front fender, sending the rider over the handlebars, tumbling head over heels as his limbs broke from the high-speed collision. The motorcycle continued on, riderless, for a dozen yards before crashing over and skidding into a building.

Jet goosed the accelerator again and resumed her run as the second motorcycle slowed. She watched in the side mirror as the rider stopped by his fallen companion and then tore off after them again.

Another hard turn onto another street, and after five harrowing seconds Jet locked up the brakes and wrenched the steering wheel right, causing the car to drift sideways in a slow, balletic turn. It came to a stop and she floored the pedal, spinning the front wheels as the tires clawed for traction on the dusty pavement.

The motorcycle came around the corner and the rider braked hard when he saw the car hurtling straight at him. He slowed to a near stop as she adjusted her trajectory, and threw himself off the bike when Jet rammed it, sending it cartwheeling through the air in an explosion of plastic and metal. She didn't wait to see whether the rider had survived or not, and accelerated through the intersection while honking the horn in warning.

When she dared a look in the mirror, she saw pedestrians rushing to where the motorcycle had landed, but couldn't make out the fallen rider from the sea of islanders. Keeping her attention on the road, she reached down and tapped Hannah on the shoulder.

"You can open your eyes and sit up now."

Hannah crawled her way up into the seat and looked at her mother. Jet smiled and forced herself to slow, ignoring the screeching from the front axle, which had been damaged in the collision.

"We're fine," Jet said. "Those were bad men."

"Why?"

"They wanted to rob us, I guess."

"Rob?"

"Take our things."

Her face grew troubled. "Oh."

"Don't worry. Mommy's not going to let anything like that happen." Jet cocked her head and listened to the alarming sounds from the front of the car. "Believe me?"

Hannah nodded.

"All right. We're going to walk for a little, okay? Find another taxi. You ready?"

"Uh-huh."

Jet pulled into an alley and left the car running as she climbed from behind the wheel and rounded the hood. She opened Hannah's door and lifted her out, and then set off toward the waterfront, where she hoped she could find a cab before more of the city's miscreants mistook her for easy prey.

Two blocks later she saw one of the neon-painted pickup trucks and flagged it down. The driver looked at her in surprise as he pulled alongside. She opened the passenger door, sat beside him with Hannah on her lap, and gave him the name of the hotel. He nodded and put the truck in gear, and they bounced their way along the uneven street toward the town center and, hopefully, tranquility.

The inn proved to be a walled oasis situated on a hill overlooking the city and sea, a colonial plantation home turned into a hotel, but with all its stately charm intact. An armed guard stood at the gates and only opened the barriers for the taxi to enter after seeing Jet and Hannah in the cab.

At the front desk, a courteous clerk informed them that a room was available. Jet swallowed hard when she heard the price, but nodded. One night wouldn't break her. And she had no desire to spend another in the cramped cabin of the ship, as kind as Adrian had ultimately been.

After a shower with Hannah and a rinse of their clothes in the sink, she set their wet things on the terrace and watched as the sun dried them in minutes. Reinvigorated by bottles of juice and water from the minibar and after snacking on the fresh fruit platter left as a welcome gift, Jet led Hannah downstairs and stopped to speak with the concierge. She asked about attorneys with influence, and the concierge leaned toward her, his voice low.

"They're all liars and thieves here. But my cousin is a top name, and probably the most honest of them."

"That would be fine. Does he specialize in criminal cases?"

The concierge laughed. "Can't make a living if you don't, not here, you can't."

Jet took down the information and asked the woman to call a cab. Fifteen minutes later, she was sitting in the reception area of Frantz Aristide, Esq., under the watchful eye of a receptionist who could have moonlighted as a sumo wrestler.

Frantz proved to be jovial and competent, and immediately understood the gravity of Matt's plight. They agreed on his legal fee and spent a half hour discussing details, the first of which was Frantz accepting a diamond as his payment in full. By the end of the meeting, Jet had a better feeling, although Frantz cautioned her that the system had its problems, and not to take anything for granted. He placed a call to the magistrate while she waited in the lobby, and when he was done, invited her back into his office.

"They wanted twenty-five thousand. I got them down to ten by explaining that you aren't prosperous world travelers or you wouldn't have been on a cargo ship to begin with. He agreed." Frantz looked over his reading glasses at Jet. "So now I need the ten thousand dollars, plus my retainer, plus…the transportation we discussed. Do you have this diamond with you?"

"I can get it today, but I need to find someone to watch my daughter. I don't want her involved in anything more. She's sick and needs rest."

"My receptionist can double as a babysitter if it's only for a few hours," Frantz offered.

"That would be wonderful." She paused. "We have attorney-client privilege, right?"

"Of course. Why?"

"So if I told you about something that happened today, you couldn't discuss it with anyone?"

Frantz nodded and regarded her. "Within reason. But if you tell me you're planning on committing a crime, I'd have to alert the appropriate authorities."

"No, it's nothing like that. We were attacked by two motorcycle gunmen after leaving the jail. They killed our taxi driver. I was able to escape with Hannah, but I think I ran over one of them. Maybe both."

Frantz didn't blink. "Carjackings are a serious problem here. I'm sorry you had to experience it. If you're worried about the robbers, nobody is likely to mourn them. Most crimes go unreported due to police corruption, so the chances that anyone will volunteer that they saw anything are slim." He frowned. "You're lucky you're alive."

"That occurred to me."

"*Bon.* Come, let's introduce Hannah to Rosie, and get you on your way, shall we?"

"I appreciate this. I don't want Matt in jail a moment longer than he has to be."

Frantz nodded again. "It shall be my pleasure to act as the swift arm of justice in this case, and see him freed before nightfall."

CHAPTER 46

Matt winced in pain as the guards manhandled him to his feet, the blood-crusted bump on the back of his skull throbbing. He'd put together what had happened, and while he was furious, there was nothing he could do about the guard's brutality other than remain silent and wish him dead. Haiti was clearly not the place to file a complaint, and his justified fear was that if he did, he'd be inviting far worse.

"You. Face the wall and put your hands behind you," the nearest guard ordered, and Matt did as he was told. The man clamped handcuffs on him so tightly that they bit into his skin, but he didn't make a sound. He wouldn't give them the satisfaction of a reaction.

Matt was relieved to see that these were different guards than those on duty the night before, or he would have been in fear for his life. Once Matt was cuffed, the guard prodded him in the lower spine with his club. "Turn around, you. We're moving you to the main jail."

"What? Why?" Matt demanded.

"Because you got into a fight last night, and those are our orders," the second guard said.

"But I was attacked. They had knives. I was defending myself."

The two men looked at each other and smiled. "Right. Prisons everywhere are full of innocent men, they are."

"Ask him," Matt said, inclining his head to one of his two cellmates.

"I don't know nothing, I don't," the prisoner said, averting his eyes.

"You saw the whole thing," Matt accused.

"I don't want no trouble wit' nobody."

"There you go, white bread. Now come on and move, or I'll have to make you. You really don't want me to do that," the first guard said with an evil grin.

The other guard laughed. "Not unless you wanna be peeing red for a week, you."

Matt shuffled down the hall, past the bloodstains that had yet to be cleaned up from the night before, a guard on either side of him. They moved him from the cellblock to a waiting van and, after passing a chain through the cuffs and locking him to a filthy steel bench in the rear of the vehicle, slammed the door closed.

The ride in the unventilated hotbox was mercifully short, but Matt's heart sank when he was pulled out into the sun, blinking against the glare. The building looked like a condemned industrial warehouse, the walls partially collapsed in one place and everything coated in grime.

The new guards were just as unfriendly as the ones at the port jail. After processing him, they led him down the cellblock corridor past chambers packed with humanity to the last cell on the end. The maintenance crew responsible for keeping it clean was apparently the same one in charge of doing so at the port. The cell was as noxious as the last, only with eight occupants in a space intended for two.

Once the cuffs were removed and the door locked behind him, Matt gave his cellmates a cold stare, and was relieved when they made room for him without being forced. He could sense fear in the men, and it was quickly obvious that word of his tussle the prior night had spread because nobody met his eye, which was just as well. He didn't know how long he'd be in for, but he wanted no more trouble, and could only hope that none of his fellow captives had murderous intentions.

He sat down on the floor beside the rest of the unfortunates and, after nodding to the nearest, closed his eyes, determined to make it until Jet could arrange for his release, assuming she'd appeared before the magistrate and worked a deal. His only fear was that she'd also been attacked, but the moment he thought it, the idea made him smile inwardly – he would have undoubtedly heard about it, because anyone foolhardy enough to try it would have been carried out in a body bag.

Matt opened his eyes when footsteps approached from across the cell. He glanced up to find himself looking at a powerfully muscled islander with full-sleeve tattoos and a shaved head. The man glared at Matt and then spat on the floor near his feet.

"Don't look so tough to me, he don't," he said, his Creole accent thick.

Matt didn't say anything.

"You hear me, you? I said you don't look tough at all. After hearing 'bout how you laid out two of Renoir's boys, I figured you'd be a badass. But you ain't shit, you."

The other men were staring at him, waiting for a response. Matt didn't rise to the bait. The bully was clearly trying to establish his dominance over the cell, and anything Matt said would escalate the confrontation. So he remained quiet and kept his expression neutral.

The islander spat again, but no closer, and addressed his cellmates. "See? Ain't no thing at all. This boy ain't going to cause no trouble long as I'm around, he ain't." A few of the men nodded, and the big man moved back to his corner, his position at the top of the cell pecking order reconfirmed.

Matt closed his eyes again, glad he'd made the right call. His head was splitting and he didn't need to get into another fight. But now he had a puzzle and a name: Renoir.

And the question was, who was this Renoir, and why had his men tried to skewer Matt in his sleep?

CHAPTER 47

Adrian waited on the fishing boat for Drago to climb aboard, taking care to keep his hands where they were visible at all times and not make any sudden moves that might set the gunman off. The captain had been in his share of dangerous situations, after a lifetime spent in lowlife ports in Central and South America, and was still breathing. Whatever the man wanted, Adrian intended to give him, because he wasn't ready to willingly shed his mortal coil quite yet.

The hull shifted and the rotting floorboards creaked as Drago stepped onto the aging vessel. Adrian eyed him nervously. "So here we are. What do you want to discuss that requires all this?" he asked.

"I'm interested in your passengers. I have a bone to pick with them, and I need to know when they're planning to return to the ship."

Dawning awareness crept across Adrian's face. "You're...you're the one who was after them..."

"*Is.* I'm the one who *is* after them. And you're going to tell me what I need to know."

"I have no idea. The Haitians took them. Ask the coast guard."

Drago nodded, expecting the response. "Yes, I heard. But I also know that you're their way off the island, which means you expect them back."

Adrian shook his head. "No. As soon as we're allowed, we're leaving. They can fend for themselves."

Drago's eyes narrowed. "You know, one of the things I'm really good at is telling when someone's lying. It's like a sixth sense or something. Been that way my entire life. And I know you're lying. I don't blame you for it or take it personally, but you will tell me the truth or you won't be getting off this boat."

"I'm telling you the truth. But you don't have to believe me. You can just watch the gangplank until we head out to sea."

"I intend to. However, it would be most helpful to understand exactly when they're going to arrive."

"I swear I don't know."

Drago shook his head as though disappointed, and cocked the hammer back on the pistol. "I can see you're not taking this seriously. That's a shame. If you're not going to help me, you're my enemy, and I see no reason not to end this now. Make your peace with whatever God you pray to, because you're about to meet him."

Adrian believed the gunman. His eyes met Drago's, and it was like looking into an open grave. He shuddered and looked away. "She called earlier. She's coming sometime today. That's all I can tell you. I swear I'm telling the truth."

"Why's she coming?"

"To get her kid's pills."

"Where's your crew? Be specific."

"Everyone's hanging out up in the galley. It's air-conditioned."

"Where is that on the boat?"

"Up two levels from the cabin level, in the superstructure – one level below the bridge and my cabin."

"So the lower part of the boat is empty?"

"Yes."

"Nobody in the cargo area?"

"No. Everyone stays in the superstructure, where it's cool."

Drago moved so quickly he was a blur. The gun butt caught Adrian on the temple, stunning him. He dropped to his knees and Drago hit him again at the base of the neck. Adrian's breath blew from his mouth like a muffled sneeze and he fell to the deck, unconscious.

Twenty minutes later Adrian was bleeding, his wrists and legs bound, his fingers broken and twisted at impossible angles. His face was a mass of contusions and cuts, and he was missing most of his teeth.

Drago stood over him with a rusting gaff in his hand, studying him dispassionately. Adrian looked up at him, the pain from the torture excruciating, and coughed, wincing at the pain his broken ribs sent searing through his body.

"I…tol…you…every…"

"Shh. Don't try to talk. I believe you now. But I had to make sure."

"I…"

Drago took a step forward and slammed the heavy gaff handle against Adrian's head. Adrian struggled against his bindings and Drago hit him again, and then moved behind him and jerked the point of the metal hook through the captain's left eye, up into his brain.

"Did you know that two doctors won the Nobel Prize in medicine in 1949 for basically this procedure? The frontal lobotomy. They came up with the idea of driving a surgical instrument into the front of the brain, through the eye socket, and wiggling it around until enough of the prefrontal cortex was so scrambled the patient wasn't a problem anymore. Of course, nowadays it's viewed as barbaric, but at the time it was hailed as the latest thing in psychiatric medicine." Drago eyed Adrian's stiffening form and shrugged. "Times change, I suppose. But regardless of your views on medical ethics, nobody would question its effectiveness in keeping you quiet for the duration. Of course, you'll bleed to death from your other wounds eventually, or at your age, more likely will suffer a heart attack, but you won't realize it's happening. Or maybe you will."

Drago stepped away from Adrian, pulled the gaff free, and tossed it onto the deck. Adrian tumbled over onto his side. Drago looked down at the front of his pants and shirt to ensure there was no blood splattered on them, and closed his eyes as a wave of dizziness swept over him. He froze and waited for the spell to end and, when it did, glanced back at Adrian. "Now, I'm afraid, charming as the company's been, I have other fish to fry. A date with the woman. Which I've been looking forward to for some time." Drago looked to the stern where he'd come aboard. "Don't get up on my account. I know my way off the boat."

Drago stopped himself with a muttered oath and then relaxed. It really wasn't talking to himself if he had an audience. That seemed self-evident. Even if the other party had the comprehension of a starfish, it didn't violate his rule – not the spirit of it, anyway. His head throbbed with a dull ache as he rationalized, and then he shook it off and gave Adrian a flip salute.

"Try to stay out of trouble, Captain."

The boat rocked slightly as he moved to the rear deck, stepping cautiously around the collected bird droppings that encrusted the deck. The woman was within reach now, and although Matt was in jail, Drago could attend to him after he'd amused himself with her. Whenever Matt was released, assuming he ever was, Drago would be waiting – and a few pops of his pistol would end Matt's life as surely as stepping on a bug.

Now it was just a matter of time. He'd sit and watch, and when she appeared, he'd follow her onto the boat, incapacitate her, and have his way with her in the bowels of the ship, her daughter broken in front of her, her last moments spent begging for her life.

He smiled and moved onto the jetty.

It wouldn't be long now.

Not long at all.

CHAPTER 48

Ramón limped along the street, ignoring the stares from the islanders, to where Clyde had said he'd pick him up, near a shantytown a block away from the destroyed National Palace. Renoir's man had been reluctant to get too close to the site of the motorcycle accidents, because even in Haiti, the police would be scouring the neighborhood for witnesses, and his face was too known among law enforcement to risk being stopped.

He withdrew his cell phone when he arrived and shook his head at the sight of the massive white building, its domes collapsed in the big earthquake of 2010, which had demolished so much of the city and delivered a death blow to the already struggling nation. He leaned against the corroding green wrought-iron fence and dialed Mosises.

"Yes?"

"It's me. We had a problem. Felix is dead."

"What?"

Ramón gave him a brief report of the motorcycle chase and their ultimate failure. When he finished, Mosises remained quiet for an ominous stretch before speaking so softly Ramón had to strain to hear him.

"The man is still in jail?" Mosises asked.

"That's correct. But they moved him out of the port facility into the main prison complex."

Another wait. "What is your plan?"

"I'll have Renoir put out the word to see if he can locate her, but in the meantime, I'll watch the prison. She's going to have to show up to pay his fine and get him released, and when she does, I'll be there. If she uses an intermediary, I'll follow the man once he's free and take them all out at once."

"What about having Renoir's men try again while he's inside?"

"I think we can expect the same result as the last time."

"It's not like you've met with much success."

"True, but that's because Felix didn't follow my instructions. He went charging in instead of waiting until they arrived at their destination. You know he was a hothead. The plan was to discover where they were going and make our play once they were out in the open."

Mosises sighed. "I don't have to tell you how disappointed I am with this."

"No. We both are."

"I'm going to fly some more people there. Sounds like you need help."

"I don't, but I appreciate anything you can do. It's a big city, and Renoir only has so many resources."

"Yes, that was one of my fears. Everyone seems to overestimate their own competence…and underestimate that of our quarry."

Ramón's ears grew hot at the barb, but he remained calm. "I won't let you down."

"I've heard that assurance before. This time, see that you don't."

Mosises hung up without saying anything else, his warning resonating long after the line went dead. Ramón knew the cartel boss well enough, and when he grew impatient, as he was now, he became dangerously unpredictable.

A multicolored tap-tap, which passed for an island bus but was in reality a van or truck with room for a dozen riders on two benches in the rear, slowed to see whether he wanted a ride, but he waved it off.

Clyde's SUV appeared out of a cloud of dust at the end of the block and barreled toward Ramón, slowing at only the last moment to let him aboard. Ramón did his best to hop into the high vehicle without showing he was hurt, but it was no good, and he winced as he sat down.

Clyde took in Ramón's abraded trousers and shook his head. "Didn't go so good, huh? Shoulda let the boss take care of it, you should. He's got guys would do it, no questions asked."

"Too late now."

"Where's your buddy?"

"He didn't make it."

Clyde nodded. "Where to, then, boss?"

"I need a car."

"I can drive you around, I can."

"I want my own car. As soon as possible."

"Easy enough." Clyde placed a call and relayed the request.

"Take me to the main jail," Ramón said, when Clyde had disconnected.

Clyde turned onto a smaller street. "Hell, boss, you coulda walked there, you could. Isn't more than two blocks away."

Ramón tried to stop the groan that escaped from his lips, but it was too late. A minute later they were passing two U.N. peacekeeping force armored personnel carriers parked in front of the high prison periphery wall. Island women made their way along the Rue de Centre with baskets and pots perched atop their heads, seemingly oblivious to the war machines mere footsteps from them, the soldiers appearing bored at the monotonous duty.

Ramón opened the door at the corner and got out. Clyde glanced at him out of the corner of his eye. "You sure you all right here, you? You look a little rough, know what I mean?"

"I'll fit right in. Just bring me a car. And try to be quick about it."

"We're stealing it as we speak. Shouldn't be that long." Clyde grinned. "Want some new pants, at least? What size are you? Look to be about a thirty-two waist, you."

"That would be good. And make it thirty-four."

"You got it, boss."

Ramón watched him drive off and patted the pistol in his pocket, its weight not nearly as reassuring as it had been earlier in the day. The main prison doors were forty meters away, and he could easily make out the few visitors entering to commiserate with the inmates. A market with a tattered awning down the block had set three circular plastic tables out on the sidewalk, and he pulled up a chair, resigned to waiting as long as it took for the woman to show or Matt to come out.

He called Renoir. "Do you have anyone inside the main jail who can alert me when the man is scheduled to be released?"

"I do." Renoir paused. "Clyde tells me that you had some…problems. Sorry to hear that."

"Appreciate it. Please call when you hear something about the prisoner. Clyde's getting me a car. Put it on our tab."

"Yeah, that and the motorcycles."

"Charge Mosises whatever you think they're worth."

Renoir laughed. "Oh, I will, you can be sure of that."

"Not my concern. But the prisoner is."

"I understand."

CHAPTER 49

Jet walked along the waterfront toward the *Milan*'s ebony hull at the far end of the main jetty. In her hand she had a white plastic bag of take-out food she'd bought at a stand where the taxi had dropped her off, and to anyone watching, she hoped she looked like a delivery person, wearing a cheap baseball cap with an embroidered marlin on it in rainbow colors pulled low over her brow and a pair of sunglasses bought from a street vendor for the equivalent of six dollars shielding her eyes from the sun's glare.

She moved with an unhurried gait, eyes roving over the area, alert for any watchers. She wanted to believe that the attack on the taxi had been a carjacking gone wrong, but her operational instincts told her it hadn't been. Somehow their pursuers had tracked them to Haiti, and she had to assume that the boat was compromised.

Jet spotted a figure sitting at a building on the far side of the field as she neared the *Milan* and recognition flooded her. It was the assassin she'd shot to pieces in Chile, whom she'd assumed had died in the river. But she was now committed, and it would look suspicious if she didn't follow through. Her pace didn't change as she neared the gangplank, expecting to be challenged by a crew member or Haitian military, and she was surprised when there was nobody guarding it. She looked around, as a delivery person might do, and then proceeded up the ramp.

Once on deck she dared a final peek at the man from the corner of her eye and rushed to her cabin, anxious to retrieve the diamonds and the gun. When she neared the door, she slowed – it was possible the assassin had an accomplice waiting inside. She listened, ears alert for any hint of movement, but didn't hear anything. Jet stood, frozen, but detected no signs of life – she was alone on the cabin level. A nervous glance at her watch confirmed that too much time had already gone by – the killer could even now be making his approach.

She swung her cabin door open and stepped into the stateroom, looking for any evidence that it had been searched, but saw nothing out of place. She quickly moved into the bathroom, located the gun, and then pulled the leather lanyard with the diamond pouch over her head. Hannah's pills went into her small bag along with her own few things, and after slipping on Matt's windbreaker, she was out in the corridor, a round chambered in the pistol.

At the superstructure entry she crept down the length of the ship to where she could see the café. A peek over the edge of the gunwale confirmed her fear – the killer was no longer there, nor was he on the gangplank.

Which meant he was on the ship, having recognized her in spite of her improvised disguise.

Now she had two options: she could make a break for it and hope he didn't gun her down as she descended the gangplank; or go on the offensive and hunt him down.

She straightened and took soft steps back to the superstructure. If she could wound the assassin, she might be able to learn who had hired him. That would be optimal, although not necessary – in the end, that someone wanted them dead was enough, and any of her or Matt's enemies were lethal enough to pose an ongoing threat.

Jet continued past the superstructure entry and rounded the stern, doing her best to keep her steps silent on the steel plating. The killer was probably inside the ship, having entered while she'd been retrieving her things. Which meant that he thought he had the upper hand – a slim advantage for her, but hopefully sufficient.

She neared the starboard-side superstructure entry and spotted what she'd remembered – a steel ladder up to the second-level deck, where there was another watertight door. Jet slipped the gun into her windbreaker pocket and clambered up the rungs, keenly aware that while she was doing so, she was exposed. When she reached the upper deck, she stopped. The crew dining area was to her right, and she could hear a radio and good-natured joking about sexual exploits drifting from the galley, including physically impossible suggestions from a crewman with a resonant deep voice.

Jet crept past the galley's watertight entrance and continued to the opposite side, remaining below the level of the windows. At the next door, she twisted the lever handle and frowned when the hinges protested like a wounded bird.

Committed in spite of the noise, she pulled the door open, stepped silently to the stairwell, and descended again to the cabin level. Her room was at the far end of the corridor, with four crew quarters doors between hers and the stairs. She moved on silent feet, her running shoes soft against the unyielding nonskid of the deck, and spotted one of the crew cabin doors open. She was nearly to the door when a voice hissed from behind her.

"Looking for something?"

She froze, hands in her pockets, and slowly turned to find herself facing the assassin. He held a pistol easily in one hand, a smirk on his face, and…something more frightening in his leaden eyes.

"Who are you?" she demanded, stalling for time.

"My feelings are hurt that you don't remember me. Chile? A river? Nighttime?" He took a step toward her, reaching up to touch the back of his head with his free hand for a moment before slowly lowering it.

She shrugged. "Oh. But you're alive. I'll have to work on my marksmanship."

"Maybe in your next life. Where's your little one?"

"Safe. Who are you working for? Whatever they're paying, I'll triple it."

Drago appeared to consider the proposition. "Sorry. Professional ethics prevent me from accepting. I'm sure you understand."

"That's a shame. We could both have walked away from this, no harm done."

"Afraid that's not how it works, as you well know." Drago paused and took another step toward her. "Your skills are exceptional. Where were you trained?"

"Moscow."

He smiled. "Liar."

She shrugged. "How about you?"

"I'm a citizen of the world. Let's just say I've been through many experiences that have molded me."

Jet understood that if the man had intended to simply kill her, he'd have already made his move. No, his expression revealed that he wanted something more.

Something worse.

His eyes flicked to the side in sudden awareness. "Remove your hands from your pockets, slowly," he ordered. The muscles in his gun hand tensed, a telltale sign that the exchange was over.

Three shots exploded through Matt's windbreaker from Jet's pistol. All hit Drago squarely in the chest.

The assassin fired wildly and his bullet grazed Jet's arm. The gun drifted to the side and his mouth worked as though he was trying to speak, but nothing came forth but a burble of bloody froth. She ducked as he struggled again to steady his weapon to shoot her, and she pulled her pistol from the shredded pocket and fired a final shot using a two-handed combat grip. The parabellum slug took most of his skull off, and he dropped like a felled tree.

She moved nearer, her pistol trained on his inert corpse, and kicked his weapon away. "You lost your edge in the river. Should have stayed in whatever hole you crawled into," she murmured, and then looked at the far stairwell. The crew would be down within moments to see what the racket was – the gunshots wouldn't be audible outside the ship, but would certainly have been heard above, even with the radio and two stories of dense superstructure between the galley and the cabins.

After a final glance at the dead assassin, Jet sprinted for the stairwell as she heard footsteps clomping down the far stairs. She took the steps three at a time and vanished from the stateroom level before anyone spotted her. Once on deck, she confirmed that nobody was around to see her depart and then made her way down the gangplank. After she'd gone fifty meters along the waterfront without any pursuit, she veered off to the busy street across the field, where she disappeared into the throng of islanders going about their business.

Once the cops arrived, it would mean hours of questioning to establish what had happened, and since nobody had seen anything, all they could ultimately have were suspicions. At the speed the locals worked, it would take the better part of the day and evening.

She hoped that would be long enough.

CHAPTER 50

Jet sat in front of Frantz with Hannah by her side. The office was quiet except for the soft whirring of the ceiling fan spinning lazily overhead. His friend Emmanuel, a local jeweler, inspected the diamond she'd placed on the desk, turning it in the light, then laying it on a sheet of white paper and examining its color. He fished a loupe from his pocket and studied the stone for several minutes before straightening and placing the diamond back on the paper.

"It's as represented," he said in French.

Frantz nodded. "*Bon*. Then we have a deal. I'll arrange for the fine to be paid, and for all the rest of it to be taken care of."

"How long will it take for him to be released?" Jet asked.

"No more than a few hours, I wouldn't think. Once they have the money, you're of no more interest to them."

"So we could be at the airport by evening?"

"I would think so. Why?"

"I've called in a favor for transportation off the island. The sooner we're rid of the place, the better. No offense," she said.

"None taken. You haven't seen our best side, I'll grant you that."

"There's a better one?"

Frantz sighed. "There used to be. Sadly, circumstances have degraded to the point where you now find us. What the future holds, nobody knows, but it likely isn't good."

"Why do you stay?" she asked.

"Where else would a broken-down lawyer go? I'm too old to start over someplace else. And my whole family is here. My whole life." Frantz shook his head. "I was born here, and I'll die here. On Judgment Day, none of it will matter."

"I like to think there's more than that," Jet said, smoothing Hannah's hair.

"The wonder of belief is that at the end, one of us will be right. I hope you are, but I'm afraid I am. I've seen too much to believe otherwise."

Jet nodded. "When will you have confirmation that this is done?"

"I'll call your hotel and alert you. Trust me. Everything is in motion now that Emmanuel here has given your bauble his benediction." He gave her a shrewd look. "It must pain you to have to give the diamond up."

"If it gets him out of jail, it's worth it."

"I'm glad you see it that way."

Jet shrugged. "I want to put this behind us and move on."

Frantz stood, shook hands with Emmanuel, and slid the diamond into his vest pocket. "Thanks, my friend."

"Any time."

After Emmanuel left, Frantz knelt unsteadily in front of Hannah. "She has your eyes," he said to Jet.

"I like to think she got all of the good and none of the bad."

He offered her a smile and patted Hannah's shoulder. "And now, allow me to go to work on freeing your husband. Much as I enjoy the company, there's business to attend to."

Jet rose and took Hannah's hand. "One question – can immigration stop us from leaving on some trumped-up charge?"

Frantz looked thoughtful. "Anything's possible, but I'll exert my influence with the gentleman working the evening shift at the airport – he's a fixture there, and we know each other well. I've handled some sensitive matters for him, so I think it's safe to say you'll make it through without delay."

"Thank you. I'll be waiting by the phone."

"You'll be the first to hear."

~ ~ ~

A pair of guards marched down the prison corridor amidst catcalls and hoots and stopped in front of Matt's cell. He looked up, and one of the men pointed his truncheon at him.

"Stand up, you."

"Why? What's going on?" Matt asked.

"Stand up and step away from the door. And the rest of you, anyone move and you get your head cracked open right quick, you hear?"

Matt did as instructed and waited as one of the guards unlocked the door.

"Come with us," he ordered.

"Where?"

"You're being processed out, you are. Your fine was paid."

"Really?"

"Best get moving quick, or they might change their mind," the guard warned.

Matt didn't have to be told twice. He followed the two guards out and they made their way to the administrative section, leaving the cells behind in favor of air-conditioned bureaucratic comfort.

Matt took a seat where indicated in a shabby office and signed a sheaf of papers. The woman processing him handed him a manila envelope with his few possessions in it. He took them, counted the money, and grunted acceptance.

"Sign here," she said, stabbing a sausage-like finger at a line on a form. Matt did so.

"Anything else?"

"No. You're free to go."

"Is there anyone waiting for me?" Matt asked, suddenly suspicious.

"A boy out in the lobby."

"A boy?" Matt repeated.

"That's what I said, isn't it? Hard of hearing or something, you?"

Matt didn't linger to continue the interaction, instead pushing through the double doors to the front of the building. Inside the lobby, which lacked so much as a fan, a boy no more than eleven waited, shifting his weight from foot to foot.

"You here to see me?" Matt asked, approaching him.

The boy looked around nervously at the islanders sitting on wood benches and drew close. Matt leaned down and the boy whispered in his ear. When he finished, Matt nodded, withdrew a few bills, and handed him a ten.

The boy's eyes lit up and he smiled. "Thank you, boss."

"No, thank *you*. Now why don't we go see about that car?"

CHAPTER 51

Ramón waved away an annoying fly that had singled him out for persecution and checked his phone. Clyde's man would be by within minutes with the car Ramón had requested. That would be welcome, because Ramón's leg was aching pretty badly now that the adrenaline from the chase had burned off and the tumble from the motorcycle was making itself known, and sitting on something softer than a hard plastic seat had considerable appeal – especially if the air conditioner worked.

He'd been waiting for four hours, but nobody but islanders had entered or left the prison. After baking in the heat most of the afternoon, he'd had his fill of Port-au-Prince's dusty allure and was ready to shoot whoever needed shooting and get on the first plane out.

His phone rang softly and he raised it to his ear. "*Sí?*"

"It's Jon. I just received word that your man is being released within the hour."

"Where's the car I was promised?"

"It should be there any second."

"Any further detail on the release?"

"No, just that the fine was paid and he's being processed out, *tout de suite* island time."

"I haven't seen the woman."

"Nor has anyone. My contact at court says he hears a prominent lawyer manhandled the fine for her, so she's lying low. Which, after your motorcycle chase this morning, makes sense, no?"

"Yes, that was my fear. But he'll lead me to her."

"Good luck. Call me if you need anything more."

Ramón hung up as a gold Isuzu sedan eased to a stop beside him and a gangly young islander wearing a T-shirt emblazoned with a cartoon dog playing pool on it stepped out. "Dis your car, mon," he announced, handing Ramón the keys. "Compliments of Jon. It full up on petrol, so you good to go, you."

Ramón slid behind the wheel and started the car, and was relieved to find that the climate control did anything besides blow hot air around the interior. He probed his sore leg with his fingers and made a mental note to see a doctor before he left the island – the hard landing had done more than bruise him, and he could feel a subdural hematoma in the ominous swelling near his hip. Nothing fatal, and he realized he'd been extremely fortunate, given Felix's twisted remains – but still painful.

His pulse quickened when a taxi with windows tinted black glided to a halt in front of the prison's main entrance and sat as though waiting for someone. If there was one thing Ramón had learned by watching the flow for the day, it was that cars didn't stop for long, for any reason, on that street, lest they risk the outrage of other drivers and the harassment of the local gendarmes.

Two of those had been framing the prison doors for the entire day, apparently impervious to the temperature or the dust that swirled along the patchy pavement. Ramón felt for his pistol in his bike jacket and tapped it as he waited to see what happened next. If the taxi was there to pick up the man, it was quite possible that the woman was riding along to meet him, in which case Ramón would be able to make short work of both of them – contrary to Mosises' instructions, but Ramón suspected that at this point he'd be so delighted to have exacted his revenge that he wouldn't dwell on the details.

As if reading his thoughts, his phone rang again. The number was blocked, which was vintage Mosises.

"Sí?" Ramón answered.

"I just spoke with Renoir. He tells me the man's been discharged?"

"I'm sitting outside the prison. He hasn't been released yet, but he will be at any time."

"I'll have two men arriving this evening on a charter flight from Medellín. They're at your orders, in the event you haven't been successful by that point."

"Thank you. Hopefully the excitement will be all over by then." A thought occurred to him. "Do they have...sheets?" Many of Mosises enforcers were known to Interpol and wanted for crimes outside of Colombia as well as within its borders.

"That won't be a problem. Renoir has taken care of it."

So the answer was yes.

The prison doors opened and Matt's Caucasian face appeared.

"I've got to go. I see him," Ramón said, terminating the call. Mosises would understand, he hoped.

Matt looked around cautiously, obviously wary and looking like warmed-over crap, his close-trimmed hair insufficient to mask the discoloration from the blow to the back of his head or the dried blood. A lance of pain seared up Ramón's leg, reminding him that the gringo wasn't alone in having taken recent lumps, and he sat up straighter to relieve some weight from the damaged tissue.

Matt, spying no danger, moved quickly to the car and disappeared into the rear, pulling the door closed after him.

Ramón allowed the taxi to get a running start so he wouldn't be too obvious, and then pulled after it, ignoring the toot of a tap-tap horn behind him. The Isuzu's engine buzzed like an enraged hornet, and Ramón cursed the four-cylinder motor – it felt like it was barely generating enough horsepower to drive a lawnmower, much less a car, and flooring the gas did little but make noise.

The taxi held to a straight course for several blocks, and then ran an intersection, ignoring the traffic cop's whistle and frantic waving. Ramón growled a Spanish curse and put the pedal to the floorboards, determined not to allow the taxi to get away.

That the target had spotted him was obvious from the maneuver. He wasn't going to make the same mistake Felix had that morning, but he was going to stick with his quarry whatever it took, which right now meant narrowly avoiding being T-boned by a truck as he blew past the furious policewoman. He caught a glimpse of her in his rearview mirror, raising a handheld radio to her lips, and swore again as he sighted the taxi again, which was pulling away as it barreled down the narrow street, sending startled islanders jumping.

It made a right at the next intersection, barely slowing, and increased its speed so that by the time Ramón had followed it around the corner it had gained four more car lengths. A few seconds later and he would have missed seeing it dodge into an alley that skirted one of the numerous shantytowns littering the capital.

He made the turn and saw nothing but a dust cloud pulling away down a dirt lane barely the width of the car. A chicken dodged out of his path as he hit the gas and downshifted in an effort to coax more power from the anemic power plant. The motor whined like a spoiled child but did little to close the distance, and he slammed his hand into the steering wheel again and again in frustration, his swearing growing in intensity with each thud.

Another turn and he lost sight of the cab. By the time he rounded the corner, he was reduced to looking above the shanties for the dust cloud as evidence of its passage. He saw beige off to his right, drifting over the tarp roofs of the lean-tos, and took another turn as fast as he dared.

There. Up ahead.

The taxi's brake lights winked at him, and then he lost sight of it again as it cornered onto a paved street at the far side of what had degraded into a tent city, the inhabitants the poorest of the poor in a country that had redefined a new low at the bottom of the socioeconomic scale. He goaded the reluctant sedan to the street, only slowing as he neared it, and almost collided with two men pushing wheelbarrows filled with five-gallon water bottles.

Ramón ignored the shaking fists as one of the wheelbarrows dumped over and the bottles ruptured onto the pavement, and focused on regaining a fix on the escaping vehicle. He was guessing at this point, but thought he could make out tire marks at the next street, where the cab had skidded before taking the right turn.

He went with his instinct and grinned when he spotted the taxi – far ahead, but drawing no farther away. One of the U.N. vehicles was lumbering in front of it, crawling along at patrol speed, and the cab had no choice but to slow for a block before zagging hard left. The delay bought Ramón the precious seconds to close the distance to no more than fifty meters, and for the first time since he'd given chase, his optimism surged.

Traffic grew heavier as the taxi rolled to the town center, preventing the cab from evading him again. Ramón could taste victory. He was savoring his win when a siren keened behind him. He checked the rearview mirror and cringed at the sight of a police cruiser closing on his vehicle, perhaps a hundred meters down the street, blocked by two cars crawling along on the narrow way.

"No. No, no…no," he exclaimed before refocusing on the taxi, which slowed as it made yet another turn ahead. Ramón followed it onto the smaller street and braked hard when he came to a parking lot filled with other similarly painted taxis. His throat tightened at the sight of at least thirty cars, and then his eyes narrowed when he spotted the one he had been following – he recognized the scratches on its rear bumper after having tailed it halfway across Haiti.

He skidded to a stop and leapt from the car, adrenaline coursing through his veins as he moved toward the taxi. The driver's door opened and an islander got out, ignoring Ramón, who was rapidly approaching. The Haitian waved to a group of six other drivers lounging in a group, a pall of cigarette smoke hovering over them, and strolled unhurriedly toward his friends. Ramón reached the taxi and, keeping the pistol in the bike jacket, pulled the door open, his finger on the trigger.

To see an empty car.

"What?" he hissed. He whipped around to where the drivers were gathered, the newcomer grinning while the others laughed. The driver leaned over to get his cigarette lit and Ramón called out to him, enraged, his voice hoarse.

"Where are they?"

The drivers looked at Ramón like he was mad, and the one who'd led him on the chase made a face.

"Whatchou talking about, mon?"

"You picked a man up at the jail," Ramón spat as he stalked toward them.

"Yeah. And?"

"Where is he?"

"He jumped outta the car back by the church, he did. What's it to you?"

Ramón's pulse thudded in his ears and his face flushed. "You little bastard," he growled, and unable to control his rage, drew the gun from his pocket and leveled it at the man's head. "You think this is funny?"

The man's eyes widened in alarm, and then his smile returned. Ramón hesitated, anger urging him to pull the trigger, and then he understood the driver's demeanor as a siren whooped behind him and a voice called out, "You. Drop tha gun, you. Now, or I'll shoot, I will."

Ramón held both hands up slowly and dropped the pistol onto the dirt. When he turned to see the speaker, he was unsurprised to see two police, their guns at the ready, drawing a bead on him as they moved slowly toward him. "Keep your hands up. Don't move or you gonna be fish food, you."

Ramón understood instantly what had happened – he'd been lured into a trap and had fallen for it. By the time Renoir could pull enough strings to get him released, the targets would be long gone, and there was nothing he could do.

"Officers, please, I can explain," Ramón tried, but seeing the expressions on the cops' faces, stopped talking. As the larger of the two men neared, Ramón made one final attempt. "At least let me call my lawyer. Please."

The cops made short work of cuffing him, and one led Ramón to the cruiser while the other slipped Ramón's dropped pistol into a plastic bag using a pencil in the barrel to lift it. Ramón spoke in a low voice to the cop as he opened the rear door.

"I'll give you five hundred dollars to let me make a call. It's important. Five hundred for one call." He hated how pleading his voice sounded, but swallowed his pride. He had to get hold of

Renoir. The clock was ticking.

"Yeah? You got dat on you, do you?"

Ramón nodded. "In my front pocket. That and more."

The officer removed Ramón's money, thumbed through it, and slipped it into the pocket of his shirt. "I don't see any money," he said, and Ramón's stomach flipped.

"You're going to regret this," Ramón snarled, and then his head snapped to the side as the cop slammed his club into his skull.

"Oh, yeah?" the big man growled. "You almost killed a buncha people with your crazy-ass driving, you pull a gun on my man there, and then you lip off to me, you? Bruddah, you in a world a hurt, resistin' arrest an' all. You lucky we don't feed you to the sharks with that mouth a yours."

Most of this was lost on Ramón, who had lost consciousness a third of the way through the warning.

~ ~ ~

Matt held Jet in his arms for a long minute before releasing her and kissing the top of Hannah's head. Jet gave him a dazzling smile and led him to a waiting car driven by Frantz. Jet made the introductions, and they got in. Matt turned to her with a quizzical expression.

"Where are we headed?" he asked.

"Airport," she answered, then crinkled her nose. "I'm guessing you didn't shower with the fellas while you were locked up?" She tilted his head away from her and eyed the bump on his head. "Ow. That looks like it hurt."

"You should have seen the other guy." He tried a grin. "How are we getting off the island?"

"Your friend pulled a rabbit out of his hat. A big one."

"Yeah?"

"You'll see."

Frantz negotiated the winding streets and they sat in silence watching the ruined buildings glide by, many of them half demolished, casualties of the earthquake and pervasive poverty. Jet gave Matt a bottle of water and he drank greedily, draining most of it before handing the bottle back to her with an apologetic shrug.

"Did they feed you anything while you were locked up?" Frantz asked.

"No. But truthfully, I wasn't hungry. Something about sleep deprivation and then having your head bashed in dampens the appetite."

Jet took his good hand. "That and being in close proximity to a few dozen hardened felons, I'll bet."

Matt nodded. "Let's just say it's an experience I hope to never repeat." He studied her profile. "How about you? How's Hannah's fever?"

"We're fine. And back together. That's the most important thing."

"Anything happen while I was indisposed?" Matt asked.

Jet gave the back of Frantz's head a glance and shook hers. "Nothing important. I'll tell you later."

He squeezed her hand. "Fair enough. Thanks for coming up with whatever the fine was."

"You owe me big now. I plan to have you make it up to me for some time."

He smiled. "Fair's fair."

The sun was setting as they reached the prop plane terminal. Frantz parked at the end of the nearly deserted lot and they got out together. Jet had disassembled her pistol and disposed of it in trash cans around the hotel, so all that remained was to go through immigration and board the plane.

Frantz escorted them into the terminal and to the door leading out to the tarmac. An older man with hunched shoulders and a dour expression eyeballed them and then perked up when he spotted Frantz. The two men shook hands, and Jet saw a few bills, carefully folded, change hands. "Alban, these are my friends. They're in a frightful hurry. Could you see to it that they make it to their plane undisturbed?"

"Of course, Mr. Frantz. My pleasure." Alban turned to Jet. "You going out on the military transport, right?"

She nodded, and Matt struggled to keep the surprise off his face. "That's right. It's here, isn't it?"

"Can't miss it, you can't. Right out there with the engines running. Been on the ground for half an hour. Just finished refueling." He shook his head. "Don't get a lot of Cuban Air Force planes here, we don't. That's a first for me. An Antonov AN-32. Seen one from Mexico, but never from Cuba."

Alban directed them to the waiting plane, a white twin prop sitting on the tarmac with its fuselage door open and the unmistakable Cuban colors on its tail. A uniformed Cuban officer stood at the bottom of the stairs and, when they reached the plane, helped them aboard. After they were seated, he closed the door and tapped on the cockpit wall and called out in Spanish, "Take us up."

The plane rolled down the runway and lifted into the sky. The interior of the plane was bare except for overhead netting and some primitive seating. The officer turned to them once they were soaring above the Caribbean and introduced himself. "I'm Lieutenant Costa. We'll be landing at a base outside Havana. I'm afraid I don't have much to offer you, but we have some water and nuts, if you want them."

Jet gave Matt's hand a squeeze and smiled. "We do. And thank you for the ride."

Once they were at cruising altitude, Costa went forward, and Jet told Matt about the motorcycle incident and Drago. When she finished, his face was lined with worry. "That had to be about me, not you. An American, you say? I knew it. First Tara, then this guy…"

"Who we don't need to worry about anymore. But what's still troubling is that he wasn't working alone. The car chase from the jail proves that."

"Yes," he agreed. "Bastards. They'll never give up."

"Oh, I think the ones who were chasing you will. Frantz arranged for the police to detain them. Whoever they are will have to tip their hand to get out. If it's your old gang, we'll know. Frantz said he'd let me know. I'm to call him in a day or two."

"Frantz seems like a godsend."

"I think he feels guilty about the stone I traded him. It was almost three carats. Worth an easy fifty anywhere in the world. Maybe more."

"So it's not because you entranced him with your womanly charm?"

She smiled and looked at Hannah, who had dozed off from the monotonous drone of the engines, and then took his hand in hers. "Let's get you a shower and we'll see how that's working."

Matt leaned his head back and closed his eyes. "I don't think I've ever heard a better offer in my life."

"I expect a lot for my fifty."

His eyes opened before fluttering closed again. "You're on."

CHAPTER 52

Ramón looked up when the guards arrived to free him. He'd only been behind bars for twelve hours, but it was twelve more than he'd ever wanted to be, and his head hurt almost as much as his bruised thigh. He endured the cuffing and escorting without saying a word, and when he was released with only his watch, phone, and passport, he resisted the impulse to spit in the clerk's face and instead made his way to the discharge area.

The tall youth who'd dropped the car off was waiting, and led him silently to an idling vehicle. Clyde sat behind the wheel, a knockoff Louis Vuitton baseball cap on his head at a precarious angle.

"Hey, boss. Sorry it took so long. They wanted to hold on to you like nobody's bidness, they did," Clyde said as Ramón climbed aboard.

"Let's go see Renoir."

"He expecting you, boss. We on our way, *tout de suite.*"

The drive took fifteen agonizing minutes, and Ramón noted that his phone was dead, the battery having drained while he was incarcerated. The eastern sky was blushed with streaks of salmon and tangerine as dawn broke over the sea, and he wished he could appreciate the sight with anything but simmering hate.

When they arrived at Renoir's compound, the big man was sitting behind his desk, drinking coffee, obviously awake before his usual time, looking disgruntled and groggy. Renoir motioned to an empty chair and Ramón lowered himself cautiously into it, pain flaring through his hip before it faded into a background throb.

"Coffee?" Renoir asked, and pointed to a cup. Clyde filled it without waiting to hear Ramón's answer and brought him a china cup on a saucer, and then quietly slipped out of the room. Ramón drank half the cup before he spoke, relishing the taste of the rich brew.

"We know it was a setup. Everything. The cab, the cops, the whole thing."

Renoir nodded. "Seems that way."

"They had to have inside information," Ramón said, looking Renoir straight in the eyes.

Renoir leaned forward, and when he spoke, his tone was dangerous. "No, they just had to be smarter than you. They figured someone was gunning for them, so they laid a trap. It worked. No inside job required to explain it."

"I need to find out where they went."

"We're working on that, but it'll take time, you know? Nobody saw anything. The trail, it ends at the taxi depot, and the driver took a week's vacation to go fishing. So have the cops who arrested you."

"That's convenient. One of them robbed me. Lifted three grand."

Renoir shrugged. "A couple of your men are waiting for you at a hotel near the town center. I can have Clyde take you there. Get some rest. We'll know more when we do."

"That's not good enough. Mosises is going to be livid. I need to pick up their scent, and quick."

"Yes, well, Mosises isn't happy, that's true enough. I had to call when I got word about your...situation."

Ramón blanched. "You spoke to him?"

"Yes, and I explained things. I think you'd better call him sooner than later."

"My phone's dead," Ramón spat, anger dripping from every syllable.

"You can use mine. I'll step out."

"No, I can call from the hotel."

Renoir shrugged. "Fine by me."

"What steps have you taken to locate them?"

"My people are talking with the harbor patrol and at the airport. They don't show up on any logs, so they haven't left the country."

"How reliable is that?"

Renoir laughed and his whole frame shook. "Look around you. How reliable do you think it is?"

"So it's meaningless."

"Well, let's just say I haven't stopped there." Renoir locked eyes with him. "Ramón, you're a guest, and Mosises is like a brother to me, so I'll say this once to you, and once only. Don't you ever come into my home, my territory, and throw around talk about me selling you out, or you'll leave the island in a box. No hard feelings, but you don't disrespect me. *Comprende?*"

Ramón held his stare and then looked away. This wasn't the hill he wanted to die on. "I apologize. It was a long night with no sleep, and I took a hard spill on the motorcycle. And I'm still shaken from Felix's death. I meant no offense."

Renoir nodded, mollified. "We all had some long days. Apology accepted. Now go with Clyde, and hopefully by the time you wake, we'll know more." He paused. "But I'd definitely call Mosises before you sleep."

"I understand. Thank you for all your help."

Renoir waved a hand the size of a ping-pong paddle. "We'll talk soon." He tilted his head back and called out at the top of his considerable voice. "Clyde? Come on in here."

Clyde hurried into the room, trailing cigarette smoke, and Renoir sat back like a medieval king. "Take Ramón here to the hotel right quick."

"Yes, boss."

"And then pick up some spicy eggs and plantains, would you? I'm wasting away to nothing here. Got an appetite today."

Clyde's face didn't even twitch as he surveyed Renoir's corpulent form.

"You got it, boss."

CHAPTER 53

Havana, Cuba

The big prop plane banked on final approach to the military airfield on the outskirts of Havana, the lights of the city a glimmering tapestry stretching to the sea. Costa had warned Jet and Matt that they would be landing shortly, and everyone was strapped in, Hannah now awake as the aircraft bounced toward the airstrip.

Once the plane touched down, it slowed and taxied to a collection of hangars, where Jet could see through her small window that a military SUV was waiting, along with a dark green army van and a recent-model white Honda Accord. The airplane braked to a halt and the turbines shut down, and then Costa was opening the fuselage door and lowering the stairs.

A row of palms ringing the airfield swayed in the trade wind as Jet carried Hannah down the stairs. Matt led them toward the vehicles, where an army officer stood beside a white-haired man in a pastel blue seersucker suit, a cigar the size of a baguette clamped between his teeth. Matt grinned as he approached, and shook hands with the cigar smoker.

Matt turned to Jet. "This is Carl. Carl, meet Victoria and Hannah."

Carl took Jet's hand and kissed it lightly, his eyes twinkling in the moonlight. "Pleased to meet you." He straightened and turned to the officer. "This is Major Luis Fuentes. You have him to thank for your flight. He will also be facilitating your paperwork."

"Charmed," Fuentes said, clicking his heels together and offering a small bow.

"And now for the formalities. I believe you have something for me?" Carl asked Jet, who nodded and placed three diamonds in his hand.

"The down payment, as agreed," Matt said. "Your expert will find nothing to complain about. They're flawless, and worth easily double what you're giving us in credit."

Carl gazed down at the stones and dropped them into his jacket pocket. "I would expect nothing less. I'll have them verified, but we can proceed as though they already have been. For now, I've arranged lodging for you at a very private bed and breakfast located in the Miramar district. Tomorrow morning we'll have photographs taken, and then the major here will work his magic while you take in the sights of Havana."

"That's very kind," Jet said, pulling Hannah near. "Hopefully there's a restaurant nearby?"

"Several of the best in town," Carl confirmed with a flamboyant hand wave and a smile to Fuentes. "Which, no offense, Major, isn't saying much."

"None taken," Fuentes said, clearly accustomed to Carl's digs. "I'm painfully aware of our island paradise's shortcomings. I'd recommend plentiful mojitos to mitigate any disappointment."

"We brought a van for you, unless you'd prefer to ride in my car," Carl said, indicating the Honda.

"Whichever is easiest," Matt said.

"If you can all squeeze into the rear seat, mine's more comfortable. My driver is excellent. I, on the other hand, can't be trusted after dark," Carl joked, and winked at Jet.

"I'll be sure to keep that in mind," she responded.

"You want anything for the trip into town? I picked up this excellent cigar in one of the stands just outside the grounds. They also sell food, alcohol, sodas," Carl asked as they climbed into the Accord.

"No, thanks. We'll be fine. I think right now a shower at the hotel's the most pressing thing," Jet said with a look at Matt, who nodded in agreement.

The ride from the airfield took an hour, during which time Carl regaled them with tidbits of information about Cuban culture and everyday life. As they traversed the hodgepodge of streets leading to the city center, his account turned to history.

"Havana was the most important Spanish hub in the New World for centuries. The fort you'll see as we near the water was built to protect the harbor. A massive iron chain still runs from Havana to the fort across the harbor mouth, and every evening a cannon's fired in a ceremony, which used to signal the closing of the harbor by the chain drawing tight. An effective, if crude, barrier, it worked for hundreds of years."

"How long have you lived here?" Jet asked.

"Oh, what, now, going on…fifteen years? When I chucked my old life and went walkabout, I didn't have to look far. I wanted someplace that wasn't in the U.S.'s pocket, and it was either Iran, North Korea, Myanmar, Venezuela, or Cuba. I'm not a Sharia law kind of guy, couldn't warm up to starvation conditions in the Far East, nor did I like what I saw developing in Venezuela…so that left Cuba. On balance, I'm happy with the choice, although the sanctions have obviously taken their toll on the country."

"But overall, you like it?" Matt asked.

"Yes, but you have to understand that I'm in a very different position from most Cubans. On the positive side, they have an excellent educational system, and it's free for everyone, so if you want to become a doctor or a lawyer or a professor, there are no limitations. The problem is that once they graduate, there are no opportunities, which is why any jobs dealing with tourists are prized positions. You'll find young women with specialized physician's degrees working as cocktail waitresses or escorts, because they can't make a decent living as doctors. It's sad, but the country's a train wreck economically, as are all communist regimes. Note I don't count China among those, because it's really a capitalist oligarchy, with only some loose trappings of socialism still in place." He paused. "But I, because I was fortunate enough to sock away money for a rainy day, can live like a king on a fraction of what it would cost elsewhere. And of course, my little hobby brings in an occasional dollar."

Carl's voice drifted off and the car was silent.

"Tell us about the passport process," Matt said.

"Nothing to it. We get photos taken, and you'll have legally issued Cuban passports within forty-eight hours in the names of your choosing. Birth certificates for you will appear in the system, and never be questioned."

"And those are safe to travel on?" Jet asked.

"Of course. That's the entire point, isn't it? Depending on where you want to go, you might need to get visas, but that's the only hassle, and it's really no big deal. Because of the way the passports will be coded, you won't be subject to any of the exit constraints the less fortunate here have to contend with."

"We haven't decided where we're off to next," Matt said, his glance darting to Jet for an instant.

"No problem. I don't need or want to know. My role is that of a conduit. The major is the one who makes it all happen. I'm just a small cog in a big machine."

"Why do I get the sense that you're being too modest?" Jet asked.

Carl laughed and twisted in the passenger seat to look back at her. "My dear, if I were about fifty years younger and you weren't frittering your time away with this no-goodnick, you could have had your way with me and I'd have been the luckiest man alive for it."

She reached across Hannah and took Matt's hand. "No accounting for taste, is there?"

"I'm rarely envious, but in this case, Victor here has the honor of having awakened the green-eyed monster in me."

The inn turned out to be an old mansion two blocks from the shore, in a neighborhood of stately homes, many in disrepair, but most in some form of rehabilitation.

Carl pointed to the black wrought-iron fence that ran along the street. "Built in the 1880s by a wealthy plantation owner, it fell on hard times after the revolution. The current owner bought it a decade ago and refurbished it. Be sure to let me know what you think of the service and the furnishings."

"Why? Are you friends with him?" Matt asked.

"In a manner of speaking. I own it."

Jet smiled. "I see. You're a man of many surprises, aren't you, Carl?"

"You've seen my best ones. It's all downhill from here."

"Why do I think that might be an exaggeration?"

"You have excellent intuition. If you rethink your commitment to this scoundrel, we might have a short but glorious future together. At least for me it will be."

"I'll take that under advisement in case he doesn't behave," Jet said as she opened her door. "On that note, thank you for everything. You mentioned there were restaurants nearby?"

"Yes. Ask Gloria, the manager. She'll arrange transportation. It's not recommended that you walk around after dark, even in this neighborhood."

"I see. Thanks again," Matt said.

"I'll be by at nine tomorrow, sharp, to get your photos done. We're a bit old-fashioned here, so everything takes twice as long as it should. But I know a shop that does decent work." He paused. "I own it as well."

Jet leaned into Matt as Carl's car drove off.

"Your friend's a peacock, isn't he?" she whispered.

"He's gotten worse in his winter years, obviously. Apparently he enjoys the attention. I imagine he's an *enfant terrible* on the social scene."

"He certainly isn't shy."

"No, he makes an impression wherever he goes. That's his style."

They mounted the stairs and approached the ornately carved mahogany entry door, which glided open as if by magic. A handsome woman with her hair pulled back in a tight bun stood with a small bouquet of flowers and a beaming smile of welcome.

"Good evening. I'm so glad you made it," she said. "I'm Gloria." She stooped down and handed Hannah the bouquet. Hannah's face broke into a happy grin. "Aren't you gorgeous?" Gloria said, studying the little girl.

"Thank you," Jet said.

Gloria stood and motioned for them to enter. "I'll show you to your rooms – Carl said you're to have the honeymoon suite, which is two large rooms with a sliver view of the sea. Your little one should be comfortable in the sitting area – there's a daybed in it for her use."

"Lead the way," Matt said, his voice tired, and Jet nodded approval.

Gloria gave them an orientation and, after promising to book dinner at a nearby restaurant in an hour, left them to freshen up. Jet stood on her tiptoes and kissed Matt before detaching from him and giving Hannah's shoulder a squeeze. "This will do just fine, Mr. Victor."

"You know what they say. To the victor go the spoils…"

"We can negotiate the truce over dinner."

"I can't wait."

CHAPTER 54

"Cuba? On a military transport?" Ramón repeated, incredulous.

Jon Renoir nodded his massive head. "That's what I said."

"How?" Ramón was trying to digest the information. Suddenly his desperate fugitives, on the run and nearly cornered, could commandeer military flights? What was he missing? He had the same sense of dislocation he'd had when he'd found Fernanda's body in the bell tower, the feeling that the situation was more complex than Mosises understood – and that he was in way over his head.

"Simple. The pilot filed a flight plan and gained approval to refuel here. He wasn't authorized to, but apparently he took on three passengers – none of which made it into the books, of course." Renoir shrugged. "It happens, you know. This is Haiti," he said, as though that explained everything.

Ramón had spent a difficult night after talking to Mosises and meeting with the two killers he'd sent, one of whom he knew from Colombia. Mosises had been seething at Ramón's failure, but had eventually calmed down and authorized Ramón to do whatever it took to continue the pursuit.

That morning he'd seen a doctor about his injuries, and the man had done a quick inspection of his wounds and pronounced him fit, if badly bruised. As Ramón had suspected, he had a hematoma on his thigh that would require months of physical therapy to treat, so the clot would eventually dissolve and be absorbed into the surrounding tissue, but it wouldn't incapacitate him – it was just painful. The doctor also said he showed all the signs of a minor concussion from the blow to his head, but with rest that would also pass.

Ramón nodded and rose from his chair. "The flight was eighteen – no, nineteen hours ago. By now, they could be anywhere."

"Maybe. But I wonder why Cuba?"

"It's nearby, and that's where the boat they were on was headed when it ran out of fuel."

"So there's something there that's drawing them."

"Or someone."

Clyde took him back to the hotel, and he called Mosises and reported the new development. Mosises didn't hesitate. "I want you on the first flight to Havana."

"Mosises, with all due respect, the military transport changes things, doesn't it? I mean, it's starting to look like the situation is more complicated than we originally assumed."

"Complicated in what way? These people killed my son. I want them dead. That seems simple to me."

"Yes, of course. I'm just saying that the involvement of a government, rather than private individuals, means that Jaime could have stepped into something far bigger than he was expecting…and that's why he died. I never liked or trusted Fernanda. Seems like she might have left out some important information in order to gain your cooperation."

"Such as?"

"We don't know who she was working for, do we? What if it was a government agency?"

"So what? They still killed Jaime."

"True. And they should pay. But if this is one government battling another, it could be a war we want to stay out of, or at least know more about before we rush in. That's all I'm saying."

Mosises voice grew quiet. "I want you to fly to Havana and do whatever it takes to kill them. Leave the strategizing to me. Is that clear?"

"Of course. I was just–"

"Your concerns are noted. Let me make a call or two. I'll be in touch."

Ramón found himself listening to a dial tone. He hadn't expected

Mosises to back down, but wanted to go on record with his concerns. Throughout this nightmare he'd had misgivings, and they'd grown as the trio had escaped time and time again from impossible situations.

Whatever, or whoever, these people were, they were definitely not the typical nuclear family caught in something ugly. Which Mosises didn't appear to care about, but Ramón had to if he was to succeed.

And survive.

He pulled up a travel site on his phone and scanned the flights. There was one in the late afternoon. He booked a reservation for himself and turned to more practical matters. The men Mosises had sent to help wouldn't be able to breeze through Cuban immigration, he knew from his prior visit, so they'd be of no use. But he'd wait until hearing back from Mosises to break the news to them.

In the meantime, there was nothing he could do but be patient and hope that Mosises' contact in Cuba could pick up the scent. Ramón would have had a lot more confidence if it had been anywhere else – he'd seen firsthand that the Cubans were secretive, paranoid, and highly centralized, the system far harder to game than a wide-open regime like Haiti. Securing meaningful information might be all but impossible. It would depend on how high up Mosises' source was, and of course, the amount of money he was willing to spread around.

Which right now was limitless, Ramón guessed, based on the resolve in the drug lord's voice.

He popped a pain pill, lowered himself onto the bed, and set the phone beside him, his eyes half closed as he waited for instructions on what to do next.

It seemed like only moments had passed when his phone jarred him from a light narcotic slumber. He fumbled for it with fingers numbed by the medicine and answered it on the third ring.

"I spoke with our contact," Mosises said. "He's turning over rocks. He hopes to have more by tonight. But he says there aren't that many private parties who could arrange for a military transport. He also warned that if it's not a private party, there's little he can do, because the administration rules the island with an iron fist. And if it's some sort of an intelligence operation, we're out of luck."

"I have a flight booked. I should be there this evening."

"Good."

Ramón shared his concerns about the two hired guns, and Mosises understood. "Then it's just you, with some local support in Havana. Don't let me down." He didn't have to say "again."

"I won't. If they're still in Cuba, they're as good as dead…or I will be."

"Let's hope it's the former."

"I'll let you know when I arrive. I'm booked on the Air Caraïbes flight from Port-au-Prince."

"He'll have someone get in touch once you're in Havana. He has your number."

CHAPTER 55

Havana, Cuba

Ramón looked around the spacious lobby of the Meliá hotel as the reservation clerk checked him in, and he did his best to shake off the grogginess from the pain medication. The doctor had told him that he might experience blurred vision and light-headedness, but he'd hoped to avoid the worst of it. Unfortunately, the waves of nausea he had been feeling since getting off the plane were severe, and if he didn't get better by the following morning, he was afraid he might not be up to his task.

His room was hot and stuffy when he opened the door, which didn't help, and he lay in misery on the bed as the air conditioner groaned to life. As far as he was concerned, the next day couldn't come soon enough, and he dismissed any idea of having a medicinal rum in the bar in favor of a glass of water, another pain pill, and a night of uneasy, pained sleep.

Ramón's phone jangled the next morning as the sun was barely beginning its ascent. It was Mosises.

"Yes?" Ramón answered, hoping he didn't sound too out of it.

"Our man has been working all night, but nothing yet. Renoir learned that the plane's flight plan called for it to return to its base – a military outpost in the middle of the country."

"That's what I was afraid of when I heard it was an army plane."

"Revolutionary Air Force," Mosises corrected.

"Of course."

"Your weapons are waiting for you."

"Perfect. When do I pick them up?"

"Later. When he has news. He's pulling out all the stops for me, but he didn't sound hopeful."

"Maybe he can bribe someone at the airfield?"

Mosises grunted. "That occurred to us."

"Ah. All right, then."

Ramón signed off and rolled over, willing away the sunlight seeping beneath the blinds. When that didn't work, he rose slowly, closed the blackout curtains, and felt his way to the bathroom, where he washed down another pain pill and staggered back to bed.

Three hours later, another call woke him. The Cuban.

"We have made some progress. A description of a car and of one of the passengers, from last night. We're trying to put a name to a face. Should have something by this evening."

"I don't understand. Why would that be relevant?"

"It's a remote airfield. There's nothing there but a military encampment. But this was a civilian. One of the vendors nearby remarked on it when we questioned them. He bought a cigar."

"That's why you're calling? Because a man bought a cigar in Cuba?"

"It's our only lead. Nobody on the base will talk. We tried. Whoever their commanding officer is, they're terrified of him, and nobody wanted to risk his wrath for any amount of money. But this cigar buyer was there when the vendor heard a plane land. Find the man with the cigar, and you've likely found the people you seek," the Cuban finished, sounding annoyed at Ramón's question.

Ramón digested the information and nodded to himself, then winced at the pain the movement caused. "I got it. Fine. When would you like to get together to hand over the weapons?"

"At the end of the day. There aren't that many relatively new Honda sedans on the island, and that's what our cigar buyer got out of. Once we have a list, we'll look for someone matching his description, and there's your first stop."

"Sounds reasonable. I'll leave my phone on."

~ ~ ~

Carl, true to his word, was waiting for Jet and Matt in the downstairs lobby at nine, wearing another lightweight tropical suit, this one mustard-colored, with a blue shirt and bright yellow tie. He'd topped the ensemble with a Panama hat and carried an ebony walking stick.

"Good morning. I trust you slept comfortably?" he boomed as they came down the stairs.

"Yes, thanks. It was marvelous," Jet assured him.

"Glad to hear it. Are you ready, or do you want to get something to eat?"

"We already had a light breakfast," Matt said.

"Very well, then. Let's get this over with." He peered down at Hannah, who stood shyly by Jet's side, holding her hand. "Ready for your modeling audition?"

Hannah blinked at him in puzzled confusion. He straightened and smiled at Jet. "Breathtaking child, really. She'll stop hearts when she's older. Takes after her mother in that regard."

"Thank you. Hannah's a wonderful little girl. Aren't you, sweetheart?"

Hannah smiled, unsure of what was expected of her.

"How far to the shop?" Matt asked.

"Oh. Ten minutes. Over by the university," Carl said, leading them outside to where his car waited.

"No driver?" Matt asked.

"Don't worry. I'm not much of a menace during the day."

"That's reassuring," Matt said doubtfully.

"Hush up, young man, and open the door for the ladies."

The drive took twice as long due to flooding of the waterfront road and congestion on the approach from a tunnel that ran below the Rio Almendares. As they rolled to the curb in front of a brightly colored building, Matt eyed the sign.

"Yankee Pride? Not particularly subtle, is it?" he said.

"I abandoned subtlety lifetimes ago. Way overrated. Besides, the locals are enraptured by anything American. The government says they're to hate it, but that's worn thin over the years, and now more want an iPhone and a big-screen television than revolutionary solidarity."

"How much of the town do you own, Carl?" Jet asked.

"Oh, just this and that, my dear, this and that. I try to keep my fingers in a number of pies. Someone must do the devil's work, after all," he said with another wink.

Jet offered him a dazzling white smile. She was getting used to Carl's odd charm, a sort of cross between Santa Claus and Truman Capote that she found strangely endearing.

"Idle hands," she agreed.

"Let's go see if the shiftless thieves I overpay to run the place have shown up for work yet, shall we?" he said, opening the driver's door and, without waiting for an answer, slammed it and marched to the shop entrance, toting his cane like a rifle.

The photographs were finished in fifteen minutes. Matt eyed the street out of habit as they left the studio. Urchins were kicking a battered soccer ball at the far end of the block, their thin frames and baggy shorts moving in a blur as they vied for a goal. "What now?"

Carl waved his cane at nothing in particular. "I had my expert appraise the stones, and they are as you represented. Not that I for a moment doubted your veracity. But it's official. And may I say that they are of remarkable quality."

"I'm glad you think so, Carl," Matt said.

"From here I'll leave you to wander the town; or if you like, I can drop you off at the inn. I have a meeting with Fuentes at ten, and I don't want to be any later than usual."

"We can walk, if you think it's safe," Jet said.

"During the day, no question. At night's a different story."

"You really believe the passports will only take forty-eight hours?" Matt asked.

"I do. Fuentes is a good lad. Rock solid, although he shares my sin: the love of money. But he can work magic, and will, for me. We have intertwined holdings, so I get special consideration. And I've made it very clear you're a priority." Carl patted his pocket, where he had the forms they'd filled out in the photo shop with their new names and ages written on it. "Victor and Alicia Campeno. And their little marvel, Ana. Oh, and if you're in the mood, tomorrow is my weekly dinner at the best restaurant in all Cuba, with breathtaking views of the water. Another restored home in a lovely location. I'd be delighted if you'd be my guest."

"That sounds wonderful, Carl," Jet said.

"See if you can talk this cheapskate into buying you something suitable to wear. It's not formal but, well, those clothes look like they've seen some duty."

"I will," Jet assured him.

"What about me?" Matt asked.

"With her on your arm, nobody will be looking at you," Carl said. "You can wear a towel if you like."

Everyone laughed, and Carl bid them goodbye as he returned to the car. Matt motioned to the waterfront a few blocks away and glanced at Jet.

"Up for a walk?"

"I'd follow you anywhere. But he's probably right about finding some decent clothes."

"Something tells me Cuba's not going to have a lot of choices."

"We're only looking for one outfit. And of course, something for Hannah."

"Perhaps we should see about having Gloria look after her during dinner? One of Carl's affairs doesn't sound like her kind of thing."

"We'll see. Lead the way, oh great white hunter."

"I thought I was the victor."

"That was last night. Today we're on the hunt for something to wear."

CHAPTER 56

Ramón met Mosises' Cuban contact, Salvador, at a café in the old town at dusk, near Hemingway's old hangout, La Bodeguita del Medio. The area was jammed with European and Canadian tourists, distinctive in their floppy Tilley hats and hiking sandals, pink sunburned skin a badge of honor in the tropical heat. They sat together at a tiny circular table, Salvador smoking, while a comely waitress with a quick smile for them both brought coffee and a snifter of rum on the side for Salvador. Ramón stuck to water, not wanting to further impair himself with additional chemicals, the pain pills more than sufficiently altering his state.

Salvador waited until the woman had set their drinks down and moved to another table before sliding an envelope to Ramón. "In there you'll find a photograph of the man who bought the cigar, as well as a brief dossier on him. He came from nowhere and has become a colorful addition to the Havana scene. He's rumored to be a high-level fixer."

"Fixer?"

"In a regimented society like ours, there's always a need for those who can get things done unofficially, who can secure forbidden fruit. He has that reputation."

Ramón opened the envelope and peeked inside. "How do I find him?"

"He has a mansion by the water…but I checked, and it's well guarded."

"Is that typical here?"

"If one has sufficient financial wherewithal, it's not unknown.

He's got a contingent of armed ex-military on his grounds, and they tend to be rather good at what they do, so I wouldn't try to tackle him there."

"Do you have someone watching the house?"

Salvador tossed back half the rum and washed it down with coffee. "No. It's not practical in that neighborhood. The police patrol it very regularly, and they're sensitive about nonresidents loitering around."

"Then what do you suggest?"

"He owns a number of businesses. Actually, a dozen that I was able to find, and probably more where he's a silent partner. You can look for him at his known establishments."

"That sounds like a lot of ground to cover."

"I am happy to assist, if you'd like me to."

"I would."

They finished their drinks and Salvador led Ramón to his vehicle, where he opened the trunk and retrieved a green tote bag and handed it to him. "Your pistol and ammunition are in there."

"Perfect. I'll wait to hear from you. Time is of the essence in this matter."

"Mosises made that very clear."

Ramón walked back toward the main plaza, where taxis lined the block, and read the brief paragraph on the subject as he went. Carl Rodgers, ostensibly Canadian, man about town, bon vivant, entrepreneur. A list of his enterprises, which included three cafés, an art studio, two tour companies, and a handful of other miscellaneous ventures.

Not a lot to go on. But their only thread.

And Carl had bought a cigar in the wrong place, at the wrong time.

Which was enough.

Tomorrow, Ramón would make a tour of as many of the man's businesses as he could. From the picture, it wouldn't be hard to spot him. The man was the size of a polar bear, judging from the weight on the driver's license copy Salvador provided, and his Lincolnic beard and leonine head of platinum hair were distinctive even in the small photograph.

In the meantime, more meds and another night's sleep would set Ramón right. He was already healing; with every hour he felt surer of himself, his limp now a mere nuisance, the pills taking the worst of the edge off the pain.

Tomorrow he'd be ready for battle. He just hoped that there would be an enemy to fight, because with every hour the trail grew colder, and he knew that eventually it would disappear altogether.

~ ~ ~

Major Fuentes stood in the doorway of his friend and sometimes lover Solana, who was in charge of the Havana passport department – a job she'd held for over a decade and which had earned her a tidy sum, working in conjunction with him. Fuentes had dropped off the photos that morning, and stopped in after hours to confirm that progress was being made.

"You're an angel for helping with this, Solana."

"I know. Of course, the money helps my divine intervention in the matter."

Fuentes nodded. "We must seize opportunity when we find it."

She smiled up at him from her desk. "Speaking of which, why are you here so late?"

"I was thinking you might want to have a daiquiri with me somewhere quiet."

Solana eyed the pile of documents on her desk. "Can we do it some other time? I have a lot on my plate."

"Sure. Just name a time and place. Perhaps when I pick the documents up the day after tomorrow?"

"Ah, so this is your way of reminding me I need to come in early to get them. I see. Don't worry, *mi amor*, I want my payday as much as you. Although a daiquiri sounds…interesting. Shall we say noon, Friday, at La Floridita? I'll bring the passports, you bring the second half of the payment, and we'll see if we can find something to discuss other than business. I shall tell the staff I'm feeling under the weather that morning, so we'll have the afternoon to ourselves."

"Sounds like a date."

She watched him walk down the corridor and out the front entrance and sighed. "Oh, Luis. What am I going to do with you?" She placed a hand on the pile of documents and eyed her ring finger, and then took up her work again, the clock behind her ticking inexorably, a reminder that time was creeping by in tiny increments that added up to a life waiting for another woman's husband to buy her a drink.

CHAPTER 57

Ramón's phone rang as he was making his way back to the hotel at the end of the next day. His entire afternoon had been a wash, Carl nowhere in evidence at any of his businesses. Ramón wasn't looking forward to having to tell Mosises that there had been no progress, and his mood wasn't being improved by the body aches that lingered from the accident. He fished in his pocket and dry-swallowed another pain pill, figuring it wouldn't matter since he was just going to be in his hotel room the rest of the night.

It rang one more time before he managed to press the right button. Salvador.

"Yes?" Ramón answered.

"One of my men learned that this Carl has a standing reservation every Thursday night at La Golondrina. That's where you'll find him tonight."

"La Golondrina?"

"On the water down by the Hotel Occidental Miramar." Salvador gave him an address.

"How did you find out?"

"It's no secret. Apparently he hosts a who's who of Havana society there. A regular event. Imported wine, gourmet food, musicians, very hedonistic. Not at all in the spirit of austerity that the regime preaches, but then again, hypocrisy's the national pastime."

"What time?"

"Eight o'clock."

Ramón checked his watch. He had fifteen minutes. "Okay, thanks. I'll get over there and see if I can convince him to spend a few minutes with me."

"I should caution you that in that neighborhood, you won't be allowed to stand around. The security will be tight. These are the wealthiest people in Havana, and they don't encourage the locals to hang out there. So you'll need a better plan than that, or you'll be told to move along."

"I'll figure something out."

Ramón flagged a passing taxi and gave him the address. The old driver grinned – it would be a good fare on a slow evening for him. Ramón fingered the butt of the pistol in his windbreaker pocket. This Carl fellow was about to have the worst night of his life.

~ ~ ~

Jet twirled with her arms outstretched and Hannah clapped her hands in delight, both giggling as Matt looked on. They'd eventually found a dress for Jet the day before, and had spent that morning converting the smallest of the diamonds, a one-and-a-half carat princess cut, into dollars at a black market jeweler Carl had introduced them to. Now, after a relaxing day lounging around the courtyard wading pool, they were preparing to meet Carl for dinner.

"You look gorgeous, as always," Matt said approvingly.

"I'm glad I can still get your attention."

Matt's gaze drifted from her caramel skin to her sparkling jade eyes and smiled. "The most beautiful woman in the world has nothing to worry about."

"That's the kind of talk I can get used to." She studied him for a moment. "You look very handsome."

He fingered the lapel of the jacket they'd bought him, a lightweight linen outfit with matching crème pants. "I feel a little like a pimp in this getup."

"It's Havana. Go with it."

"Something in the water?"

"Exactly."

Jet locked the diamonds in the room safe, and they descended to the ground level. Hannah went running to where Gloria's daughter, Jamie, stood beside her mother in the entry hallway. Jamie was a year older than Hannah, and they'd spent most of the day playing by the wading pool and were now new best friends. Jet smiled at Gloria as they approached. "Thanks for watching her. We shouldn't be more than two hours. Just in time to put her to bed."

"It's my pleasure," Gloria assured them.

"Don't let her have too much sugar or her head will spin around," Matt warned.

Gloria smiled. "I think I've got it under control."

"Famous last words," Matt said, and they all chuckled.

"Your taxi's here," Gloria said, tilting her chin at the front door.

Jet glanced at the entry. "Oh, good."

The ride to the restaurant was mercifully brief, and when they pulled down the cobblestone drive past two stern-faced guards, Jet took Matt's good hand and squeezed. "Wow. Tell me this isn't nice," she said as they neared the huge waterfront villa.

Matt nodded. "Carl doesn't do things small, I'll give him that." He turned to her and kissed her lightly on the cheek. "You ready?"

"I'm starving."

~ ~ ~

Ramón reached the restaurant with four minutes to spare. He tossed the cab a few pesos before climbing out and moving to the entrance. A beautiful young woman with a low-cut black evening gown stood with a clipboard, checking off names as diners arrived. Ramón approached and gave her his most charming smile.

"Good evening. I'm just in from out of town and heard about your place. Do you have a table for one?"

"Oh, no, sir, I'm sorry. We're usually booked several nights in advance."

He turned on the charisma. "Are you sure you can't find something? Even in a quiet corner somewhere?" He let her see the twenty-dollar bill in his hand.

"If it were up to me, I'd do my best, but no, I'm afraid there's nothing."

"I hate to go home hungry."

"I can recommend some other very good places."

It was obvious to him she was a dead end. "No, that's fine."

He turned and almost collided with a mountain of a man wearing a lime green tropical-weight suit, replete with vest, hand-stitched shirt, and matching cravat. Ramón recognized Carl, his white mane unmistakable, but all he could do was step aside. Ramón would have to wait for him to finish dinner and then make his move – there was no way to do it in a crowd of diners.

Carl pushed past him and Ramón caught a glimpse of the Accord accelerating away, a valet behind the wheel, and watched as its taillights disappeared around a corner. Carl's voice boomed behind him as Ramón stepped off the porch and made his way toward the street. "Andreina! You look positively edible tonight! Is my table ready?"

Ramón didn't wait to hear any more, his attention drawn by a taxi in front of the restaurant whose doors were opening. Recognition surged through him like an electric jolt as a stunning woman emerged from the car, followed by a Caucasian man – with a cast on his hand.

It was them.

His fingers drifted to the pistol in his pocket as he calculated how he'd make his escape after gunning them down, but he was too slow, and before he could act, they were inside, leaving him gaping at them from a dozen yards away. He swore under his breath – doubling up on the pain medicine had slowed his reactions, and that had just cost him his opportunity.

Movement down the drive caught his eye. He turned to where four musicians in street clothes were tuning their instruments near a circular fountain in the center of the driveway. An idea formed as he ambled in their direction, and by the time he made it to where they stood, his confidence had returned.

"How are you fellows doing tonight?" he asked.

"Good, *Señor*. And you?"

"Excellent. It's a special night for me, and I'm hoping you can help make it a success."

"Would you like us to play you a song?" the leader asked, strumming his guitar.

"Not exactly."

"Then…how can we help you?"

Ramón stepped closer and withdrew his money clip fat with hundred-dollar bills.

"My friend's having dinner in there and I want to surprise him. Do something special. I'm thinking a little deception would be perfect."

"A deception?"

"Yes," Ramón said, peeling off four hundred dollars. The musicians' eyes widened at the sight of the bills as Ramón held them loosely in his hand. "Let me explain."

CHAPTER 58

Carl rose from his seat at the tablecloth-draped table as Matt and Jet followed the hostess through the restaurant. A few of the other diners murmured appreciatively, and Carl held his arms out like he hadn't seen them in years.

"You're lucky I brought my heart medicine. Such a vision of loveliness takes my breath away," he declared theatrically, and then nodded to Matt. "You clean up pretty good, too."

Jet flashed a smile at him and offered a small hug, and Matt waited dutifully and shook his hand. Carl indicated two chairs. "Please, have a seat. What do you think of the joint?"

"It's spectacular," Jet answered honestly. The high ceilings accented the mansion's colonial charm, the paint a creamy yellow with white accents, and the chandelier overhead glittered like a thousand diamonds.

"I like it. And the food's not half bad," Carl assured them. A waiter wearing black pants and vest over a crisp white dress shirt approached and cleared his throat discreetly.

"Ah, there you are, my good man! The young goddess will have…" Carl paused, eyeing Jet. "A…mojito. Am I right?"

Jet nodded. "That sounds wonderful."

"And my friend and I would like a generous portion of your finest aged rum. Havana Club Añejo, of course."

"Of course, sir. Would you like an appetizer while you wait?"

Carl leaned toward Jet like he was confiding in her. "They have brilliant sashimi. Fresh line-caught yellowfin tuna." He turned his attention to the server. "The tuna is fresh today, is it not?"

The man nodded stiffly. "Yes, as always. Caught a few hours ago."

Carl beamed at Matt and Jet. "Then you absolutely must try it. Bring us a platter to share."

The waiter made a note and hurried to the ornate dark wood bar near the entrance as Carl waved a bear-paw-sized hand at the sea. "It's the closest thing to paradise I've found. Except during storm season, when anyone sensible gets the hell off the island."

"Where do you go?" Matt asked.

"I favor Tulum, on the Mexican Riviera. I have an interest in a little place there."

Matt smirked. "Seems like the private life has treated you all right since you left the company."

Carl returned the smile. "Well, there's considerable power in knowing where the bodies are buried. You'd be surprised at how helpful the guilty can be when offered a proposition they can hardly refuse."

"I'll just bet," Jet said.

"I didn't invent the world. I'm merely trying to make my way in it, as are we all." Carl patted his stomach, his vest buttons straining at the challenge of containing his girth.

"Some with more good fortune than others," Matt observed wryly.

"What's that old song? Something about a little help from my friends?" He stopped as a thought flashed across his face. "Speaking of which, Fuentes confirmed that he'll have your passports tomorrow in the early afternoon. He'll bring them by the inn. I already paid him the second chunk, anticipating that you'd do so once you had them in hand."

"Of course. We can get together for cocktails in the early evening. Our treat," Jet said.

Carl smoothed his hair and an emerald pinkie ring twinkled on his chubby hand. "Have you decided where you're going to go after Cuba?"

"Not yet. We're exploring our options," Matt hedged.

"You could do worse than stick around here for a spell. I could use some honest help with some of my projects. It would be invaluable to have someone with your field background," Carl said to Matt.

"I'll definitely consider it."

The server returned with their drinks and they toasted. "To a bright new future," Carl said, and they clinked their glasses together.

The musicians moved into the dining room from the waterfront French doors, which were thrown wide to allow the ocean breeze to cool the large area. They wove their way between the tables, the leader bowing to a few regulars as they made their way toward the bar, and then the last member of the group broke away, lingering as the troupe passed Carl's table.

A pistol appeared in Ramón's hand and he pointed it at Jet's head from only a few feet away, his eyes flat as pools of oil. A woman at an adjacent table screamed and another gasped, and then a stampede of the privileged ensued as the patrons scrambled for the entrance.

"You killed the wrong man, bitch," Ramón hissed, the gun steady. He pulled his iPhone from his pocket and held it up to film so Mosises could watch the execution in real time. He sneered in triumph as his finger tightened on the trigger, and then a pop only slightly louder than a champagne cork rang through the restaurant, and the crowd shrieked at the sound.

Puzzlement flashed across Ramón's face and his eyes dropped to his chest, where a tiny hole had burned through his shirt, crimson spreading around it like spilled ink. He looked up at Carl, who was holding a small derringer. Carl fired again, the.22-caliber round punching beneath the first, and anger flushed Ramón's face as he shifted the gun toward Carl.

"You…you shot me," Ramón growled, and pulled the trigger, blowing a hole in Carl's forehead, the shot as loud as a cannon in the high-ceilinged salon. Carl fell back in the chair and crashed against the ground.

Jet sprang toward Ramón, a sterling silver steak knife in her hand.

Ramón swung the gun back toward her, but he was a split second too late. His eyes widened in shock as Jet, a blur with the knife, drove the point up through his jaw and into his brain with all her strength.

He convulsed and the gun fired again, the slug drilling into the ancient polished wood floor, and then he collapsed in a heap, his appendages trembling as life drained from his body.

"Everybody freeze!" a male voice screamed from the entry. Jet and Matt slowly raised their hands over their heads and turned to where three suited guards approached, guns trained unwaveringly on them, their stares hard.

Jet's gaze flitted to Matt and a silent message passed between them. They couldn't take all three of the guards, especially not with them armed and maintaining a safe distance. The men moved like professionals, probably ex-military, and to make a try would be suicide.

She cleared her throat and spoke in an even tone. "This man attacked us. He has a gun. It's on the floor beside him. He shot our friend in the head."

The lead guard held up a hand and stopped his companions from getting any closer. "That's for the police to figure out. Just everybody stay calm and keep your hands up."

"But we didn't do anything except defend ourselves," Matt protested.

"Then you have nothing to worry about. The police should be here any minute. For now, just keep quiet and no sudden moves, or I'll be forced to shoot."

Jet nodded, the crash of surf on the rocks outside a rhythmic accompaniment to the singsong of distant sirens that were growing louder with each passing second.

CHAPTER 59

Jet sat in the holding cell with three prostitutes suspected of mugging their johns in collusion with their pimps, a woman accused of trying to kill her husband, and two middle-aged women who had been caught breaking into a house. The mood was largely civil, everyone's problems large enough that creating more drama in jail wasn't on their agendas.

At one point during the night one of the prostitutes, whose dilated pupils and fixed expression told Jet she was high on something powerful, tried to pick a fight with her, but a few carefully chosen words of warning from Jet threatening to break her arms settled the matter, and peace reigned for the rest of the evening.

When the police had arrived at the restaurant, they'd studied the scene, begun taking statements from witnesses, and held Matt and Jet while the forensics crew and the coroner went about their business. Eventually Matt was released, having been guilty of nothing but sitting at the table, but Jet wasn't so fortunate. An apologetic detective had placed her under arrest pending further investigation, assuring her that it was purely a formality.

Jet's biggest concern was with immigration, because she didn't appear on any entry documents, which could trigger alarms. Her explanation would be that she had no idea why the clerk at the airport hadn't stamped her passport – she couldn't be held responsible for the lack of competence of Cuban personnel, after all. It wasn't a bad stance to take, but it was decidedly adversarial, and she wasn't looking forward to having the discussion.

The detective was treating it as a robbery gone wrong, but she'd heard him muttering to an associate about Carl having attracted the wrong kind of attention, of making himself a target, perhaps by business competitors, or jealous lovers, or envious miscreants who wished him dead. Jet was sure that his reputation as dabbling in less than aboveboard activities was also known, or if it wasn't, soon would be, providing more motives.

The still of the morning was broken as a door creaked open somewhere out of Jet's field of vision. Two guards approached along the concrete corridor and called her alias and, when she stepped forward, warned the other prisoners to back off. They unlocked the door and led her to an interview room, the same one where she'd spent several hours of her night answering questions over and over.

She sat in a steel chair that was bolted to the floor and waited for whatever was to come, but was surprised when Major Fuentes appeared moments later with the fatigued-looking chief detective who'd escorted her to the jail. The detective took a seat opposite her while Fuentes stood in a corner, watching silently. The cop scratched at the stubble on his face and leaned forward.

"We've cleared you of all wrongdoing," he announced.

"That's good to know, considering all I did was defend myself," Jet countered.

"Yes, well, it's unusual to see such a...spirited defense. But the footage on the phone and the statements from the diners established that you reacted to the gunman's shooting of your friend, nothing more."

"Am I free to go?"

"Yes. However, I do have a question. The gunman appeared to be targeting you, and insulted and threatened you. Any idea why?"

"No."

"Specifically, he accused you of killing the wrong man. Several of the diners confirmed that."

"They heard wrong. The man was mad."

"And you didn't know him?"

"I've never seen him before in my life." She paused. "Who was he?"

The detective looked to Fuentes. "He was Colombian. That's all we know at this point."

"Probably on drugs."

The detective nodded. "Probably." He sighed. "My condolences on the death of your friend. He was highly regarded by many. That's become clear as we've continued our investigation."

"Thank you."

There was nothing left to say. The detective rose and moved to the door, and Fuentes nodded to her, his eyes flashing a warning. She understood – don't talk, because without a doubt the walls had ears.

Jet followed Fuentes out and remained silent as she was released, signing the paperwork quickly, anxious to be rid of the prison, which, although terrible, was nevertheless a five-star resort compared to Haiti.

Once they were outside and walking to Fuentes' vehicle, she turned to him. "Thanks. I presume you had something to do with that?"

"I accelerated the process and smoothed over a few open issues. Nothing big."

"Can you give me a lift to the inn? I'm afraid I don't have any money for a cab. All I have is what I'm wearing and my watch."

"Of course. I planned to. And I have your passports. Everything's in the system, so you can travel whenever you like."

"That's wonderful."

"It's probably not a bad idea to do so sooner than later. We both know that was no madman."

"We weren't planning to dawdle in Havana."

"Let me know if you need any help getting off the island. Many of Carl's contacts are also mine."

"He mentioned you were involved in some of his businesses."

"Yes, there will be much to sort out in the coming months. It's unfortunate, but life moves on. And he went out like he would have wanted – in a high-profile blaze of glory that will be discussed for months. If there was one thing he hated, it was to be ignored."

"Sad that this is how he'll be remembered."

"Yes, it is."

They were quiet on the way to the inn, both lost in their thoughts.

When they pulled up outside, Fuentes handed her a manila envelope with the passports in it. "He already paid me for everything, so our business is concluded."

"Wait here," Jet said, and hurried into the mansion. She returned in a few minutes. She leaned into the car and placed a three-carat stone in Fuentes' hand with a smile. "Honesty is too rare. This is for you. I owed it to Carl for the last payment."

Fuentes watched as she returned to the big house's entryway, where her daughter was standing with her husband, and slipped the diamond into the breast pocket of his uniform.

"*Vaya con Dios*, Victoria, or whatever your name is. Go with God, because I have a feeling you're going to need all the help you can get," he whispered. He put the car in gear and drove away, his bonus bittersweet but appreciated, the stone another step toward leaving the service and picking up where Carl had left off.

Epilogue

Pristina, Kosovo

A crisp wind blew off the mountains as Jet and Hannah hurried down the sidewalk to the small house they'd called home for three weeks. The rental had been laughably cheap, in a good neighborhood. Their neighbors were mostly of Albanian descent: physicians, shop owners, lawyers, and other professionals.

Matt and Jet had decided to try Kosovo because it was far off the beaten path, and after their experiences in South America, that continent was decidedly unappealing. Neither Jet nor Matt had ever been to the beleaguered city before, which meant they wouldn't be recognized accidentally – a huge consideration.

Jet's only real complaint was the weather, which was colder than she was used to, but which she could grow accustomed to if it meant living in safety. They'd researched everything from health care to schools and were confident that it would work for them, at least for a year or two. The bargain they'd made with each other was to give it a reasonable try, and if they didn't like it, they'd move on, perhaps to Sicily – someplace warmer, where a secluded lifestyle could be had without intrusive inquiries from nosy officials.

But for now Pristina was home, and for the first time Jet felt like it could last. There had been no sign of anyone attempting to follow them from Cuba, and she'd stayed in touch with Fuentes in case he was approached. So far, nothing, which was cause for relief.

Jet unlocked the heavy oak door's deadbolt and twisted it open. "We're home," she called, and dropped her keys into a clay bowl on a side table in the entry hall. She hefted the shopping bag in her hand

and looked down at her daughter, her little cheeks pink from the chill.

"Go wash your hands like I showed you. Lunch will be ready in a few minutes, so don't take all day, sweetie."

"Okay, Mama."

Jet's heart tugged at the words, and she flooded with the simple joy of seeing herself reflected in her daughter, who was filled with wonder at her new home. The troubling events of the prior months had been largely forgotten, although she still woke up in the middle of the night sometimes, crying and calling out for her mother. Jet and Matt had chosen the house largely due to the layout, and Hannah's bedroom was right next to theirs on the second floor, so Jet could rush to comfort the little girl at a moment's notice.

Jet didn't kid herself that everything would be storybook perfect in Hannah's life, but she also knew from experience that she wouldn't remember much of what had taken place. Jet's first memory was of her fifth birthday, and Matt's was around the same age, so perhaps nature would compensate for a brutal upbringing by blocking the worst of it. That was the hope, and perhaps it was overly optimistic, but they'd have to play it by ear and adjust accordingly.

The remainder of the diamonds were safely stored in Uruguay, and it would be years before they ran low on money from the two and a half million worth she carried in her pouch. She'd found a dealer in Montenegro who could convert the smaller stones for her at a fair price, and she would make trips to Antwerp when required – one of the benefits of living in Europe was that little was farther than an hour or two plane trip.

For now, she was enjoying being just a mother and homebody, learning the layout of the city, the best shops for produce and food, and spending quality time with her daughter and Matt. It seemed almost surreal to have no greater concerns than the price of carrots or wine, but she was adjusting, reveling in her morning runs and renewed workout regimen, and nights in Matt's arms.

She tried not to think about the two guns they'd hidden around the house, purchased on the black market and readily available due to the tens of thousands of weapons that had entered the region during the troubled times. But was now considered ancient history, and peace had been restored, if a precarious one. There was little danger of more violence breaking out, and as with all things, humanity went on with its business, trying to normalize after a period of atrocities that were the bane of the region's existence.

"Did you get some bread?" Matt called from the kitchen.

"Yeah. And some more jam. We're almost out." She shrugged off her jacket and hung it on a hook. "Getting colder every day."

"Wait till it starts snowing. Hannah will love that. I'll show her how to throw snowballs. She'll be a menace in no time."

Jet smiled at his enthusiasm and felt her face flush with warmth. He was a fine man and, in spite of everything, was more focused on the future and a possibility of a life together than his troubled past.

She turned as Hannah came clomping down the hall from the bathroom. Jet's breath caught in her throat at the thought that flooded her when she saw her little girl's smile, free of fear or guile or anything but sweet goodness.

They were safe.

Finally.

This was real.

And nothing had ever felt so good.

ABOUT THE AUTHOR

Featured in *The Wall Street Journal*, *The Times*, and *The Chicago Tribune*, Russell Blake is *The NY Times* and *USA Today* bestselling author of over forty novels.

Blake is co-author of *The Eye of Heaven* and *The Solomon Curse*, with legendary author Clive Cussler. Blake's novel *King of Swords* has been translated into German, *The Voynich Cypher* into Bulgarian, and his JET novels into Spanish, German, and Czech.

Blake writes under the moniker R.E. Blake in the NA/YA/Contemporary Romance genres. Novels include *Less Than Nothing*, *More Than Anything*, and *Best Of Everything*.

Having resided in Mexico for a dozen years, Blake enjoys his dogs, fishing, boating, tequila and writing, while battling world domination by clowns. His thoughts, such as they are, can be found at his blog: RussellBlake.com

☼

Visit RussellBlake.com for updates

or subscribe to: RussellBlake.com/contact/mailing-list

The JET Series

JET

JET II – BETRAYAL

JET III – VENGEANCE

JET IV – RECKONING

JET V – LEGACY

JET VI – JUSTICE

JET VII – SANCTUARY

JET VIII – SURVIVAL

JET IX – ESCAPE

JET – OPS FILES (prequel)

JET – OPS FILES; TERROR ALERT

The BLACK Series

BLACK

BLACK IS BACK

BLACK IS THE NEW BLACK

BLACK TO REALITY

BLACK IN THE BOX

Non Fiction by Russell Blake

AN ANGEL WITH FUR

HOW TO SELL A GAZILLION EBOOKS

(while drunk, high or incarcerated)

CPSIA information can be obtained at www.ICGtesting.com
Printed in the USA
LVOW11s1927031215

465241LV00002B/182/P